Song of the Trumpet

Charles G. Coleman

Zeezok™
PUBLISHING

Elyria, OH

Song of the Trumpet

by Charles G. Coleman

ISBN 978-1-933573-30-4

Cover Art by Renee Wilcox

Published by:
Zeezok Publishing, LLC
PO Box 1960
Elyria, OH 44036

www.Zeezok.com
1-800-749-1681

Contents

The Land of Man

Including
Broad Valley
and the
Great Mountains

Valley of Despair

Cleft of the Rock

Grassy Knoll

The Village

The Tower

King's Castle

The Path

The Outpost

CHAPTER 1

Akara Receives a Gift

The call for help came loud and clear, but only one person was near enough to hear it. On this spring afternoon, the road beside the river was deserted except for a young girl in her teens. She was walking slowly, pulling behind her a wooden cart piled high with homespun cloth bags. The cry jolted her out of a pleasant daydream, and she stopped and looked around. It had come from somewhere near at hand, but where? Just ahead, and screened from her by bushes, was a place where the river tumbled over huge rocks into a turbulent pool. The call seemed to come from that direction. She knew that people sometimes crossed the river on those rocks, but the crossing was difficult.

She ran forward, still dragging the cart, past the barrier of bushes. Her guess was right; there was someone in the water! She could see a head bobbing above the surface.

"Help!" The call came again, a man's voice! She looked around wildly. There was no one else in sight. Dropping the handle of the cart, she ran toward the bank.

The man was clinging with one hand to a piece of wood that kept his head above the swirling water. He was weighed down by a pack strapped to his back, and with his free hand, he struggled with the straps that held it. He stopped calling when he caught sight of the girl running toward him.

She had no idea how to help him. Then, as she ran, she caught sight of a large tree limb lying on the ground. That might do it! She veered toward it, seized one end, and with all her strength began tugging it toward the pool. When she reached the water's edge, she dropped her end of the limb and ran panting to the other end. She lifted it and pushed with all her might. The unwieldy piece of wood slid on the soft mud at the shoreline, then floated into the stream.

The man's head was still above water. The girl kicked off her shoes and waded in behind the limb, pushing it toward him. She was knee-deep in water when he was able to stretch out an arm and grasp its other end. When he did so, the girl backed toward the shore, pulling the limb after her. A few moments later, the man found a firm bottom for his feet and waded ashore. He took off his pack and dropped down at full length on the grass, where he lay breathing heavily.

The girl looked down at him for a moment, then ran to her cart, opened one of the sacks, and pulled out two crumpled towels. By the time she returned, he had caught his breath and was sitting up. She handed one of the towels to him, then dried her feet with the other before slipping on her worn shoes.

The man stood up. He was tall, lean, and broad-shouldered, with a deeply tanned face. He was not young, his hair was streaked with gray, but his movements were sure and vigorous. Blue eyes twinkled down at his rescuer. "You saved my life, young lady," he said with a courtly bow. "I'm very grateful."

The girl flushed and looked at the ground. "I'm glad," she said, shyly. "I'm glad I happened to be passing by."

His eyes took in her straight figure, her well-shaped face, and the patched and faded dress she wore. He thought, she can't be older than fourteen, but she is certainly a quick-thinking young person. She doesn't much look like a local girl; down at this end of the valley, the people are mostly short and stocky. She is not. Aloud, he said, "Let me introduce myself. People call me 'Wenk the Wanderer'. I can swim, but not in that rough water with my heavy pack! If you hadn't come when you did, my wandering days might be over!"

He glanced toward the river and gave a sudden exclamation, "My hat! It's floated ashore!" Off he went with long strides to the water's edge, lifted something black and shapeless from the shallows, and shook it vigorously. It was a broad-brimmed hat. He looked at it fondly, then clapped it on his head and strode back to where the girl stood. She smiled at his enthusiasm, her shyness gone for the moment.

He returned her smile. "You must be one of Dame Dessit's orphans," he said. She nodded, and he continued, "That means you live up the river at the orphan home, that white house on the hill. And I'll wager that cart is full of dirty laundry you're taking from the village of Palloweth to the home, where you and the other orphans will slave away washing it."

Again, the girl nodded. Wenk turned and rummaged in his pack. "Let me give you something as a sort of 'thank you' for saving my life." He held out a small, silver-colored object. "It's not much, but a wanderer like me doesn't have much to give."

She put both hands behind her. "I don't want a reward, I was happy to help."

"It's not a reward. It's just a little gift I want to give you because I'm thankful. Please accept it!"

The girl hesitated, then slowly reached out and took the object. It was small, only a little longer than the man's hand. "It looks like a little horn," she said,

"People call it a trumpet. I think it is silver, though it's old and battered. It was given to me by an old man in another village. There are a few of these trumpets scattered around this valley. They come from somewhere in the Great Mountains. Some folks believe that in some magical way they bring good fortune."

The girl only half heard this explanation. To imagine how she felt, you must understand that she had never owned anything in her entire life except her clothes. The children who lived in the house on the hill were not allowed to have possessions of their own. So even though the little trumpet was scratched and dented, the girl thought it a most wonderful gift.

"It's beautiful! Thank you! Thank you!" she said. She paused for a moment, uncertainly, "Does it make music?"

He shook his head. "I'm afraid not. At least, I haven't been able to get a sound from it. Perhaps it will do better for you. Try!" Encouraged by Wenk's gentle smile, the girl raised the trumpet to her lips and blew through it softly. Her breath went freely through it, but no sound emerged. She blew again with the same result.

"Have you ever blown a trumpet?"

"No."

"A trumpet — any trumpet — is just a tube of metal. Air will go right through it, as you just found out. To make a sound with a trumpet you must press your lips together and then blow through it. The problem is, this trumpet won't let you do that. Try it and you'll see!"

The girl squeezed her lips together and blew, but now she could force no breath through the trumpet at all. It was as if a little door inside the instrument had closed. She relaxed her lips, and again her breath flowed through easily.

Wenk watched her, still smiling in his gentle way. "Strange, isn't it? You're finding, as I did, that it won't make a sound whichever way you blow it. I'm sorry. I wish it would."

"It's all right," she reassured him. "I like it anyway!" She stopped suddenly and her eyes widened. "Oh! I must get back with the laundry or Dame Dessit will be angry!"

Wenk looked northward toward the white house. "I'd go with you to pull the cart and to explain the delay to Dame Dessit, but she knows me and disapproves of me." He shook his head. "It's best she doesn't even see me; it would just make matters worse."

The girl smiled. "I'll be all right. I'll try to slip in through the back way. Thank you so much for my trumpet, and I...I..." She paused, not knowing how to finish, then burst out, "I hope your clothes dry!"

She scooped up the towels, turned and dashed for her cart. There she stuffed them into the sack they had come from, then tucked the silver trumpet in after them.

"You haven't told me your name!" Wenk called after her.

"It's Akara. Good-bye!" She waved a farewell and picked up the handle of the cart.

Wenk stood watching until the girl with her cart reached the top of the hill. There she turned and passed out of his sight toward the rear of the house. "No sign of Dame Dessit," he muttered. "I hope she doesn't catch the girl. I wish I could give her a better gift than the little trumpet." He sighed, slung his wet pack over his shoulder, and set off in the other direction toward Palloweth.

CHAPTER 2

At the Orphan Home

The girl Akara lived in a place called Broad Valley, in a land far away from the one in which you live. At the southern end of this valley stood the village of Palloweth. Farther on, the green fields of the valley gave way to barren desert.

Life was not easy for the orphans who lived there. Dame Dessit kept them hard at work, and she was quick to punish those who worked slowly. As a result, most were sad-faced young people who lived in fear, though a few got special treatment by spying on others.

Akara was not a spy, nor was she one of the fearful ones. Even as a small child, she realized that Dame Dessit did not like her, and she became stubbornly independent. Now, as a teenager, she worked hard when she had to but disobeyed whenever she thought she could get away with it. Dame Dessit realized this and responded by giving her the most difficult jobs to do.

The gift of the silver trumpet was the most exciting thing that had ever happened to Akara. She had brought her new treasure into the house in the bag of laundry. She had then managed to smuggle it upstairs to the attic room she shared with three other girls, and to hide it behind a loose board in the wall beside her bed. She longed to use her trumpet freely, but of course, could not do so since she had to keep its existence secret. Only when her roommates were asleep did she dare to take it quietly from its hiding place, hold it close, and blow through it softly.

One night she became brave enough to slip out of bed, take the silver trumpet from its hiding place, and tiptoe out the door and down a back stairway. She felt her way along a dark passage and opened a door leading down to a seldom-used cellar. Closing the door quietly behind her, she crept halfway down this stairway to a landing where there was a casement window. She unlocked it and swung it open.

The window was close to the ground, and she climbed through it, closing it behind her. She emerged behind a row of bushes. These bushes formed a leafy tunnel close against the side of the house, which ended under a big bush beside the front porch. This was one of Akara's favorite hiding places. Here she could sit comfortably, her back against the house, with the drooping branches forming a screen in front of her.

On this night, she seated herself, then raised her little trumpet, pressed her lips together, and tried to blow. As before, an invisible door inside the little instrument seemed to close so that no air could pass. She blew again, without compressing her lips, and her breath flowed through freely. After repeating this test several times, she gave up. "You are mine, little trumpet," she whispered, hugging it close. "I love you whether you make a noise or not!"

She tilted her head back against the wall. What would the trumpet sound like if it did play, she wondered? Closing her eyes, she again breathed through the trumpet, imagining a succession of lively notes.

She lowered her trumpet but kept her eyes closed. In her mind the music continued, changing from the original light tune to a deep, thrilling melody. As she drifted into a half-sleeping, half-awake state, she seemed to see before her a dimly lit, open area where several misty figures, one bright and others dark, twirled and swayed in time to the music.

This vision lasted only a moment, then it faded and the music ceased. Akara opened her eyes. She knew that what she had heard and seen existed only in her imagination, but it had seemed real. Was it possible there was some special power in the silver trumpet? She blew through it again, trying to recover the strange music, but without success. Finally, she gave up and made her way back into the house.

After this experience, the habit of breathing softly through the little trumpet each night while her roommates slept became very important to her. She began to notice that, no matter how hard the day had been, this process brought her a sense of peace.

While at first she told no one about her trumpet, she eventually decided to confide in old Burkon, the gardener. Dame Dessit often assigned her to help in the garden. The work was hard, and most of the children disliked the assignment. Akara secretly enjoyed it. She liked working with growing things, and she found that Burkon, under his crusty exterior, was honest and kind. So one sunny spring day when she was helping Burkon prepare the ground for planting vegetables, she told him about her trumpet and how she had gotten it.

Burkon nodded without looking up from his work. "I've heard about those little trumpets," he said.

"Wenk the Wanderer told me some folks believe they bring good fortune."

Burkon dug his spade into the ground. "Has it done anything for you?"

Akara hesitated. "It hasn't changed anything around me, but I think it has made me different."

"How?"

"Well, when I go to bed discouraged or troubled and blow through it quietly, I feel more content." She bent to pull up a weed. "But it does something I don't always like. When I'm angry with Dame Dessit, it seems to cool my anger!"

Burkon straightened up and chuckled. "In that case, it's probably good for you. You spend a lot of time being angry at Dame Dessit."

Akara laughed too. Then a wistful note crept into her voice. "There's one more thing. I sometimes think that, when I blow through the trumpet, someone is listening, someone far away, who understands and sympathizes with my problems. I know it would be easy for me to imagine this, but the feeling has become stronger and stronger." She looked at the gardener appealingly, "You told me you've heard things about these trumpets. Do you think it's at all possible that I'm right?"

Burkon stared at the ground. While he doubted that the battered little instrument had special powers, he knew Akara needed all the support she could get. "I don't know," he said at last. "I will say you've seemed to be more content in the last few weeks. If the trumpet seems to help you, don't question it."

He turned back to his work, spading the soft soil while Akara wielded a rake, breaking up the lumps. A short time later, Burkon spoke again. "Do you know how old you are, Akara?"

The girl looked up in surprise. "I'm not sure."

"You were brought to the orphan home almost fifteen years ago, though no one knows your exact birthday. Anyway, you've reached the age where I think I should show you something."

He dropped his spade and led the way into the little shed where he kept his tools. There he reached up to a high shelf, brought down a folded cloth packet, and shook it out. It was a sturdy blue bag. It had carrying handles made of brightly colored cords woven together.

He laid it out on his worktable. "This bag was found with you, Akara. It had your baby clothes in it." He gave her a little grin. "I hid it from Dame Dessit because I thought you should have it. She would, I'm sure, have taken it for herself." Akara's eyes sparkled as she fingered the cloth. "It's beautiful! Thank you so much for saving it."

Burkon folded the bag again and returned it to the shelf. "You'd better leave it here until the time comes when you have to leave the orphan home."

Akara knew, of course, that the older orphans were sent away from the orphan home, but she had not thought about this happening to her. "Where will I go when I leave here?"

"You won't just be turned loose. The boys are usually sent to farmers in the area to help in the fields. The girls become servants in the more well-to-do homes near Palloweth."

"That might be worse than working for Dame Dessit."

Burkon shrugged, turned, and led the way out of the shed. "At least you would be paid for your work. Anyway, there is nothing you or I can do about where you will be sent. But don't worry about it now. That won't happen for many months."

CHAPTER 3

A Daring Escape

Burkon was wrong. It was only two days later that Dame Dessit sent for Akara after the noon meal. "You've reached the age when you must leave us, Akara," she told the girl. "I'm sorry not to give you more notice, but you must be ready to go tonight."

With an effort, Akara kept her voice calm. "Where are you sending me?"

Dame Dessit gave her a tight little smile. "You'll learn all about it this evening. Right now, you must get a sack from the laundry and pack your clothes in it. Then be in the front hall after the evening meal."

Akara did as she was told. But when the bell rang for the evening meal that day, she did not go to the dining room. The turmoil inside her had destroyed her appetite. She certainly wanted to get away from Dame Dessit and the orphan home. At the same time, she realized that Dame Dessit might well choose to send her to some place even more unpleasant. So she waited until everyone else had entered the hall. Then she slipped quietly down the basement stairs to the side casement window, crawled through it and on to her hiding place under the front porch. She had no plan in mind. She only wanted some quiet time to prepare herself for what was going to happen.

Beside her, as she sat with her back against the wall of the house, was her sack of belongings. In it were her few clothes, her silver trumpet, and, folded in the bottom, the blue bag Burkon had kept for her. The old gardener had brought it to her when he heard the news.

Dusk was settling over the fields and villages of Broad Valley. As she looked out between the branches of the bush and down the hill, she could see the lights of the village winking on one by one. She thought of the silver trumpet nestled in the bottom of the sack beside her. While blowing through it always comforted her, it also softened her anger toward Dame Dessit. Tonight she wanted to stay angry. Being angry kept her from giving way to fear, and she was determined to be strong. She decided the trumpet would stay where it was. As the dusk deepened, a cool breeze swept across the yard, and she wrapped her old cloak more tightly around her. The evening meal, she thought, was surely over by now. Above her, she heard the sound of a door opening and closing. Then came the sharp click of Dame Dessit's heels on the stone porch, followed by a second pair of heels, less firm. Fendilla, the housekeeper, had joined her employer.

The two sets of heels clicked back and forth together, then came Dame Dessit's voice. "Where can the girl be?" The tone was low, but Akara could hear the anger beneath it. "I told her to pack her things and wait in the front hall."

Fendilla gave a dry laugh. "She's hidden herself away somewhere."

"I don't know why. She should be as glad to leave as I am to have her go!"

"Oh, she wants to leave, all right. Maybe she just doesn't want to be turned over to the Tall Woman."

This was a new name to Akara, and she strained to hear more. "How could she find out about the Tall Woman?" snapped Dame Dessit. "We've kept that a secret." Then, in a different tone, "Unless that old fool Burkon heard of it and told her. Well, what she knows makes no difference. She's old enough, and it's time for her to go!"

"Maybe you're right, though I think Akara has changed recently. She works harder and is less troublesome than she was. Maybe she deserves something better."

The clicking stopped. Evidently, the two women were now standing near Akara's end of the porch. Dame Dessit said, "There's no use trying to place her as a servant in one of the village homes. It wouldn't work. She's too independent."

"Well, if I were Akara, I'd rather be a servant than be turned over to the Tall Woman. I've never seen that creature, but I've heard odd things about her!"

"I've never met her, but I've heard stories too. Anyway, the matter is out of my hands. One of the village elders arranged for the Tall Woman to take her."

"What does she want with the girl?"

"I don't know and I don't care. She'll take her away north somewhere and put her to work, I suppose." Dame Dessit's voice took on an impatient edge. "My job is to take care of orphans from Palloweth. Akara wasn't born here and doesn't belong here."

"I wasn't with you when she came, so I don't know the whole story. Wasn't she found near Palloweth as a baby?"

"Yes, just north of here by the Akara Creek. That's why she was given that name. She was lying on a blanket in the back of an old wagon. A horse was grazing nearby. In the wagon was also the body of a wrinkled old woman — too old to have been her mother — who had apparently died in her sleep. That wagon must have come from somewhere in the north. The elders should have traced her and sent her back, but instead, they made me take her. Now, when the Tall Woman comes, we'll find her, wherever she's hiding, and I'll be rid of her. Come, I've had enough air."

The heels moved again, the door opened and closed, and the women were gone. Akara drew a deep breath. It was just as bad as she thought. She was being given away like a bag of potatoes. And to a woman even Dame Dessit thought was bad!

She considered running away, but she knew that wouldn't work. Children who had tried to run away in the past were always caught. They would be seen on the road, or they would stop at a farmhouse to ask for food. Someone would guess the truth, and they would be brought back and punished. And Akara knew that, even though Dame Dessit wanted to be rid of her, she wouldn't let her escape if she could help it. The best plan, Akara decided, was to stay hidden until the Tall Woman had come and gone. She would be beaten, of course, but maybe the Tall Woman would be discouraged and not come back!

Just then the clop, clop, clop of a horse's hooves broke into her thoughts. Peering between the branches in the gathering darkness, she saw the dark form of a two-wheeled cart coming up the curved drive in front of the house. It stopped. A figure in a long, hooded cloak swung down to the ground and stood for a moment, apparently scanning the darkened yard. Terror gripped Akara's heart. She felt as though the eyes under the hood were piercing the screen of branches to see her where she sat. She closed her eyes tightly, and when she opened them, the figure was gone. She heard a knock at the door over her head. It opened and closed. The Tall Woman had come!

Akara drew a deep breath. Soon the search would begin. Would they find her? As these thoughts raced through her head, she heard the sound of a second horse, coming at a slow walk up the road from the village. As it came closer, a creaking and rattling sound told her it was the wagon of Trask the peddler, a fox-like old man who traveled the valley selling pots and pans. Several times a year his travels would bring him south to Palloweth.

The peddler's wagon did not turn into the entrance to the orphan home but stopped on the road. Akara remembered that the old man liked to fill his pail with water from the well beside the house when he could do so without Dame Dessit's seeing him.

A wild idea came to her. Trask was evidently heading north up the valley. Could she escape by hiding in his wagon? The idea did not seem to make much more sense than running away on foot, but at least it was different. The peddler would probably camp for the night soon, and she would be discovered in the morning. On the other hand, if he drove through the night, his wagon might carry her past the area where she was most likely to be seen and captured. Then, if she could slip out of the wagon without his seeing her, she might more safely make her way northward on foot.

Desperate as she was, Akara decided to take the chance. She parted the branches of the bush and looked around. No one was in sight. She knew the peddler was at the well, for she could hear the windlass creak. She drew a deep breath, picked up her bag, and — running like a deer — sped across the grass and out to the wagon. There she slid her bag over the low tailgate beneath the canvas that covered the peddler's wares, and wriggled in after it. A moment later, she was lying completely hidden among stacks of pots and pans!

Soon she heard the old peddler come stumping back. Akara held her breath fearing that at the last minute he would turn back the canvas and discover her, but to her relief she heard him climb again to his seat. The wheels rumbled and turned, and she felt her bed beginning to move.

As the wagon jolted up the road through the night, her fears subsided. Let Dame Dessit and the Tall Woman search for her all they wanted. For the time being at least, she was free! She lay quietly, listening to the creaks of the old wagon. Finally she slept.

CHAPTER 4

Discovered!

Akara awoke suddenly with a feeling of panic. Why was she not in her own bed, and where was she? She raised her hands and felt something strange and rough stretched a foot or so above her. Then she remembered. She was in the back of Trask's wagon, under its canvas cover, traveling north up the valley.

But why was everything quiet? Of course! The motion had stopped. It was this change that had awakened her. As she strained her ears in the darkness, she heard the wagon seat squeak as the peddler climbed down. She heard him fumbling under the wagon, then came the sound of flint striking steel. He was making a light of some sort. There were shuffling footsteps, then his voice came. To her horror, she realized he was speaking to her!

"Well, whoever you are, I guess this is far enough to travel."

The cover was jerked back, and Akara found herself looking up into a sky full of stars. She sat up, clutching her sack. The man's head and shoulders in front of her were a dark blur. Then he raised his arm and the flickering flame of a small oil lamp cast its light on his face and her own.

The peddler snorted. "Well, young lady, you might as well get out. I'm going to build a fire and then we'll talk."

Akara climbed down, clutching her bag, and stood shivering with fear and the night chill. She pulled her cloak around her and listened to the peddler's grunts as he moved around, the little flame moving with him. A small fire sprang up. Trask, a short, wrinkled man, squatted beside it. He blew out the lamp, then lit his pipe with a burning twig. Akara came forward hesitantly to the other side of the fire and crouched down, her bag beside her.

Trask blew a cloud of smoke. His eyes flicked up to her face, then down again. "I know you," he said gruffly. "You're one of the older ones at the orphan home. What's your name?"

"Akara."

Again came the quick glance. "Why are you hiding in my wagon? Don't you know I could be thrown in prison for helping you run away?"

Akara hung her head. "No, I didn't know. I just had to get away." She looked up earnestly. "I don't want to make trouble. If you'll tell me which direction is north, I'll walk."

"Humph!" he grunted. "Not so fast! If you go off by yourself, you'll be caught. Then you'll tell them how you escaped, and I'll get into trouble. Now I want to see what you've stolen and hid in that bag! If it's not enough to risk prison for, I'll take you back. Maybe they'll give me a reward!"

"But I haven't stolen anything. The bag has only my own things in it."

"You ran away without stealing anything?" Surprise and disappointment were in the peddler's voice.

"That's right. And please! I can't go back."

"Why not? What's so bad about the orphan home? At least you get food there, which you won't find if you go wandering in the valley." He gave her another quick, furtive glance, and it came to her suddenly that he was uncertain what to do.

Her courage began to return. "I can't stay there. Dame Dessit wants to get rid of me. She plans to give me to the Tall Woman."

"The Tall Woman!" There was a new note in Trask's voice. "What does she want with you?"

"I don't know." Akara felt tears coming to her eyes. "I don't know anything about her. Do you know her?"

"Humph! No, but I've heard about her. I don't hold with her and her kind."

He sat for a few moments, puffing his pipe and staring into the fire. Finally Akara gathered her courage and broke the silence. "I'm sure

Dame Dessit won't give you a reward for taking me back."

The peddler nodded. "You're probably right. And if you don't have any of Dame Dessit's silver, you're not worth anything to me! I should have dragged you out of my wagon at the start! Now I don't want to drive all the way back for nothing, and I've told you I can't let you go off by yourself." There was a long pause while he puffed at his pipe. Finally he said, "I'll have to take you with me, for a while anyhow."

Akara brushed the tears from her eyes with her sleeve, and gave him a trembling smile. "Oh, thank you!"

"It won't be all that easy," said the peddler roughly. "You're going to be riding in my wagon and eating my food. Do you have any money?"

"Only a little that I earned in the village and hid from Dame Dessit." She fumbled in her sack, pulled out a small, cloth-wrapped package and handed him the few coins inside.

"Little enough," he grumbled as he tucked them into the pouch at his waist. "What else do you have?" He seized the sack and dumped the contents out on the ground. "Humph! Only a few clothes and a cloth bag. Wait a minute! Where did you get this?" He held up the battered silver trumpet.

"That's my trumpet! You mustn't take that!"

"Where did you get it?"

"It was given to me by a man who came to the village. I helped him when he fell into the river, and he gave it to me."

Trask held the trumpet at arm's length and glared at it. "I know what this is. It's one of those horns that silly folk think have some sort of magic power. I don't like them, and I don't want this one around!" His expression changed, and he added in another tone, "Maybe I can get a few coins for it from some fool in the next village."

While Trask's rough voice and harsh words had frightened Akara, the thought of losing her beloved trumpet made her angry. She jumped to her feet. "No! You can't have it. It's mine, and I won't let you sell it!"

The peddler glared up at her. She met his gaze, standing with hands on hips, though inwardly she was quaking with fear. Then to her surprise he dropped his eyes and tossed the little trumpet onto the pile of her clothing.

"Got a temper, have you?" he grumbled. "Well, I may sell it or I may not, but you can keep it for now. Put it away! I'm going to eat my supper, and I don't like looking at it."

He got up and shambled off to the wagon. Akara lost no time stuffing her possessions back into the sack. In a few minutes he returned, carrying a pot , a clay jug, and several bags. He set the pot on the coals, poured in water from the jug, then threw in two handfuls of chopped vegetables from one bag, chunks of dried beef from another, and a pinch of salt from a third. He carried the bags and the jug away and returned with two wooden bowls and two spoons.

During this time Akara had stood watching. When Trask finished, he sat down again by the fire, relit his pipe, and glared up at her. "Sit down, I'm not through talking to you."

Obediently, Akara seated herself. She was still frightened, but the fact that Trask had backed down a moment before gave her confidence. She reminded herself that she could certainly run faster than the old man and could escape if things became ugly. After a few preliminary grunts, he spoke.

"I'll take you with me if you behave yourself and do what I say. But that money you brought won't pay for your food. You must earn more. When we get farther up the valley, I'll find you work in houses or on farms. If anyone asks questions, you must say you're my granddaughter."

This arrangement suited Akara, and she quickly agreed. She was used to working. Her labor would surely bring in more than enough money to feed her. More important from her point of view, she would be safe from capture, and each day would take her farther from Dame Dessit and the Tall Woman.

The peddler had nothing more to say, and they remained silent while the pot bubbled merrily. He poked at the vegetables from time to time with his knife, and when they were done, emptied the contents of the pot into the wooden bowls. He gave one bowl and a battered spoon to the girl. Akara was hungry, since she hadn't eaten since noon. The peddler's stew was a crude mixture, but she found it nourishing.

When they had eaten, Trask showed her how to scrub out the pot and bowl using water and tufts of grass. "Cooking and cleaning up will be part of your job," he told her.

From the wagon he got a ragged blanket and a rolled-up hammock.

He slung the hammock from two hooks under the wagon. "This is where I sleep," he said. "You can roll up in the blanket and sleep in the wagon if you lie still. If you rattle the pots and wake me up, you'll sleep out on the ground!"

He turned away and sat down again by the fire. She took the blanket, climbed into the wagon, then glanced back at the peddler. He was paying no further attention to her. Akara took a deep breath. Things had certainly turned out well! Sitting cross-legged in the wagon, she emptied her belongings out of the homespun sack, opened the blue bag with the colored handles that Burkon had given her, and transferred her belongings into it.

When she reached the silver trumpet, she began to lift it to her lips as was her habit every night. Then she stopped. What if Trask looked up and saw her? He had ordered her to keep it out of sight. Besides, did she really need its comfort tonight? After all, she had escaped from Dame Dessit and won her argument with the peddler, too, without its support. Now she was headed northward to freedom! Maybe the trumpet, helpful as it had been, had served its purpose. While she would always cherish it, maybe it was no longer as important as it had been. She caressed the little instrument gently, then tucked it into her blue bag. Then she rolled up the empty homespun sack and stuffed it into a corner of the wagon.

Akara rolled up in the blanket, pulled the canvas cover over herself, and settled down to sleep. As drowsiness stole over her, she smiled in the darkness. Tomorrow was a new day and the beginning of a new life!

CHAPTER 5

Akara Meets the Miller

In the morning, Akara awoke to the song of birds and the rough voice of the peddler calling her name. She climbed out of the wagon to find a new fire burning where the old one had been.

Trask's disposition had not been improved by a night's sleep, judging from the glare he gave her. "It's time you were up," he said. "If you travel with me, you must be out of bed early. You must learn how to cook porridge in the morning and stew in the evening. Now go wash up and come back quickly!"

Akara darted off to a nearby stream. When she returned, the peddler showed her how to combine meal, water, and a pinch of salt in a pot and cook the mixture over the fire. She watched this process closely for she realized that the more helpful she was, the easier her life with Trask would be.

They ate the porridge, along with hard, black bread. Afterward, Akara washed the pot, bowls, and spoons in the stream, rubbed them dry with a cloth Trask gave her, and stored them in the wagon. Trask hitched up the horse, which had been grazing nearby, climbed on the wagon seat, and motioned for Akara to sit beside him. He shook out the reins, and with many groans and rattles, the old wagon moved up the grassy bank onto the road.

It was a glorious morning, sunny with white clouds overhead. The purple mountains that bordered the valley on the east stood out clearly against the sky. Akara was a naturally high-spirited girl, and the fresh air and sunshine made her feel like jumping down to dance along beside the wagon. However, a glance at the grim-faced man beside her convinced her it was wiser to sit still.

They traveled some distance before the peddler spoke. "A little later we'll pass some houses, and then you'll lie under the canvas where no one can see you. By tonight, we'll be far enough away from Palloweth so it won't matter. Tomorrow we'll reach some places where you might be able to work."

His words gave Akara an idea. "If you find someone who would like to hire a full-time housekeeper or maid, you can leave me there."

Trask grunted disdainfully. "That won't do. You'd decide you didn't like it, and run off again. Then you'd be caught, the whole story would come out, and I'd be blamed." He shook the reins impatiently. "Get these foolish ideas out of your head!"

Akara wisely said no more but turned her attention to the sights and sounds around her. Since she had never traveled, every view was a new one. She was especially fascinated by the Great Mountains and after a while, she ventured a question about them.

"Sir, have you ever climbed those mountains? And are there people who live up there?"

The old man's face flushed with anger. "No one lives in the mountains — no one with any sense, that is. I haven't been there, and I'm not going! Now be quiet!"

They drove on in silence. Several times during the day, Trask ordered her to hide under the cover while they stopped at farmhouses or passed through villages. At noon, they stopped beside the road to lunch on bread and an apple apiece, then they pressed on, camping at dusk in a little wood. They ate their evening meal in silence, then Akara crawled into the wagon and wrapped herself in the blanket, leaving the peddler sitting by the fire.

On the second day, Trask drove steadily for several hours, then stopped before a farmhouse. Leaving Akara in the wagon, he went to the door. After speaking briefly to the woman who answered his knock, he waved to Akara to join him.

"She's my granddaughter," he was saying as Akara arrived. "Her mother just died, and she doesn't want to talk, so don't ask her questions. She's a hard worker and will do a good job for you."

The peddler's tactic was effective, for the woman spoke to Akara only to tell her what to do. Akara worked steadily, scrubbing floors and washing windows, stopping only long enough to eat a lunch, which the woman provided. The peddler returned in mid-afternoon and collected the coins the woman dropped into his hand. Then he and Akara climbed to the wagon seat for another hour of driving before stopping for the night.

With some variation, this became their daily pattern. They would take to the road early each morning. When they came to a village, the peddler would find a house where Akara could work while he was off peddling his wares or doing other business. In the afternoon, he would pick her up and drive on.

Some of the people she worked for were pleasant, others were not. A few asked her about herself in spite of the peddler's request not to do so. When that happened, she said as little as possible. The work was often hard, but Akara did not mind, since each day took her farther from Dame Dessit.

Then one morning Trask turned from the main valley road onto a narrower one that slanted eastward toward the Great Mountains. Soon the scenery changed. They traveled past empty fields and rocky wastelands where the only vegetation was small, scrubby bushes. There were few houses, and those they passed were poorly kept. The peddler stopped at none of them. As the sun went down, they came to a drab-looking village that lay at the very foot of the mountains.

On its outskirts stood an old mill. It was unpainted, and its windows were dark. The only sign of activity was a great wooden wheel at one end of the structure that turned slowly as a stream of water from behind the building flowed over it. From the mill, the stream ran out to the road, under a wooden bridge, and into the fields beyond.

Trask turned into the mill yard. "We'll stay here tonight," he told Akara. "The miller will probably give you some work to do tomorrow."

The wagon came to a stop beside a large, flat rock in the center of the yard. Trask climbed stiffly down, pulled some sticks of wood from a bin on the side of the wagon, and built a small fire on the rock. "Start cooking our supper while I talk to the miller," he told the girl. "Be sure to draw water from the cask in the wagon for the stew. I don't like the water from this stream, though the miller drinks it."

He stumped off toward the mill. Akara stood, staring at the gloomy building. For some reason it frightened her. It reminded her of something dead, and its windows seemed like blind eyes. The whole area was strangely silent, with no bird songs or insect noises.

Reluctantly, she began preparing their meal. As she put the pot of meat, vegetables, and water on the fire, the mill door opened. Two figures came toward her through the growing dusk. The peddler's uneven gait made him easy to recognize. With him was a taller man, someone who moved smoothly, almost seeming to glide across the yard. Akara, her heart beating quickly, rose to her feet. As they approached, she saw that the stranger was an old man, though he gave the impression of strength. He had white hair, a long face, and deep-set eyes that seemed to pierce through Akara.

"So this is your little runaway, Trask," he said in a soft voice that was somehow more disturbing than the peddler's loud one. Seeing Akara's surprise, he went on, "Yes, Akara, I've heard all about you. I am the miller. Trask keeps nothing from me, do you, Trask?"

The peddler mumbled something, and the miller smiled, a small smile that made no change in the expression of his eyes. "He tells me you are a good worker. Since we grind no grain tomorrow, my sister will be pleased to have the working areas of the mill swept and scrubbed." He turned to Trask. "Bring her in the morning."

He nodded, turned, and was gone, gliding into the dusk as he had come. Akara drew a deep breath. She stood looking after the miller until Trask's voice came. "You don't like him, do you? I'm not fond of him either, or of his sister, Dame Dreng. Well, don't worry. We'll be here only for one day. So stop staring at the mill and watch that stew so it doesn't burn."

After their meal that evening, the peddler went off to the mill. Akara crawled into her bed in the wagon where she lay, tense and uneasy. The miller's brief visit had somehow shattered her self-confidence. Her thoughts turned to the silver trumpet. It had lain unused in her blue bag since the night she left the orphan home. Now she needed its comfort!

She slipped her hand into the bag, pulled it out, and blew through it softly.

Something was wrong! The trumpet was strangely dead! It seemed no more than a metal tube through which her breath passed. Akara felt a surge of anger, then sudden panic! Whatever the cause, the trumpet's magic — Akara did not know what else to call it — was gone!

Perhaps the atmosphere of this place had affected it. Then came an even more disturbing thought. Could this deadness be the result of her own neglect? She had thought about using it on the evening of her escape when she was hiding under the bush, but had not done so. Later that night in the peddler's wagon, she had foolishly decided she did not need it. Now she wanted its reassurance!

Again and again, she sent her breath through the silver trumpet, but the result was the same. Was its magic lost to her forever? Urgently, she began sending thoughts through the trumpet with each breath. Her message was, "I'm sorry! I'm sorry! Please forgive me." As she persisted, a faint touch of life seemed to return to the little instrument. Soon afterward, exhaustion overtook Akara and she fell asleep.

CHAPTER 6

The Miller's Trumpet

In the morning after breakfast, Akara walked with Trask to the mill. The unease she had felt the day before still oppressed her. She had seized a moment while the peddler was building the fire to breathe through her trumpet. While it seemed a little more responsive, it had not taken away her fears. Not wanting to be separated from the silver trumpet and her other possessions, she carried her blue bag with her. Also in it was a packet of bread and cheese. Remembering Trask's warning against drinking water from the millstream, she also took along a leather bottle of water.

The peddler's instructions, mumbled around his pipe at breakfast time, still rang in her ears. "I'll be gone most of the day. The miller and his sister, Dame Dreng, will also be going to the village, so they aren't likely to bother you. When you finish your work, wait for me by the flat rock."

The mill looked as gloomy as it had the evening before, and Akara had to force herself to follow the peddler inside. Trask led her up a flight of steps to a large, open room. Its center was occupied by a round, massive object that, Akara correctly guessed, was the millstone that ground the grain. A series of heavy rope belts connected it to a horizontal shaft above, which extended across the room and through the wall. Akara guessed it was connected to the mill wheel. None of the machinery was moving.

A door in the far wall opened, and a gaunt, gray-haired woman entered. She had a long face like her brother's and a mouth that looked as though it had never smiled.

"So you are the runaway girl," she said. "I'm Dame Dreng. I'll show you the rooms that must be cleaned and where the cleaning materials are. You must sweep and scrub the floors, dust the furniture, and wash the windows. Be sure to do it well!"

Trask left, and Dame Dreng gave Akara a list of detailed instructions. Then she, too, disappeared through the door she had entered by. Left alone, Akara shrugged off her uneasy feelings, dropped her bag in a corner, picked up a broom, and went to work. In addition to the big, open space where the milling was done, there were several smaller rooms that Akara was to clean. After sweeping these areas, she was to scrub the floors. For this, she needed water from the stream behind the mill. A door in the corner of the big room looked as though it would lead outside, and she picked up a pail and headed for it, carrying her blue bag with her.

She found herself in a level area behind the mill. Ahead, on the other side of this area, was a large millpond, and beyond it, rocky cliffs towered upward. The cliffs were broken by a deep gorge with vertical sides — a great gash running back into the mountain. Out of this gorge flowed the dark river that filled the pond.

To her left, Akara could see the top of a dam that held the water in the millpond. At its end closest to the mill was a lower section over which the water flowed out through some sort of channel, disappearing around the corner of the building. She guessed that this channel led to the mill wheel. A wooden fence extended from the mill across the top of the dam to the cliffs. To her right, a similar fence ran from the far corner of the mill past the pond to the cliff beyond, so that the area was completely enclosed.

The most striking feature of this scene was the gorge. She crossed the grassy area to the edge of the pond and stared at it. Its rock walls rose so high on each side that little light penetrated it. Far back in its depths, a black fog hung over the water. As she looked into it, Akara was suddenly fearful. She felt trapped between the dark gorge and the silent building behind. On an impulse, she reached down, slipped her hand into the bag, and drew out her silver trumpet.

At that moment there came a soft voice behind her. "Are you enjoying the view, Akara?"

She spun around. There, a short distance away, stood the miller! He was smiling slightly, though above the smile his eyes were watchful as they had been the night before. "I'm sorry if I startled you," he said. "I returned from the village earlier than I expected."

As he finished speaking, he caught sight of the trumpet in her hand. His face changed, but just as quickly, the new expression vanished and the small smile was back. "I didn't know you were a woman of the trumpet!"

Remembering the anger of the peddler when he first saw the trumpet, Akara spoke quickly. "I'm sorry!" she said. "I'll put it away."

She made a move toward her bag, but the miller's voice stopped her. "No, don't. I'm glad to see it. Trask didn't tell me about it."

"He doesn't like it. He says it's useless, and I must keep it out of sight."

"The peddler is a fool!" said the miller in the same soft voice. "He doesn't believe in the Great Powers. Come, sound your trumpet for me."

Akara hadn't the faintest idea what he meant by the 'Great Powers', and she certainly didn't intend to blow her trumpet for the miller. "It... it doesn't make any sound when I blow it."

The miller nodded. "It is good that you realize this. Some say it has a voice, but I doubt that this is so. Come, let us talk about it."

He came forward and seated himself at a stone bench near the water's edge that Akara had not previously noticed. In front of it was a stone table. The miller waved her to a place on the same bench. She sat down reluctantly. Both were now facing the pond.

Resting his hands, palms down, on the table, the miller stared across the water at the gorge. He spoke. "As one who carries the silver trumpet, Akara, you have been told that there is a powerful being known as the 'King'. You have been taught that through the trumpet you can call on him for help."

Akara had not, of course, been taught anything of the sort, but she thought it best to say nothing. The miller continued, "Part of what you have been told is true. There is such a being, but he is not as powerful as you think." He turned his head to look at her, a glint in his deep-set eyes. "Since you are honest enough to admit your trumpet is silent, you may also suspect that the stories about your King are exaggerated."

His eyes went back to the gorge. "Listen, then, to the truth," he said in a deeper voice. "The Dark Power whom I serve is the true ruler of the valley and is stronger than your King. I believe the water in the gorge flows from the home of the Dark Power, beneath the Great Mountains. It sinks into the ground beyond the road and mixes with the other waters of Broad Valley. The black fog guards the water's source."

He took a key from his belt, unlocked a small door beneath the stone table, and took out a box of dark polished wood, placed it on the stone table, opened it, and to Akara's surprise, lifted out another trumpet! It was almost twice the size of Akara's silver trumpet and was made of a dull gray metal. Dancing flecks of red, like sparks of fire, shone from it.

The trumpet bell bore the image of a snake's head, with the mouth open wide. The rest of the instrument was engraved with scales like those of a snake's body. The workmanship was beautiful, and Akara had a strong desire to touch it. At the same time, it repelled her.

The miller lifted it reverently. "The serpent is the sign of Broad Valley. Unlike your trumpet, this one does make music. Listen and watch!"

He put the trumpet to his lips and blew. Its tones were low and penetrating, and the strange melody he played both disturbed and attracted Akara. As it continued, she saw to her amazement that the black fog in the gorge swirled as though caught in a twisting wind! She watched, fascinated, until the tones ceased and the miller lowered the trumpet. The movement of the fog also subsided.

The miller wiped the instrument carefully with a cloth, replaced it in its box, put the box away, and turned to her. "I have shown you a little of my trumpet's power. There are other things for you to learn if you wish." He rose to his feet, turned abruptly, and walked toward the building.

Akara watched him go, her brain in a whirl. She was confused and terrified by what she had seen and heard. As the man moved on, she became aware that the silver trumpet, which she still held in her hand, was giving off a gentle warmth. At the same time, she felt an overwhelming urge to raise it to her lips and breathe through it.

She did so. At that instant, something unexpected happened! The miller's gliding walk faltered, and his body seemed to jerk to a stop, as though some invisible force had seized and held him. Only for a second did he halt, then he moved on at the same smooth pace. It seemed he had noticed nothing. However, as he reached the door into the building, he glanced over his shoulder. His eyes met Akara's and held for a brief moment, then he went on into the building.

The girl lowered the trumpet and stared wide-eyed after him. Had she seen his sudden halt, or only imagined it? If it did occur, was it possible that her trumpet call was the cause? Or could his foot simply have landed on an uneven bit of ground? She ran to the spot. It was smooth and level. There was no natural reason for the miller to stumble! Thoughtfully, she returned to where she had left her pail.

Although she was still confused, her terror was somehow gone. Akara filled the pail from the millpond, carried it to the building, and began scrubbing, determined to finish her work as soon as possible. She had seen more than enough of the miller! At noon, she paused only long enough for a few bites of bread and cheese and a drink from the water bottle, then went back to work. Just as she finished her tasks, she heard the peddler's wagon. She picked up her bag and ran quickly to meet him.

Trask had a brown earthenware jug beside him on the wagon seat, and his uncertain movements as he unhitched the horse suggested that he had been drinking something stronger than water. His manner as he greeted Akara was almost jovial. He even smiled when she told him she had finished the tasks Dame Dreng assigned her.

"No cooking for us tonight, girl," he said. "I brought hot food from the village. I'll build a fire while you get it ready."

In the back of the wagon, Akara found pots containing slices of hot meat, gravy, potatoes, and vegetables. She scooped some of each into their wooden bowls. There was also a fresh loaf of black bread from which she sliced several pieces.

Hungry after her hard day's work, Akara ate heartily. The peddler alternated bites of his food with sips from the brown jug. When the meal was finished, he settled himself with his back against a large log, the jug by his side and a pipe in his mouth. Akara cleaned up, then sat down on the other side of the fire.

The peddler looked at her shrewdly, then said, "You don't like it here, do you?" Without waiting for an answer, he went on, "Well, the miller is useful to me, but I don't like him either. We'll leave in the morning as soon as I collect the money you've earned."

A great weight was lifted from Akara's mind. Though her body ached from the hard day's work, she was happy as she crawled into her bed under the canvas cover.

In her mind she tried to sort out the things the miller told her. How much of what he said could she believe? She took the silver trumpet from her bag and breathed through it. Its deadness was entirely gone! Once again, she felt that someone was hearing her call. As she took it from her lips, a contented drowsiness crept over her. Her final thought before falling asleep was that, if there really was a Dark Power, she wanted nothing to do with it!

Chapter 7

On the Run

"Where's the girl?"

The quiet voice cut through Akara's confused dream. She awakened slowly and lay staring upward into the darkness, wondering if she had heard those words or just imagined them. Then the words came again, just as quietly, "Where's the girl?"

It was the miller's voice, and he was near at hand. Akara came fully awake. Taking care not to make a noise, she lifted the edge of the wagon cover and peered out. The fire had burned down to a few glowing coals, but she could see the shadowy form of the peddler, sitting where she had left him. On the other side of the fire stood another dim figure, the miller.

Trask spoke. His voice was also soft and the words were blurred. He had evidently been drinking from his jug freely. "She's in the wagon, asleep."

"You're drunk." The miller's voice was still low, but there was a harder edge to it.

"Just a little, just a little, but not enough that I can't count silver. Did you bring the money for the girl's work?"

"Be quiet! Yes, I have it, but I want to talk to you."

"Talk away. Did she work hard?"

"Yes, but that's not what I want to talk about. Let's walk over to the stream."

"Why not here?"

"Because I said so! I want to speak privately."

Grumbling, the peddler struggled to his feet, and the two figures disappeared into the darkness. Akara dropped the wagon cover and rested her head once more on her blue bag, which she used as a pillow. Since they were going to leave in the morning, she really didn't care what private things the miller and the peddler talked about. She breathed through her silver trumpet, then hugged it to her chest and waited for sleep to steal over her again.

As she relaxed her grip on the trumpet, it slid to the wagon bed with a soft thump. The noise jarred her awake again, and it was then that a disquieting thought struck her. If the miller wanted to talk privately, it must mean he didn't want Akara to hear. She was now fully alert. Perhaps he was going to talk about her. If so, she wanted to hear what he said!

Though she was afraid, she did not hesitate. She slipped quietly out of the wagon and set off in the direction the men had gone, her bare feet making no sound on the hard ground. Keeping the dark mass of the mill building to her right, she headed for the stream beyond it.

As she neared the water, she went more slowly. From somewhere ahead, she heard the murmur of voices, then she saw the glow from Trask's pipe. He and the miller had gone down a low bank and were standing near the water's edge. Her heart thumping, Akara crept toward them and crouched behind a bush at the top of the bank.

As her eyes grew accustomed to the darkness, she found she could make out the two forms. The miller was speaking, slowly and patiently. "I would think, peddler, that you'd be glad to get rid of the girl."

"Not really. There are houses up the valley where I can put her to work while I sell my wares. She brings in money that way."

"You're dreaming, Trask. You won't be able to keep her. If she ran away from the orphan home, she'll certainly run away from you!"

"She only ran away because the home doesn't keep them when they reach her age. Dame Dessit planned to give her to the person they call the 'Tall Woman'. The girl got frightened and hid in my wagon."

"The Tall Woman?" There was a change in the miller's voice.

"Do you know her?"

"I've heard of her. She's known by a different name here. What did she want with the girl?"

"I don't know." There was a short silence. Then the peddler said,

"Anyway I won't leave her here, and that's that. Just give me the money and we'll be off in the morning."

Akara, who had been holding her breath during the last few moments, breathed again. She was getting ready to tiptoe away when the miller spoke again. "You're being foolish, Trask. Someone may recognize her and you will be in trouble. Leave her here and I'll take the responsibility. I can use her to help in the mill." Trask's voice had lost its blur. His tone became angry. "I told you, no! I've decided to take her with me. And she doesn't want to stay."

For the first time, Akara heard the miller laugh, a soft laugh that somehow had no humor in it. "You're getting soft, Trask. What do Akara's wishes have to do with it? If money is your problem, I'll give you more than she'll earn for you."

"It wouldn't work. She'll surely run away from this place the first chance she gets."

"She won't run away. I'll make sure of that." The miller's words sent chills down Akara's back. He paused briefly, then went on. "I don't have to explain my reasons to you, Trask, but I will. I won't harm the girl, but she and that trumpet she carries are important to the Dark Power I serve. So she must stay!"

As the peddler remained silent, the miller continued. "You don't really want to refuse me, Trask. I'm the one who buys those silver cups and plates you pick up as you travel. I'm sure there are people in the valley who would like to know what happened to their property!"

Trask's voice was suddenly sober. "There's no call to talk like that. You are as guilty as I am. We've been partners in what I've done."

The miller laughed softly. "Maybe so, but people are more likely to believe an honest miller than a wandering peddler. His voice became cold and hard. "Look, Trask, I want to keep the girl and I'm going to! I can be generous and pay you, or call for my mill workers and take her without paying. Which shall it be?"

There was a long silence. When the peddler spoke again, his voice was low. "All right, I'll leave her. Maybe she'll be safer here than anywhere else." Then, after another pause, "How much money will you give me?"

Akara had heard enough. Sick at heart she turned quietly away. In the morning she'd be turned over to the miller and to the scary business of the Dark Power and the serpent trumpet! Then her courage returned. The men thought she was asleep. She had until morning to act! She must run away now and get as far from the mill as she could before morning!

She ran to the wagon, slipped on her shoes, and snatched up the silver trumpet, her cloak, her bag of belongings, and the leather bottle of water she had carried to the mill that day. The water bottle was only half full, but now there was no time to fill it. After a last glance toward the stream, she raced across the yard to the main road. There she paused under a large tree and listened. All was quiet. Trask and the miller were apparently still talking. She raised her little trumpet and breathed through it a plea for help and guidance. Then she tucked it into her bag, and considered what to do next. Her best plan, she decided, was to stay on the road, at least until daybreak. That meant either traveling south toward the orphan home, or toward the unknown north. The choice was an easy one. She began running swiftly northward!

Beyond the mill, the road passed through the village, a cluster of small houses. The windows of these houses seemed to stare at Akara as she ran past. She half expected at any moment to see a light spring up and to hear someone call out to her, and she breathed a sigh of relief when the last building was behind her and she was out in open countryside.

By this time the moon had risen, and the road stretched before her like a white ribbon. She ran on until she was out of breath, then changed her pace to a rapid walk. Her short sleep, together with the excitement of the escape, gave her energy, and for a while she did not feel tired. However, as the hours went by, her legs grew heavy and weariness overtook her. She stopped several times to sit by the side of the road, drink water, and rest, but each time, thoughts of the miller drove her to her feet and she began walking again.

At last she felt she could go no farther. Besides, morning was probably near, and she needed a place to hide. Ahead of her, another road crossed the one on which she traveled. Beyond this crossroads on the right was a wooded area that looked promising. She reached it, gave a last look behind her, climbed a bank, and made her way in among the trees. It was a pine wood, where the needles lay in a thick pad on the ground. She went far enough to be out of sight from the road, then dropped her bag at the base of a large pine tree. Wrapping herself in her cloak, she curled up on the cushion of pine needles and immediately fell asleep.

She awoke with the first gray light of morning. For a moment she wondered where she was, then memory came flooding back. Then she heard a sound that brought her fully awake. It was the clop, clop, clop of a horse's hooves, distant, but coming closer!

She picked up her bag and crawled forward on hands and knees until she could see the crossroads. There she dropped flat behind a small bush. It was that dusky time between night and morning, when even the shadows look strange. There was fog too, a bank of white mist that lay close to the ground along both of the roads.

She waited, her heart pounding, then she realized that the sounds came, not from the road up which she had come, but from the east–west road that crossed it. Someone was heading westward out into the valley. Soon there came into view a horse drawing a small cart. Its wheels were hidden in the mist, so that the cart itself seemed to float like a boat. There was only one occupant, a slender, hooded figure. Akara caught her breath. While carts and capes with hoods were not uncommon in the valley, to Akara's overwrought mind there was only one possibility. She was sure she was again looking at the Tall Woman! Frozen with fear, she watched as the cart and its hooded figure moved smoothly through the crossroads and disappeared westward.

Akara breathed again. She was about to get to her feet, when she again heard hoofbeats, faster ones, coming up the road from the south. A moment later she recognized the rattle of the peddler's wagon. Then out of the mist they came, the old horse going at a trot! On the wagon seat were two figures: a short one, Trask of course, and a taller one, the miller! The miller was leaning forward, and while Akara could not see his eyes, she was sure he was scanning the road ahead!

She held her breath until they passed. Afterward, she lay motionless for a time, then rose shakily to her feet. With both of her enemies abroad, how could she be safe on any of the valley roads? Panic seized her! She picked up her bag, turned, and plunged deeper into the woods!

CHAPTER 8

A Fortuitous Encounter

The ground under the trees was too uneven for running, but Akara's fear drove her on at a fast walk. She climbed hills, and slid down steep slopes. She grew tired and when the sun rose, its rays made her uncomfortably warm. Her water bottle was empty and she was thirsty.

She stumbled across a path that ran generally in the direction she was traveling and decided to follow it. A path usually leads somewhere. But this path twisted and turned, in no hurry to reach its destination. Finally she decided she could go no farther. She found a grassy spot under a tree near the path, dropped down, and almost instantly fell asleep.

A noise awakened her. She opened her eyes. There, a few feet away, stood a dark-haired, dark-eyed girl about her own age who was carrying a bundle of sticks.

She smiled at Akara. "I'm sorry if I startled you."

Akara scrambled to her feet. "That's all right, I hadn't meant to sleep. I was lost and tired and thirsty, and I just stopped here to rest."

"Maybe I can help. My name is Linka, but people call me Blink. My cabin is near here. I can give you water, and point you in the direction you want to go."

Akara gave an inward sigh of relief. She introduced herself, then picked up her bag and followed her new acquaintance. After a few moments, Blink turned off the path into a little clearing, in the middle of which stood a log cabin. On the ground in front of it sat a small boy playing with some stones, who looked up at them, surprised, as they approached. Blink waved a hand in his direction. "This is my brother, Baslin. Baslin, this is our new friend, Akara."

Akara greeted the boy, who smiled and ducked his head shyly.

"Baslin doesn't talk much," said Blink as she led the way into the cabin.

The room inside had a dirt floor. There was a stone fireplace, a wooden cupboard in one corner, a large chest in another, and in the center, an old table and four wooden chairs. Blink put down her bundle of sticks near the fireplace. She got a cup from the cupboard, filled it with water from a wooden pail, and gave it to Akara, who drank gratefully.

"It is almost time for lunch," said Blink. "You must stay and eat with us."

Akara was hungry, but from the bare appearance of the cabin she suspected that food was not in plentiful supply. She shook her head. "I couldn't take your food. I'll just rest a few minutes and go on my way."

Blink pulled a covered basket from the cupboard. "We have enough. A farmer who lives nearby gives us food. Please stay."

Having not eaten since the previous night, Akara was hungry, and with only a brief hesitation, accepted the invitation. Blink opened the basket and set out a wedge of cheese, a loaf of bread, and three red apples. She refilled Akara's empty cup, poured water into two other ones, and called Baslin to the table.

While they were eating, Akara tried to talk to Baslin but had little success. He kept his eyes on his plate and answered her questions in as few words as possible. She learned he was six years old, but not much else. As soon as the meal was over, he slipped outside again to play.

When he had gone, Blink said, "Now tell me where you're headed, Akara, and I'll try to give you directions."

"Thank you very much for the lunch. I'm...I'm traveling north."

"Well, we're on the east side of the valley in the foothills of the Great Mountains. The main valley road lies west of here. If you go west, you'll come to it."

"I want to stay off the main road. Are there any other trails north?"

Blink looked at her thoughtfully. "There's an old road that winds north through the foothills. Look, Akara, I don't want to pry into your business, but if you're in trouble, I'd like to help."

Akara hesitated. She had not intended to talk about herself, but Blink's kindness made her feel she could trust this new friend. "Thank you," she said. "I don't know that anyone can help, but if you have time to listen, I'll tell you about my problem."

At Blink's suggestion, the two girls carried chairs outside and sat together in the sunshine while Akara told her story. "So you see," she said when she had finished, "I'm not quite sure where I'm going or how to get there. If I can reach a town far enough north to be safe from both the miller and the Tall Woman, I'll stop there and try to find work. So if you'll point me toward the old road you told me about, I'll be on my way."

Blink chuckled. "Your eyelids have been drooping for the last ten minutes, Akara. If you leave now, you'll fall asleep again under the first big tree you come to. I've got an idea that may help, but first, you need a good nap. When you wake up, we can talk some more."

Akara was reluctant to impose further on Blink's hospitality, but she realized she needed sleep. She followed the other girl into the cabin and through another doorway to a small back room.

"As you see," said Blink, "our beds are two piles of straw, each covered with a blanket. Not elegant, but the best we have. Use either one."

Akara again thanked her, sank gratefully onto one of the straw beds, and was soon fast asleep.

When she awoke, it was late in the afternoon, and the rays of the sun were slanting through the small window. A moment later, Blink put her head through the doorway.

"I was afraid you were going to sleep right through the evening," she said cheerfully. "Time for another meal. I have made us some soup."

Akara scrambled to her feet. "I'm going to have to leave soon, if I'm going to get some traveling done before dark," she said.

Blink came farther into the room. "Please don't go now, Akara. You're safe here, and I really want you to stay tonight. I enjoy having someone my own age to talk to. Besides, I have a plan I want you to hear."

Blink's soup, made with fresh vegetables, was tasty and nourishing, and Akara again ate heartily. Later, after they had washed the bowls and spoons, and Baslin had gone to bed, the two girls sat in front of the fire, sipping from mugs of hot tea.

"We work well together," said Blink with a satisfied sigh. She gave Akara a sidelong glance. "That's good, because I think it would be great if the three of us travel north together."

"You are planning to travel? But I thought..."

"I know, you thought this cabin was our home. It isn't really. We're here temporarily."

"Where is your home?"

Blink stared into the fire for a moment, then said soberly, "We don't have one. Until recently, Baslin and I lived on a farm near here. My mother died shortly after Baslin was born, leaving my father, Baslin, and me. Then my father became ill and died three months ago."

Blink swallowed several times before continuing. "After he died, we learned that he owed a lot of money. The farm was taken away from us and sold to pay the debt."

"That must have been awful for you."

"Yes, but one of our kind neighbors loaned us this cabin to live in. He and other neighbors give us food, so we're well taken care of. But we can't stay here forever. My father once told me that if anything happened to him, Baslin and I should find his cousin who lives north of here, near the village of Midra. He said this cousin would help us. I've been putting off leaving this little cabin, but I think now is a good time."

Blink's face was back to its usual cheery expression. "So you see," she concluded, "it is a good thing I found you. You're traveling north to get away from someone, and Baslin and I must travel north to find someone." She paused to take a final swallow of tea. "It makes sense to go together."

"That's kind of you, but remember, I have enemies. Trask and the miller are after me, and maybe the Tall Woman too! If we travel together and one of them finds me, you or Baslin may be hurt."

"Nonsense!" Blink jumped to her feet. "Traveling will be more fun for Baslin and me if you're with us. If we follow the old road through the foothills, no one will catch us. Besides, the Tall Woman may have forgotten all about you by this time. As for your peddler and your miller, I have my father's oak walking stick, and we'll find a strong stick for you.

If they find us, we'll beat them off!"

At the thought of the two of them attacking the miller with sticks, Akara burst out laughing, and Blink joined her. Akara put down her empty mug and threw up her hands in mock surrender. "All right. We'll go together. I will certainly enjoy traveling with you and Baslin. I'll be ready to leave whenever you say."

"Good! That's settled." Blink sat down again. "Now it's time for bed. We must bring straw in from the shed and make a third bed in the back room. As for when we leave, I talked it over with Baslin while you were sleeping. We'll start tomorrow."

That night after the others were asleep, Akara lay on her bed of straw and thought about all that had happened during the past twenty-four hours. On the night before, at about this time, Trask was bartering her away to the miller. Now she was free, she had found two new friends, Blink and Baslin, and she was ready to set out on a journey which would hopefully let her keep that freedom.

As she thought over her latest escape, she realized that the silver trumpet had helped her. Its quiet thump on the wagon floor had awakened her, and blowing through it had calmed her and maybe even guided her in the right direction. She slipped it from her blue bag, raised it to her lips, and breathed a message of thanks through it. She was glad it made no noise, for she had no wish to disturb her sleeping friends.

As she finished, there ran through her mind a memory of the strains of music that had come to her that night under the bush at the orphan home. This time, while she heard no music, and saw no moving figures, she felt that the darkness around her was warm and comforting.

CHAPTER 9

The Journey Begins

When Akara awoke the next morning, the room was empty. Both Blink and Baslin were already up. Blink appeared in the doorway as she was putting the silver trumpet into her bag.

"Is that the horn you were telling me about?" she asked.

"Yes."

"May I look at it?"

Akara handed the instrument to her friend, who examined it curiously. After asking Akara's permission, she put it to her lips and blew through it, then compressed her lips and puffed vigorously. "It's just as you said. I can blow air through it, but it closes up when I try to get it to play." She handed it back to Akara. "It's a tiny thing, isn't it? It's hard to believe people think it has magic power. Perhaps it's meant to be a toy."

Akara did not reply, but her shock at hearing her precious trumpet called a toy must have shown in her face, for Blink said quickly, "I'm sorry, I shouldn't have said that."

"That's all right," answered Akara, but Blink's remark bothered her, and she quickly put the trumpet into her bag.

After breakfast, Blink went to a wooden chest in the corner and brought back several armfuls of clothing that she spread out on the table. "Baslin and I will carry only one change of clothes apiece. I've already set aside what we will take for ourselves. Since you and I are about the same size, I hope you will take whatever you want from this pile to replace your orphan-home clothes. We'll leave the rest behind. I'm sure the family who loaned us the cabin will be able to use these clothes."

Blink's clothes were of the serviceable homespun material used throughout Broad Valley, and fitted Akara well. There was a large selection, and she was happy to discard all of her own well-worn things, including her ragged cloak, and replace them from Blink's stock.

Then Blink reached into the bottom of the chest and brought out what Akara recognized as a backpack. This type of cloth bag, fitted with straps and worn on the back, was popular among valley folk. "Baslin and I each have one of these," said Blink. "I suggest you use this one to carry your things in instead of your blue bag. It will leave your hands free."

"Fine," said Akara. "I can fold my blue bag and store it in the backpack."

Blink and Baslin made a quick trip across the fields to say farewell to the farm family who helped them. Then they began packing, Baslin proudly helping to load his own small pack. The girls divided the food and cooking utensils between them. These would not fit in their backpacks, so each of the girls carried her share in a small sack tied on to her pack. Finally they swept out the cabin for the last time.

Akara wanted to breathe through her trumpet before leaving, asking for protection and guidance, but Blink's earlier remark about the trumpet's looking like a toy still bothered her. Of course, Blink would be too polite to make fun of her about it, but Akara didn't want to risk being laughed at, even secretly. So she waited until both Blink and Baslin were occupied with packing, then slipped into the back room and blew through it there.

When departure time came, Blink led the way across the clearing and into the woods, her father's oak stick in her hand. Baslin followed, and Akara brought up the rear. Blink had cut a similar stick for Akara from an oak branch found in the woods, and Baslin carried his own small walking stick. A short walk brought them to a broad path that ran in a north–south direction.

Blink turned northward. "This is the Old Trail," she explained. "We probably won't see many others on it, though I've been told that it was once well traveled. In these days most travelers go between villages in carts or wagons so they stay on the main roads."

The weather was sunny and pleasant, and the trail was mostly broad enough so they could walk abreast. Baslin was excited about the journey, and during the first hour, was forever running ahead or stopping to investigate something by the side of the road. Later, he settled into a steadier pace. Twice during the morning they met southbound travelers, and these folk greeted them pleasantly. They stopped briefly for lunch, and that evening camped on a grassy hill near the path. There they built a fire and cooked a light supper before rolling themselves in their cloaks. Akara waited until her companions slept, then blew through her trumpet before going to sleep herself. As usual, it brought her comfort, but she felt guilty about doing so secretly.

The second day's travel was equally pleasant. That night they camped beside a stream, where they refilled their water bottles.

"We'll need more food soon," Akara remarked as they broke camp the next morning.

"We should reach the village of Elsis tomorrow. It's on the main valley road, but the trail we're on runs close enough so we can cut across. We'll buy supplies there."

Sure enough, at noon on the following day they came to the crest of a small hill, from which they could see the red roofs and white walls of Elsis. They could also see the line of the main valley road, which ran past it on the western side.

Blink swept her eyes across the scene. "It's a nice little village. I was here once with my father." She turned to Akara. "I suppose it's possible Trask and the miller have come this far north looking for you. Perhaps you should wait here while Baslin and I go into the village and buy food."

Akara shook her head. "No, I'm not going to be afraid every time we come to a new village. Besides we can run away if we have to. Let's all go together."

Blink nodded and led the way forward. They entered the village cautiously, looking carefully up and down each street before showing themselves. All seemed quiet. They found a small shop where they bought biscuits, cheese, fruit and vegetables, and some dried meat. They stored these away in their bags, left the store, and headed back the way they had come.

At first, all went well. Then, as they turned a corner, Akara stopped in her tracks and grasped Blink's arm. There directly ahead and walking toward them in the narrow street, was the peddler, Trask!

Chapter 10

Pursued!

There was no doubt Trask was as surprised as Akara. He stopped a short distance away and stood staring at her, though his face did not change its expression. Then he broke the silence.

"Hello, Akara. The miller is looking for you!"

No one other than the peddler was in sight, so Akara felt in no immediate danger. She said nothing, but Blink, who recognized Trask from Akara's description, answered angrily. "Akara has friends, peddler. Stand aside and let us pass!"

The man gave a short laugh. "That won't help. The miller's men are here in Elsis. They'll catch you."

Blink's words had roused Akara, and she too became angry. "Why! Why won't the miller leave me alone?" she said angrily. "And why must you help him?" Then, as the peddler was silent, she went on, "It's because he knows about the bad things you've done, isn't it? You're afraid of him!"

Trask shrugged his shoulders. "So the miller was right. You listened to our talk that night by the stream. But that isn't why he's chasing you. He thinks you and that trumpet of yours will give him special power of some sort." He shrugged again. "Anyway, he's determined to find you."

Akara straightened her shoulders. "The miller's men may find me, but they'll have to drag me back. Move aside!"

Blink took Baslin's hand. "We've talked enough," she said. "Let's go ahead, Akara. He can't stop us."

As they started toward him, Trask spoke again in a different tone. "I won't try to stop you, but if you go down this street you'll run into the miller's men." He pointed to a narrow opening on one side of the street, halfway between himself and where Akara and her friends stood. "Take that lane. It will lead you to open country."

Blink was instantly on guard. "He's trying to trap you, Akara!"

The peddler gave another of his short laughs. "Believe me or not, I'm trying to help you. I've told you I don't like the miller, and I don't owe him anything. I hope you can get away from him. That lane is your best chance to escape. Farmers drive their cattle into the village that way, but it should be clear now."

He sounded sincere, and Akara made up her mind quickly. She nodded to the old man. "All right, we'll go — and thank you, Trask."

The three friends ran to the entrance of the lane. Akara saw that it was narrow and bounded by high stone walls on each side. It sloped gently downward, and at its far end was the green of open fields. "It looks good," said Blink. "Let's go!"

But even as she spoke the picture changed. "Look Blink," Baslin called out. "Look at the cows!"

A mass of dark bodies was moving into the far end of the lane. It was a herd of cattle on their way to pens in the village. The jostling forms of the big beasts filled the narrow way from side to side and surged toward them, shutting out the view of the fields beyond.

Akara shook her head. "We'll never be able to get past them," she said. "We'll have to take our chances the other way."

But at that moment, there came a new voice. "Say, peddler! Isn't that the girl we're looking for?"

Two rough-looking men had appeared in the street behind the peddler and were striding toward him. Akara saw that the expressionless mask was back on Trask's face. Her shoulders sagged.

Baslin clutched his sister's hand. "Blink, what will we do?" he whispered. Blink drew him close.

"You two, run!" Akara spoke urgently, her eyes on the advancing men. "It's me the miller wants."

Blink shook her head. "We're friends and we're in this together!"

By this time, the two new arrivals had come to where the peddler stood. One called out, "Hey, girl! The miller of Arn wants you. You can't get away. If you try to run, we'll catch you."

Tears stung Akara's eyes. There was no way out! Then, deep inside her, a quiet voice spoke, *The silver trumpet, Akara! Blow the trumpet!*

The words came to her clearly, though no one had spoken them aloud. Strangely, the first thing that flashed into Akara's mind was that Blink thought the silver trumpet looked like a toy. How foolish she would appear to Blink, Trask, and the miller's men if she were to stand in the street blowing through a tiny horn!

She hesitated, but the inner voice came again, more insistently, *The trumpet, Akara!*

Akara waited no longer. She set her jaw, plunged a hand into her bag, and pulled out the silver trumpet. Ignoring Blink's surprised look, she raised it to her lips.

As usual, there was no sound as she blew, but her act brought a response from the miller's men. "What's she doing?" said one. His companion laughed. "It's a horn. Listen, girl! No horn is going to help you! Give up and come quietly."

Akara herself did not expect anything to change. But as she slipped the trumpet back into her bag, she found her head turning again to the narrow lane. Her eyes were drawn to a spot along one wall. There, previously unnoticed, was a break in the stone, a small archway. Hope exploded in her mind! If the three of them could run fast enough to reach the archway before the advancing cattle, they might stay there safely until the last of the big beasts passed. Then they could race down the lane toward the open country and possibly, just possibly, escape!

There was no time to lose! She spoke quietly, so that only Blink and Baslin could hear. "Quick, let's run for that archway!" she said.

Blink's eyes followed hers, and her sharp mind grasped Akara's plan. "Right!" she said. Then, still holding her brother's hand, she said, "Come, Baslin, let's run!"

They turned and raced down the lane. Behind them they heard shouts as their enemies ran toward the lane entrance. As the three friends drew near the herd, a young man walking a few paces ahead of it waved his staff.

"Go back!" he shouted. "You'll be trampled!"

"Please!" Akara called back. "We have to reach the archway."

The young man's eyes flicked past them to the miller's men, who had turned the corner and now came shouting down the lane. Then he glanced to his right at the opening that was almost beside him. With a nod, he lowered his staff, and the three raced past him.

They tumbled into the recess just ahead of the first bull, who snorted, but otherwise paid them no attention as he surged ahead. Before his bulky body shut out the view, Akara was able to throw a quick look back up the lane. The miller's men were coming on.

"Out of the way, boy!" she heard one of them shout.

The young man had his staff up again. "You can't pass! The cattle must go through."

The noise of the passing herd prevented her from hearing more. However the steady movement of large bodies past the opening assured her that they were safe for the moment. Baslin, his fear gone, was laughing delightedly. Blink turned toward the rear of the shallow recess.

"There's a door here," she said, "and it's not locked. Let's go in."

Akara quickly agreed. She realized that the miller's men would certainly rush down the lane as soon as the cattle had passed. The door offered them another possibility of escape. Blink turned the handle and pushed. With a squeak of rusty hinges, the door swung open and the three friends passed through, closing the door behind them.

They found themselves in a large walled garden. Around them were grassy areas, shade trees, and well-tended flower beds. No human beings were in sight. To their right, the ground sloped downward to the back of a large stone house.

The girls looked at each other. "Perhaps there's no one home," whispered Blink.

Akara wrinkled her forehead. "Whether there is or not, we must get past the house and out of the village."

Blink put her arm around Baslin. "We may have to run some more, Bas. But first we're going to go quietly past the house."

The boy nodded, then the three went quickly down the slope and through the narrow passage between the house and the wall. They emerged onto a grassy lawn. This sloped downward to another wall that apparently marked the front of the property. Beyond it, they could see trees and bushes and farther away, a wooded hill.

But as they cleared the corner of the house, their flight came to a sudden stop. There, seated on chairs under a large shade tree, were three people, who stared at them in surprise. Akara, who was in the lead, hesitated an instant, undecided whether to race on past the group or to seek their help. Then one of them, a tall, gray-haired man, got to his feet. Akara gave a joyful cry. There before her stood Wenk the Wanderer!

CHAPTER 11

Wenk's Plan

Wenk's face broke into a smile, and he came quickly forward. "It's the girl who pulled me from the river!" he exclaimed, taking both of her hands. "Your name's Akara, isn't it?"

The sight of Wenk's friendly face eased Akara's fears. She gave him an answering smile. "Yes, and it's wonderful to see you again. We're sorry to burst in here, but my friends and I are running from some evil men. The cattle were coming up the lane and blocking it, so we came through the gate into your garden. We'd like to go on out your other gate, if you'll let us."

"The house and gardens aren't mine, Akara," said Wenk. "They belong to my friends, Adkar and Ortha. I am only their guest, but whoever your pursuers are, I'm sure you will be safe here." He inclined his head toward the couple who had risen and now joined him. "May I present Akara, a young woman who once saved my life."

Adkar and Ortha were both gray-haired. He was squarely built, while his wife was slender and graceful. Adkar spoke, "Welcome. Please sit down. You are indeed safe here. And if you tell us about your trouble, we may be able to help."

He turned his head toward the house. "Hais!" he called sharply.

A man appeared in the doorway. "What do you want, sir?"

"Hais, go quickly and bar all of our gates beginning with the back gate leading to the lane."

Hais disappeared. Akara introduced Blink and Baslin, then Wenk pulled the chairs into a circle and the group sat down. Baslin, shy in the presence of adults, sat on the ground at Blink's feet.

Wenk looked inquiringly at Akara. "Now tell us — who is chasing you?"

"Men who serve a person called 'the miller.'"

Ortha gave an exclamation. "The miller of Arn? I know he was here in our village, but I thought he left." She turned to Adkar. "Didn't he say he was hunting a runaway granddaughter?"

"Yes, and he asked the village leaders to assist him," added Adkar. "I don't trust the miller myself, but some of the other council members agreed to help him. There are some wild young men in our village he may have hired."

Wenk said, "I know nothing of all this, though I have heard of the miller of Arn. I'm surprised that his men are chasing you three young people."

"I'm the one he is after," said Akara. "But I'm certainly not his granddaughter. I'm an orphan, and I ran away from the orphan home in Palloweth."

"Good for you," put in Wenk heartily.

Akara acknowledged his remark with a smile. "Trask the peddler let me travel north in his wagon. I worked in homes along the way to pay for my food. We stopped at the mill in Arn, and the miller tried to force me to stay there. I ran away again, met Blink and Baslin, and here we are."

"Why is the miller determined to find you?" asked Ortha.

"I'm not sure. He is a strange old man who worships an invisible force he calls the 'Dark Power'. He wants me somehow to help him in this worship."

Blink said, "I don't know this miller, but I'm sure he's an evil man. The story about hunting a granddaughter must be something he made up so people will help him find Akara."

Adkar nodded soberly. "All of this fits with the little I know about him. Well, we will be happy to have all of you stay here tonight. We're certainly able to defy the miller or anyone else."

"Yes," said Ortha. "You'll be safe from the miller here."

Wenk had been listening intently. Now he said, "Your offer is generous, but I think it might be better to get these young people out of the village before the miller learns where they are. I don't doubt your ability to protect them, but the trouble can be avoided if they leave now."

"But they could be caught," said Adkar. "The miller's men may watch the roads!"

Wenk nodded. "You are right, and that's why they shouldn't use the roads. I'll go with them. You have invited me to stay here tonight, but I hope you will excuse me."

Wenk pointed down the slope. "Your house is on the northern edge of the village, and north is the direction they want to go. We can easily slip across the road at the bottom of your garden into the woods, climb the hill north of the village before sundown, and camp there tonight."

After a little more discussion, Adkar reluctantly agreed. But Akara objected. "Thank you, Wenk, but you mustn't leave your friends on our account. Just point us in the right direction and we'll find our way."

Wenk shook his head. "I know this area well, which you do not. Besides," he added with a smile, "I seem to remember that you once went out of your way to pull me out of a river. You must let me return the favor."

Akara had no choice but to accept, which she did gratefully. Blink woke Baslin, who had fallen asleep, and Wenk went into the house to get his pack and traveling cloak. Meanwhile, Hais reappeared with mugs of chilled fruit juice for the travelers. Also, Ortha insisted on increasing their supply of food with some choice items from her own larder.

Thanks and good-byes were said, then Wenk led the travelers down the slope to the gate below the house. A narrow road ran behind the property, and he checked it in both directions to make sure the way was clear. Then, at Wenk's signal, the little group dashed across it into the woods beyond.

A short walk among the trees took them to the foot of the hill, where they found a path leading upward. The climb was steep and for the last part, Wenk carried Baslin on his shoulders. At the top, the Wanderer called a halt, and the travelers thankfully dropped their packs on the grass.

Blink shaded her eyes and looked out over the valley. "You can see a great deal from here," she said.

"That's why I chose this place." The Wanderer swung Baslin down to the ground. "We can camp here and keep an eye on the village while we plan your journey north. I don't think the miller will press his search north of Elsis. In the morning, I'll show you a safe route north, a path that runs between the main valley road and the Old Trail through the foothills. It will take you to the next village."

Baslin tugged at Blink's arm. "Are we going to eat soon?" he asked softly. "I'm hungry."

"That's what we'll do now," Wenk told him. "You can help me build a fire over near those trees, Baslin, where neither the light nor the smoke can be seen from the village." He turned to the girls. "If the miller's men come this way, it won't be until morning, but I'll keep watch tonight anyway."

They moved to the spot Wenk had suggested, and he soon had a brisk fire going, using sticks that Baslin collected. Blink and Akara unpacked the food, and they all enjoyed a hot meal.

While they were eating, Wenk made two trips to the edge of the hill to survey the village. He returned the second time with news. "There's a man coming in this direction. He's alone so there's nothing to worry about. I'll meet him at the crest of the hill and find out who he is."

He strode away, but soon returned, wearing a smile and bringing with him someone whom both Blink and Akara recognized. It was the young man they had encountered earlier with the cattle herd.

"This is Skey," said Wenk. "Adkar sent him to us. He tells me he has already met you three."

"Yes," said Akara. "And we want to thank you for letting us go past you in the lane."

Skey grinned. "It wasn't a hard decision to make. I was sure those fellows chasing you were up to no good."

"Were they angry with you afterward?" asked Blink.

"They cursed a bit, but that was all. When they realized they couldn't get past the cattle, they left. I was curious about you, so after we got the cattle bedded down, I went to Adkar and Ortha's house. Adkar is a close friend of my father. They told me something of your problems."

"What made you decide to come up here?" asked Wenk.

"Adkar told me where you were camped. He was concerned that the men might try to follow you tonight, so I went back to the town square and listened to conversations. The miller wasn't there, but one of his men, Ruddle, said the miller is trying to find a runaway granddaughter. He offered money to anyone willing to join the hunt. Two search parties will start out early tomorrow morning. One of them may visit this hill."

"I'm the person the miller is looking for," Akara said, "but I'm not his granddaughter."

"I believe you," said Skey.

"Did anyone see you leave to come here?" asked Wenk.

"I'm sure no one did."

Wenk nodded his satisfaction. "Good, but just the same, I plan to keep watch tonight."

Skey reached behind him and brought into view a rolled-up blanket. "I came prepared to stay the night. I hope also you'll let me share the watch with you."

"Thank you, I'll be glad to have your help."

Akara and Blink both volunteered to take parts of the watch duty, but Wenk refused. "You two and Baslin have a long hike ahead of you tomorrow, so it's important that you sleep tonight."

Later that evening Akara and Wenk sat alone by the fire. Skey had volunteered to take the first watch and was out at the crest of the hill. Blink and Baslin had gone to bed.

Wenk said, "I'm glad you decided to sit with me for a while. I don't plan to sleep. You told us a little about your adventures earlier. Is there more you can tell me?"

"Yes, and there are some things I especially want to talk to you about."

Wenk put another piece of wood on the fire. "Good! I'm ready to listen."

CHAPTER 12

Conversation Around the Campfire

It was a perfect night for a campfire. The air was cool and pleasant. The moon had risen high enough to shine into the clearing where Wenk and Akara sat, touching the trees with silver. From the little fire, gray smoke spiraled upward into the darkness. The girl was perched on a log, her arms around her knees. Across the fire sat the Wanderer, his long legs stretched out toward the fire. Akara felt relaxed and safe. Tonight Wenk and Skey would keep watch, and tomorrow she, with Blink and Baslin, would strike out northward, away from the miller and his men.

Wenk listened intently as Akara gave him a more detailed account of her travels. Then he said, "Thank you for telling me. That's quite a story! Were there other things you wanted to talk about?"

"Yes. About the silver trumpet you gave me."

She reached into her bag and pulled out her trumpet. Wenk took it from her gently and examined it, turning it over in his big hands, then passed it back to her. "I'm glad you still have it. Has it brought you good fortune?"

"I think it has been the cause of some good things that have happened, but I'm not really certain. I hope you can help me."

Wenk leaned forward to put a stick on the fire. "I'm not sure I can. You may remember I had no success with the trumpet, but I'll be glad to listen."

Akara felt she could safely confide in Wenk. She put the trumpet back in her bag and sat silent for a moment, gathering her thoughts. "My first chance to use the trumpet was at night, under the big bush in the front yard of Dame Dessit's home." She described her vision of the moving figures and the strange music. Then she told him of her other experiences with the trumpet, finishing with her trumpet call earlier that day on the street in Elsis.

During this recital, Wenk sat quietly, his eyes fixed on the fire. When she finished, he said, "You are a brave girl, Akara, and I admire you. You've had some scary times, and I'm glad the little trumpet was useful."

"Do you think it really helped, or did I just imagine that it did?"

"I can't be certain, any more than you can, Akara. I know it's easy for us to believe something we want to believe. Let's think for a few minutes about those times when you used the trumpet."

He leaned forward to put another stick on the fire. "The first experience you told me about was at night under the bush at the orphan home. I have no idea what the music and moving figures meant, but they were something you weren't expecting."

"Yes, but I know I could just have imagined those things."

"That's true, but it happened, so we'll count it. Then there were three other things you said you noticed about the trumpet. Breathing through the trumpet comforted you when you felt discouraged; it cooled your anger when you were upset with Dame Dessit; and it gave you a feeling that you were sending a message through it to some invisible person."

"I hadn't counted them up like that, but you're right. About the last one, I didn't know who heard the trumpet call, but I felt it was someone who cared for me. I had never felt cared for before."

Wenk nodded understandably. "Then you told me that during your travels with Trask you neglected your trumpet. When you tried to use it again, it seemed to have become dead."

"Yes, it was like losing a close friend. I felt terrible about it, but when I asked forgiveness, the connection seemed to come back again."

"It's possible you did imagine all of those things about the trumpet. But it is harder to explain away what happened when you blew through the trumpet at Arn and Elsis. At the mill in Arn, it seemed to stop the miller in his tracks, and when you used it at Elsis, it guided you to the gate through which you escaped from the miller's men!"

Wenk paused for a moment, then continued. "I'm naturally a skeptic, so I really don't want to believe that your trumpet is any more than a little piece of metal. However, I have to admit that, taken together, those seven experiences of yours are impressive." He leaned forward again to replenish the fire, then gave her a friendly grin. "I think it's time I told you what the King's Book says about this kind of trumpet!"

"The King's Book?" Akara was puzzled.

"Yes." Wenk leaned back into a more comfortable position. "I'm not an expert on that book, Akara. I know about it and have read parts of it, but that was long ago. It is a very ancient book, and you can find copies gathering dust in some valley homes. Some say the story it tells is a fairy tale; others believe it is the true history of the valley. I favor the first view, but I'm not sure which is right."

"And this book talks about trumpets like mine?"

"Yes."

"Please tell me about it."

"Well, first of all, the book tells of an invisible being called the 'King'."

"That must be the person the miller told me about!"

Wenk nodded. "Part of what the miller told you agrees with the King's Book. Part does not. According to the book, this King is the true ruler of the valley. However, it also says that while the King is good, evil entered the valley long ago, and as a result, the people rebelled against the King. This evil might be the Dark Power the miller told you about, I don't know.

"Anyway, the book goes on to say that the King himself came to the valley long ago. He became a humble worker with wood and was known as the 'Good Carpenter'. He traveled through the valley pleading with people to turn from evil."

"Did they listen to him?"

"According to the book, they were too much under the influence of the evil power. They killed him."

Akara was shocked. "They killed the King? How could that happen?"

"I'm not certain. Remember, it's been many years since I read the King's Book. But according to the story, he rose from the dead. He came back to life."

"What did he do then?"

"He went away from the valley, but he left behind men and women who believed in him. They became known as 'Soldiers of the King.'"

The fire showed signs of dying down, and Wenk interrupted his story to add more wood, then he continued. "Even now there are people living in the Great Mountains who call themselves 'Soldiers of the King.'"

"Do you know any of them?"

"I've met a few of them traveling in the valley, but I know little about them except I've heard they carry trumpets that look like yours."

"Does the King's Book say anything about the trumpets?"

"Yes. As I remember, the book says that the King gave his followers trumpets on which they could call to him. I suspect these trumpets may be like the one I gave you."

Akara thought this over. "But even if all that is true, I'm not a follower of the King. I'd never heard of him until the miller mentioned his name. Yet, the trumpet seems to help me anyway. Why?"

Wenk stared soberly at the fire. "I don't know. Let's suppose what the book says is true. I can understand why the trumpet wouldn't work for me. You see, I knew the story and didn't really believe it. On the other hand, while you didn't know anything about the trumpet, you were ready to accept its help. Maybe that made a difference."

Akara sighed. "There are so many questions, and I wish I had answers. Don't you want to learn more about these things, Wenk?"

"I don't think so, Akara. Perhaps I'm too old to change, but I enjoy my life the way it is now. My destiny seems to be wandering, and I'm content with my destiny."

He tilted his head back to watch the gray smoke of the campfire as it curled upward. "See those stars, Akara? Away from the lights of the village, they seem especially bright. When my travel for the day is finished, and my campfire has died to coals, I lie back and look up at them. They are calm and not troubled by the things that distress us. Someone made them, just as someone made this valley with its hills and woods and streams. Perhaps that someone is the King the old book tells about. If so, I hope he will not be angry with me if, instead of seeking him, I am content to enjoy his stars."

Wenk rose to his feet, stretched, then extended a hand to Akara and helped her up. "And now it's time for me to relieve Skey."

He turned to leave, but Akara put her hand on his sleeve. There was something else she felt she must say. She swallowed hard. "Wenk, the silver trumpet came to you first. Perhaps if you had not given it to me, it would, sooner or later, have given you the same comfort and peace it has brought to me. Will you take it now as a gift from me and try it again?"

The Wanderer looked down into her earnest face. For a long moment he was silent. Then he said, "Thank you, my dear, I know what the trumpet means to you, and your offer makes me feel very humble. But it is not necessary. The silver trumpet is yours.

"You see, Akara, I know myself," Wenk continued. "If I took back the silver trumpet, it would probably lie in the bottom of my pack, unused." His face broke into a sudden grin and he added, "Unless, of course, I found another orphan to give it to!"

He turned, and in a few moments his tall figure was swallowed up by the darkness. Akara stared after him. What a wonderful person the Wanderer was. And how fortunate she was to know him. With that thought in mind, she turned from the fire and made her way to bed.

CHAPTER 13

Midra

Akara awoke in the dawn to find Baslin shaking her shoulder. "Wake up, Akara!" he said. "Blink and Wenk are making breakfast, and I've been gathering sticks for the fire." "Thank you, Baslin." Akara sat up and gave him a hug. After he left, she threw off her blanket, took a few moments to blow through her trumpet, and a short time later joined Wenk, Blink, and Baslin at the fire. Skey also joined them, and they breakfasted on thick slices of bread that Wenk had toasted over the fire on a split stick, then coated with honey from a pot Dame Ortha had provided.

As they ate, Skey reported, "No one has left the village yet, but I can see men gathering in the village square. There will probably be search parties out soon."

Wenk nodded. "One group may come this way, but we have time to finish eating." He turned to the three travelers. "Skey has offered to lead you down the slope on the side away from the village and put you on a path leading north."

Baslin, who had been looking anxiously at Wenk, stopped chewing to ask him plaintively, "Can't you come with us too?"

Wenk smiled at him. "I wish I could. I had planned to walk with you partway, but I think I had better wait here by the fire to welcome the searchers."

"Won't they be angry if they suspect you've helped us get away?" asked Akara anxiously.

"I'll come to no harm," Wenk reassured her. "I know some of the men of the village. I'll either persuade them to go back or send them off in the wrong direction." He swallowed a bite of bread. "Do either of you girls know how far north you plan to travel?"

Akara said, "I'll stay with Blink and Baslin until they reach their destination, wherever that is. After that, I'll decide what to do."

Wenk looked at Blink, who said, "Baslin and I are traveling to the home of my cousin Kelidon and his wife, Delsa. They live on a farm near the village of Midra."

"Midra is a day's journey to the north," said Wenk. "A friend of mine named Zemla lives there. He probably knows your relatives, Blink. And I'm sure he will be glad to help you too, Akara, in any way he can. I'll write a note for you to give him."

He took a small box from his pack, and from it pulled a quill pen, a tiny clay bottle that apparently contained ink, and a scrap of parchment. He pulled the cork from the bottle, dipped the pen in it, and began to write. When he finished, he rolled the parchment and gave it to Akara, who put it away in her blue bag. "You should reach Midra tomorrow," he said as they rose from the fire. "It is called 'Midra' because it lies midway between the southern and northern ends of the valley. It is marked by a high grassy knoll that rises near it."

It was time to say good-bye. Akara held Wenk's hands and looked up at him with tears in her eyes. "I don't know how we can thank you," she said. "And I do want to see you again."

Wenk smiled down at her. "You will. Leave word with Zemla about where you finally come to rest. He'll let me know and I'll visit you."

The travelers fastened on their packs and followed Skey off the hilltop, leaving Wenk standing by the fire. Down the hill they went, until they reached valley level, where they came upon a path. Skey pointed northward. "Midra lies in that direction," he said. "This path is narrower than the Old Trail, but you are less likely to find searchers on it. I must leave you here, for I have a day's work waiting for me at my father's farm."

Akara and Blink thanked him warmly, then watched as he headed south at an easy jog and disappeared around a turn in the path. Then they set off in the opposite direction.

This path was a pleasant one, winding through woodland and occasionally past open fields. As they went, Akara repeated to Blink some of the things Wenk had told her. Blink was skeptical. "I haven't heard of the King's Book Wenk spoke about, and I have trouble believing in either of these so-called 'invisible powers'. Maybe people imagine them." Then, with a mischievous grin, she added, "As wicked as the miller is, I wouldn't be surprised if he dreamed up an evil power to believe in!"

Akara couldn't help laughing at this idea, but then asked seriously, "Do you think there are any powers greater than human beings?"

"I don't know," answered Blink frankly. "I was raised to believe that we must depend on ourselves, and that we shouldn't need magic to solve our problems." She grinned again. "However, if we get into more trouble, I'll accept any help your good power can give us!"

They camped that night in a grove of trees, then started off again early the next morning. Soon after midday, they came out of the woods into a broad expanse of fields and orchards. In front of them, a grassy knoll rose from the valley floor, and to their right were the white walls and red roofs of a large village.

"Midra," said Blink briefly.

Baslin took his sister's hand. "Will there be bad men in this village too?" he asked anxiously.

"I think we're safe here, Bas. This is the village Wenk told us to come to, and he has a good friend here. But we'll be careful anyway."

Just ahead, their path joined the Old Trail, then the main valley road, which had curved to enter the village. A young man working in a field directed them to Zemla's house, describing it as a handsome stone dwelling, on the main street of the village, with a red-painted door.

They had no trouble locating the house. Akara's knock was answered by a middle-aged woman with a pleasant face.

"Good day, Mistress," said Akara, using the valley formula for addressing a mature woman. "We are travelers who would like to speak to Zemla." She took Wenk's note from her bag and held it out. "Wenk the Wanderer sent us."

At the mention of Wenk's name, the woman's doubtful look vanished. She smiled, and swung the door open. "I'm Dame Leck, Zemla's wife," she said. "Step in and I'll take this note to him."

She asked them their names, then led them into a large front room and invited them to sit down. She disappeared through another door, returning in a few minutes with a tray on which were three mugs of cold milk and a plate of cakes. "I've told Zemla you're here," she said. "He'll be with you soon."

They had just finished the refreshments when the door opened and Zemla entered. He was a slender man of medium height with a thin, pleasant face and piercing black eyes. His gray hair was swept back from his forehead. He carried Wenk's note in his hand. The travelers stood respectfully while Dame Leck made the introductions. Zemla waved them back to their seats and drew up a chair facing them, while Dame Leck slipped into a seat near the door.

"I've read what Wenk the Wanderer says about you, and I'm glad you came," Zemla began. "I'll do all I can to help you, but first I would like to learn more about each of you."

Akara and Blink told their stories briefly. Zemla nodded. "You seem to be resourceful young people. Akara, I see no reason why we at Midra cannot offer you protection from your enemies. Linka, I know your cousin Kelidon and his wife, Delsa. They live on a small farm not far from Midra. I'll send word to them that you are here."

Blink smiled happily and hugged her brother. "Thank you, sir! We may have a new home, Baslin, isn't that wonderful?"

Baslin's face was troubled. "Can Akara stay there with us?"

It was Akara who answered, "That would be nice, Baslin, but it wouldn't be right to ask your cousins to take me in. I'll find somewhere to live."

Zemla spoke. "There is a place not far from Kelidon and Delsa's farm where I think you can stay, Akara. It is called the 'House of the Hill Soldiers'. I know the people who live there well, and I think they would be glad to have you. I will check with them."

"Thank you. I will also have to find a way to support myself since I have no money."

"I'm sure the Hill Soldiers will have work you can do to pay for your keep. They are a fine group of people, and I think you will fit in well there. They do much good in the valley, and they follow the teachings of a person who lived long ago called the 'Good Carpenter.'"

At the mention of the Good Carpenter, Akara felt a surge of excitement. From her conversation with Wenk, she remembered that "the Good Carpenter" was a title given to the King. "Excuse me, sir, but are the Hill Soldiers the people who are also called 'Soldiers of the King'?"

"No, those are two separate groups. The ones who call themselves Soldiers of the King live high up in the Great Mountains. The Hill Soldiers live in the foothills and in my opinion, are more sensible people."

He leaned back in his chair and put his fingertips together. "Now let's talk about the people you are running away from. Wenk believes that you had good reason to escape from the orphan home in Palloweth. I don't think the elders of that village will inquire about you, but if they do, once we get you settled, I can assure them that you are well and happy here."

Zemla continued, "I've never heard of anyone called the Tall Woman, so I doubt she will turn up in Midra. As for the miller of Arn, he may be powerful in his own village, but he has no influence here. If he were to come to Midra claiming that you were his granddaughter, we would give him a fair hearing, but since his claim is false, he couldn't win."

"But I can't prove he's lying!"

"You wouldn't have to. He would have to prove he is your grandfather. As long as he can't do that, you are safe."

Dame Leck spoke from her corner. "Of course, if you could find out who your parents were, it would solve the problem. Do you know anything about them?"

"No. I was found as a baby in a wagon near Palloweth. I could have come from anywhere north of that village. The only clue I have is this blue bag that was found with me."

"Let me see it," said Zemla. He and Dame Leck both examined it.

"This is beautiful needlework," said Dame Leck. "I'm sure I haven't seen it before."

"Neither have I," said Zemla, "but keep searching. It is possible someone will recognize it." He returned the bag to Akara. "I'll send a man on horseback with letters to the Hill Soldiers and to Kelidon and Delsa. Until we receive answers, you are invited to stay here in my home."

"Thank you, but we don't want to impose," said Blink. "We have food with us, and we are quite used to sleeping outside."

Zemla smiled and raised a hand. "No, it's all arranged. We'll enjoy having you." He rose to his feet. "Dame Leck will show you to your room."

CHAPTER 14

New Beginnings

Dame Leck led the travelers upstairs to a large airy room under the eaves. "This is where you will sleep tonight. You will have time before the evening meal to change your clothes and bathe if you wish. The bathing room is behind the kitchen."

The three were glad for this opportunity. The bathing room, like that in most of the valley homes, had a stone floor that sloped toward a central drain, and a wooden bathtub. Pails of hot and cold water had been brought in and placed there by a servant. When Akara's turn came, she scrubbed herself well, then changed into the clean clothing she carried in her pack.

Later they ate with Zemla and Dame Leck in the oak-paneled dining room. Steaming platters of meat and vegetables were brought in from the kitchen by a serving girl. While they were eating, Zemla questioned Akara in more detail about the miller of Arn.

When Akara finished, Blink said, "Sir, how is it that the miller could hold Akara captive? Isn't that against the law?"

Zemla leaned back in his chair. "It certainly is. Each of our villages is independent, so while these basic kinds of laws should be the same throughout the valley, this is not always the case. The miller is the Reeve of Arn and may be able to do as he pleases there. We are working on this problem. We have drawn up a treaty that we hope will be signed by all of the villages. Under it, all villages will work together and live by the same rules."

He turned toward Akara. "Under this treaty, Akara, if the miller tried to hold you against your will, the elders of the surrounding villages could demand a hearing. The wrong could be righted and the guilty one punished."

The three travelers were tired after their day's journey and went to bed early. When they came down to breakfast the next morning, a smiling Zemla met them. His messenger had returned bringing word that Akara would be welcome at the House of the Hill Soldiers, and that Kelidon and Delsa would be happy to have Blink and Baslin live with them.

"I will be busy this morning," Zemla said. "But after the noon meal, I will take all of you to your new homes."

Needless to say, the three young people were delighted. During the morning Blink and Akara scrubbed the clothes they had worn on the trip, and hung them to dry in the garden behind the house. After the noon meal, their bags packed and ready, they bade farewell to Dame Leck and followed Zemla outside to where a light, open carriage waited by the gate. Wahler, the driver, ushered them into the carriage, then unhitched the horse and climbed to his seat.

Akara had never ridden in a carriage, and she marveled at the way it sped along smoothly with no creaks and rattles. When they neared the foothills of the Great Mountains, Wahler turned onto a side road and stopped before a small white farmhouse.

"This is your cousin's farm, Linka," said Zemla.

Baslin gripped his sister's hand. "I'm scared, Blink!" he whispered. "Are you sure they will like us?"

Blink's face also bore an anxious look, but she gave her brother a hug and said, "Of course they will, Baslin!"

A moment later the door of the house flew open, and a squarely built, bearded man rushed out, followed by a pretty, dark-haired woman. Two young boys, both a little older than Baslin, exploded out of the doorway after them.

"Welcome!" The man's voice boomed out. "Come in, all of you!"

Introductions were made and all went inside to a small, comfortable living room. The two boys immediately settled down on the floor in one corner with Baslin, while the others found seats on couches and chairs.

Kelidon and Delsa soon made it clear that they were delighted to welcome Blink and Baslin into their family. Then Kelidon turned to

Akara. "I know that you and Linka are close friends," he said. "We will be glad to have you stay with us too for as long as you wish."

Akara was momentarily tempted to accept the offer, but she realized that the little farmhouse would probably not accommodate her as well as the other two arrivals, so she declined with thanks, telling them of the plan Zemla had made for her. Later, when she saw the tiny room off the kitchen where Blink would sleep, she knew she had made the right decision.

All too soon the time came for Zemla and Akara to leave. Good-byes were said, and the carriage rolled off. Back to the main road they went, then eastward toward the mountains. After traveling a short distance, they made another turn onto a lane that wound upward through the trees. At the top of the climb, they broke out into an open area. Akara caught her breath. There, across a grassy lawn, was a stone building, high and long, with a tile roof, chimneys, and arched windows.

Zemla smiled and waved a hand. "This is the place."

"It's bigger than I thought it would be!"

"Don't be afraid. The people here are friendly, and I'm sure you will like it."

As they drew up at the arched front doorway, a young man stepped forward to greet them. He was neatly dressed in dark green trousers and a tunic to match. Over the tunic he wore a lightweight vest covered in the front with flexible links of silver metal that gleamed in the sunlight. His polished leather belt was fastened with a silver buckle. But what caught Akara's eye was the embroidered design on the collar of his tunic. It was a tiny trumpet just like her own silver one!

"Good afternoon," he said. "We're expecting you. I'm to take you inside where our leader, Garis, will meet you."

He took Akara's bag and led them through one of the tall double doors and across a hallway into a large, high-ceilinged room. There he invited them to be seated, assured them that Garis would be there soon, and departed. Akara looked about her. The room was richly furnished. A gold rug covered the floor, and the window drapes were the same color. The chairs and couches were tastefully upholstered. On a table in the center of the room was a glass case in which was a large leather-bound book.

On the wall at one end of the room Akara saw two large pictures. One of these was a full-length painting of a young man, the other a matching picture of a young woman. Both were in uniforms like that worn by the youth who had greeted them. Facing these pictures at the other end of the room, she saw two similar paintings, but in this case, the man and woman were dressed in gleaming armor. They wore helmets, and each carried a shield and a drawn sword.

Zemla's spoke first. "Beautiful room, isn't it? It is called the 'Gold Hall'." He nodded toward the glass case on the center table. "That case contains a copy of the King's Book in which are the teachings of the Good Carpenter, and other writings."

"It's a big book. Have you read it?"

Zemla chuckled. "Only parts of it. Most of the people of Broad Valley know about it, but few have read it. The scholars among the Hill Soldiers study it, and they have written about it."

At that moment the door opened, and a tall, white-haired man entered. He was dressed in the same uniform as the young man at the entrance, except that there was an added band of silver trim on the sleeves of his tunic. He walked with a limp and leaned on a cane.

"I'm sorry to have kept you waiting," he said as he came through the door.

Zemla got to his feet, and Akara did as well. "Greetings, Garis," said Zemla. "We've enjoyed the opportunity to look at this beautiful room. As you see, I've brought your new guest. This is Akara."

Garis inclined his head graciously. "Greetings, please be seated, both of you."

Zemla said, "As I wrote you, Akara needs a place to live, at least for a time. She tells me she will be glad to work for her keep if you have things she can do."

Garis said, "We are glad to have you with us, Akara. We won't worry right now about how long you'll want to stay. Those who are members of our fellowship are called 'Hill Soldiers', but we often have others stay with us. You can also help by working in the house or garden if you wish."

"Thank you very much, sir. I'll be glad to do any kind of work you want me to do without pay."

Garis smiled. "The Good Carpenter taught that we should treat others as we would like to be treated. Your service will more than cover the cost of food and lodging, and we will pay you the difference. Is there any kind of work you would especially like to do?"

Akara hesitated for only a moment. "In the place where I grew up, I worked in the garden, and I'd be very happy doing that here. Or if you have a library and there is work to do there, I would especially enjoy that. I want to read about the Good Carpenter and also about the Hill Soldiers."

"Those are both fine ideas, and perhaps you can do both. I know Kevis our gardener can use more help. Our librarian is Oletta. I'm not sure whether or not she will have work for you to do, but I'll ask her."

At Zemla's suggestion, Akara then gave Garis a summary of her wanderings.

When she finished, Garis smiled. "Akara, you have had more experiences than most people your age. I haven't heard of the Tall Woman, but I've seen Trask the peddler a few times, and I've heard about the miller of Arn. It is sad to think that there are evil people in our beautiful valley."

At that moment, a young woman in the Hill Soldiers' uniform came into the room. Garis introduced her as Vidella, the person who was to be Akara's guide. Vidella was a sandy-haired girl, a year or two older than Akara, with a round face and ready smile. Akara liked her on the spot.

Zemla rose to go a few minutes later. Akara thanked him again for his help, and he promised to keep in touch with her. A few minutes later, Garis also excused himself, and Vidella led Akara to a small, pleasant bedroom on the top floor of the great building.

"My room is next door," she said. "It's time for dinner now. Leave your bag here, you can unpack later."

CHAPTER 15

Confidence and Confusion

The dining hall was a large room whose windows looked out on a pleasant vista of woodland. The two girls joined a large number of men and women who were filing in through the entrance. Most were in the green garb of the Hill Soldiers, but Akara was relieved to see that there were also some dressed like herself in ordinary valley clothing.

"Those not in uniform are visitors," Vidella told her. "They come to learn about our fellowship."

"Do those in uniform live here permanently?"

"Not all of them. Most of our soldiers live in their own homes in the valley. They put on their uniforms and come here for a few days or weeks at a time."

The girls joined a group of young soldiers at one of the tables. After Vidella had introduced her, Akara was content to sit quietly while the talk went on around her. When the meal was finished, Vidella turned to her. "Part of my job is to work on the team that straightens up the dining room after the meal. It will take me only a short time. Then, if you like, I'll meet you under the portico outside the front door. There are chairs there, and it's a nice place to sit in the evening."

"Can I help you with your work?"

Vidella shook her head. "Thank you, Akara, but there's not that much to do."

She hurried away. Akara left the dining hall and walked down the long corridor toward the front of the building. As she passed the door to the Gold Hall, a sudden impulse made her decide to enter. It was still early evening. The room and its rich furnishings were well illuminated by the light from the large windows. Akara looked first at the book in the glass case on the table. It was bound in a rich leather and trimmed in gold. The words "King's Book" were inscribed on its cover. She was tempted to open the case and read some of the book, but wasn't sure if this was permitted. Turning away, she went to the wall where the paintings of the Hill Soldiers hung. The figures in both pictures were life-size, and their uniforms were shown in careful detail. Their faces bore serious and determined expressions. Then she walked to the opposite end of the room to examine the paintings of the man and woman in full armor. Each of the figures wore a silver helmet and a shirt of mail in which were set gleaming breastplates. From each belt hung a short skirt made of narrow leaves of silver-colored metal linked together. Each soldier also wore metal-clad shoes and carried a shield on the left arm and a drawn sword in the right hand.

The faces of these soldiers seemed to glow with life, and Akara found them more impressive than the figures at the other end of the hall. Then she noticed something else. Around the neck of each soldier was a cord from which hung a small silver trumpet!

"They're real trumpets, and they look just like mine," she thought. "They're not just pictures of trumpets like the Hill Soldiers wear on their uniforms! And whoever these people in armor are, or were, they must have blown through their trumpets sometimes, just as I blow through mine!"

How long she stood staring at the pictures, she did not know. Finally, remembering her promise to meet Vidella, she tore herself away. Still pondering the meaning of her new discovery, she left the Gold Hall.

Outside, on the flagstone terrace, were a number of wooden chairs. A few of them were already occupied by members of the Hill Soldiers. Akara found a seat from which she had a fine view across Broad Valley to the western mountains.

A few minutes later, Vidella arrived, pulled up a chair beside Akara, and sat down. "We get a good view of the sunset from here," she said.

"Have you been waiting long?"

"No, I just arrived. I stopped for a few minutes in the Gold Hall."

She told Vidella of her interest in the paintings. Her new friend shrugged. "I remember looking at those pictures when I first arrived," she said. "Someone told me that the figures in armor at one end of the hall show how the Hill Soldiers used to dress long ago. That's all I know about them."

"I'm hoping to learn about both the past and present of the Hill Soldiers. I'm especially glad that you are followers of the Good Carpenter. I want very much to know more about him."

"You have come to the right place." Vidella settled herself more comfortably in her chair. "I too came here because I wanted to learn about the Good Carpenter."

"I'd like to read the King's Book. I saw it in the glass case in the Gold Hall."

"That copy is for display. You can get a copy from our library if you really want to spend time reading it."

"Have you read it?"

"I started. Then I found that our leaders have studied it and written about its message. We don't have to read it for ourselves."

Akara's face showed her surprise. "I thought that reading the King's Book would be the best way to learn about the Good Carpenter."

"Some people think so. I find it easier to read what others have written about it. You see, the King's Book is partly true and partly legend." She shook her head sadly. "For instance, before I came here, I thought that the Good Carpenter rose again after being killed, and that he was alive today. I wanted to believe that. Now I've learned that may not have happened."

"Quite right!" said a new voice. A young man in uniform dropped into a vacant chair beside them. Akara remembered that he had shared their table in the dining room. His name was Tazen, and she had noticed particularly his loud voice and assured manner.

He continued, "The Good Carpenter was a great person — probably the greatest that ever lived! His body didn't rise from the dead; it is his spirit that lives on. His teachings are the important things. If we put them into practice, we can make the valley a better place to live."

Akara was confused. "I was looking forward to reading the King's Book. Now I'm not sure what to do."

"I think you should read it if you'd like," said Tazen. "There are experienced people here who can tell you what parts to read and what to skip. But you can't go wrong in reading the parts that record what the Good Carpenter taught!"

The talk shifted to other topics, but what she had heard troubled Akara. As she lay in bed that night, she thought of the many things she had heard about the King and the King's Book from the miller, Wenk, Vidella, and Tazen. Obviously, there was much she had to learn. She reached for her little trumpet and breathed through it. As she did so, she asked earnestly that whatever the truth was, she would find it.

After breakfast the next morning, Vidella led Akara to the courtyard in the center of the building, where a large crowd of Hill Soldiers had assembled. There were many stone benches in the courtyard, and the two girls had no trouble finding seats. A deep-toned bell sounded and everyone stood. Then a soldier carrying a trumpet stepped out on a balcony above the crowd. The trumpet was silver in color like Akara's own instrument, but much larger. Its polished surface gleamed in the sunlight.

"That's Orben, one of our teachers," whispered Vidella.

"Let us call on the Creator," said Orben. He raised the trumpet to his lips and blew a series of beautiful resonant notes. When he finished and stepped back into the building, the audience took their seats.

Then several other Hill Soldiers rose in turn and gave short talks. They spoke of how important it was for valley people to live in peace, and how the Hill Soldiers could help them do so. The Good Carpenter was mentioned as an example of goodness, kindness, and unselfishness.

Garis spoke last. He described briefly the new treaty that Zemla hoped would be adopted by the villages of Broad Valley, and how it could promote peace.

As the two girls left the courtyard, Vidella said, "We have one of these meetings each morning. I find them inspiring, and I hope you do too."

Garis met them as they re-entered the building. "I have spoken with Oletta, our librarian, and Kevis, the gardener," he told Akara. "They'll both be happy to have you work with them. The best arrangement will be for you to alternate, one morning in the library, the next morning in the garden, with your afternoons free. You can start in the library this morning."

"Thank you, sir. That arrangement will be fine."

Vidella spoke up. "I have to go on duty shortly, but I'll take Akara to the library first."

After Garis left them, Vidella led the way to a large room on the second floor. It had many tables and chairs, and the walls were lined with shelves full of books and manuscripts. Oletta, a gray-haired woman, was seated at a desk in one corner of the room. Vidella introduced Akara to her and departed.

"Welcome," said the librarian. "Garis has told me a little about you, Akara. This is your first visit to us, isn't it?"

"Yes."

"Good. I think you will enjoy it here. Sit down and let's talk."

She explained Akara's duties. First, Akara was to become familiar with the library system. Then she was to assist people in finding the books they wanted, and she was to make sure these books were returned to their proper places on the shelves. She was also to help Oletta keep the library clean.

Akara was pleased with this arrangement. After Oletta had finished her explanation, Akara ventured a question. "I'd like to come here and do some reading on my own time. I want to learn about the Good Carpenter. Would the King's Book be the best place to start?"

"The King's Book is certainly the source of all information about the Good Carpenter. We have copies on the bottom shelf of that alcove over there. Not many of our soldiers spend time reading that book, so you'll have no trouble finding a copy available."

She looked at Akara thoughtfully. "I'd suggest that you first read some books by our own scholars. They will tell you what parts of the King's Book to read and help you to understand it. You'll find books of this kind in the same alcove. Outside the alcove are other books that tell about the Hill Soldiers and the wonderful things we do to help the people of the valley."

Before Akara left, Oletta took her to the alcove and picked out a small volume from the shelf above the King's Book.

"Here's some reading material for you to start on," she said. "Tell me when you finish and I'll have more for you."

Akara thanked her. She would, she decided, accept Oletta's guidance for some of her reading time. But she was also anxious to read the King's Book and to decide for herself whether or not it was true.

CHAPTER 16

A Midnight Meeting

That night Akara awoke suddenly from a confused dream! It had disturbed her, but she did not know why. She sat up in bed, her arms around her knees, and stared at the pattern on the floor made by the moonlight slanting through her window.

What was troubling her, she wondered? The evening had been uneventful. She had gone for a short walk, then sat for a while on the front patio chatting with Vidella before going to bed.

Then had come the dream. In it, she found herself being hurled from one scene to another. First, she was back at the orphan home, then bumping along in Trask's wagon, then scrubbing the floor at the mill of Arn, then racing through the woods with Blink and Baslin! And lurking in the background of each scene was the hooded figure of the Tall Woman. But the strangest feature of her dream — the trumpets! They were always there, dozens of them, big trumpets and little trumpets, dancing in the air around her.

As she thought about those floating instruments, her mind flashed to the trumpets pictured in the paintings that hung in the Gold Hall. Were they really duplicates of her own trumpet, or were they larger, more like the trumpet blown by Orben that morning? Making a sudden decision, she threw back the covers and got up. She pulled her traveling cloak on over her nightclothes, picked up her silver trumpet, and slipped quietly out of the room.

Most of the oil lamps in the wall brackets along the corridors had been put out. She felt her way along a shadowy passageway, down a stairway, and then on to the Gold Hall. In this large room, there were no lamps at all, but the full moon shining through the tall windows gave her more than enough light. She crossed to the wall where the portraits in armor hung, then held up her own trumpet close to each of them in turn. With a thrill of pleasure, she realized that the soldiers in the pictures carried trumpets exactly like hers.

As she stood there, her mind full of questions, a soft voice spoke from the doorway. "Is there something wrong?" Akara spun around, startled! The tall figure of Garis stepped from the shadows. "I'm sorry if I surprised you. I saw someone come in here and wondered who it might be."

"I didn't mean to disturb anything, sir. I'll leave right away."

"Don't go." Garis leaned on his cane, smiling gently. "You didn't disturb me. I'm often awake at night. But when healthy young people are wakeful, it sometimes means they are troubled about something. Is there anything you would like to talk about?"

Akara hesitated. Then, reassured by his quiet manner, she nodded. "Yes, there is."

Garis waved her to a chair and drew up another. "I'm here to listen."

"It's about my trumpet," Akara began, holding it up. "I didn't mention it to you earlier. A man named Wenk gave it to me, and while it makes no sound when I blow through it, it has brought me peace and comfort." She pointed to the pictures. "I came here tonight to look closely at the trumpets in these pictures. They seem to be exactly like this one. Can you tell me who the people in the pictures are?"

Garis nodded. "Yes. Those two are very old pictures. They show two of the first followers of the Good Carpenter. These people lived in the Great Mountains. They wore armor as you see and carried swords and shields to fight against what they believed were evil powers."

He gestured toward the opposite wall. "Later, many of these folk moved down to the foothills and founded the fellowship of the Hill Soldiers, to which we belong."

"But the Hill Soldiers don't wear armor."

"That's right. The way we dress now is shown in the pictures at the other end of the room. Since we no longer believe there are evil beings we must fight, we need neither swords nor armor. However, we honor the faith of those early soldiers by wearing the decorative chain mail on our tunics and the trumpet symbol on our jackets."

"I've heard there are followers of the Good Carpenter who still live in the mountains."

"That is true. There is a group who hold to the old beliefs and who continue to dress in armor. Their home is on the mountaintop, though they visit the valley from time to time. You may not recognize them immediately since they wear traveling cloaks over their armor. They are fine, moral folk — only, I think, mistaken in their beliefs."

"Do they carry trumpets like those in the pictures?"

"They probably still do, I'm not sure." Garis glanced down at the trumpet that Akara held in her hand. "We have one or two old trumpets like yours in our storeroom, but we can make no sound with them. That's why we designed trumpets of our own. They have a beautiful tone and add a great deal to our meetings."

"I'd like to meet some of those mountain people," said Akara thoughtfully. "I also want to learn more about the Good Carpenter. Vidella tells me your scholars have learned that he never really rose from the dead. Is that true?"

Garis spoke softly. "We can't say that for sure, Akara. Sometimes the pupils are more certain of these things than the teachers are. The Good Carpenter was a wonderful person, but my own belief is that the resurrection story is untrue. Sometimes I wish I could believe that he rose from the dead, for that idea is a powerful one."

He reached for his cane. "Keep in mind, Akara, that even wise scholars disagree on these matters. So don't simply accept as true what I think or what anyone else tells you. Listen to all points of view, then decide for yourself what to believe." He stood and gave Akara another smile. "And now, I think both of us should go to bed."

Akara parted from Garis outside the Gold Hall. She made her way back to her room, slipped out of her cloak, and climbed into bed. Her talk with Garis had given her much to think about. "It is strange," she said to herself, "that the miller, who is an enemy of the Good Carpenter, has no doubt that he is alive, while Garis, who claims to follow him, believes he is not!" Turning this thought over in her mind, she drifted off to sleep, and this time no dreams troubled her.

The next morning, while she and Vidella were eating breakfast, a short, gray-bearded man approached their table. He looked at Akara with keen blue eyes. "I'm Kevis, the gardener, and I suspect you're Akara. Garis tells me you would like to work in our garden, and I'm happy to have you. Gardening is hard work and not many of our people like it."

His manner put Akara immediately at ease. "I grew up working in a garden," she said. "I'm sure I'll enjoy yours."

"Good. I have work clothes that I am sure will fit you, gloves for you to wear, and everything you'll need. Come back to my domain when you are ready."

Akara did indeed enjoy her return to the garden. The sights and smells of fresh earth and growing things made her feel at home, and she found Kevis a pleasant person to work with. The garden, she found, was much larger than the one at the orphan home in Palloweth. In one corner, Kevis cultivated the herbs that were valued in the valley for healing purposes, and Akara learned that he also served as the doctor for the Hill Soldiers. He assigned Akara the job of weeding that area.

The morning went quickly. Shortly before noon, a farmer's wagon drove along the road behind the garden, then in toward the building, stopping outside a door that Akara guessed led to the kitchen. She paused in her work and watched idly as a young man jumped down from the seat and began unloading boxes of fruit. Then she gave a sudden gasp of surprise. The young man was Skey! Dropping her hoe, she ran to the gate, opened it, and headed toward the wagon.

Skey heard the gate swing open and looked around. His face broke into a huge smile, and he ran to meet her. "Akara! I didn't expect to see you here."

"It's a surprise to see you too. What are you doing here?"

"I come up to Midra every fortnight to deliver fruit from our orchard. But why are you here, and where are Blink and Baslin?"

Akara recounted briefly what had happened since the three travelers had left Elsis and told him the location of the farm where Blink and Baslin now lived. In answer to his questions, she described her life at the House of the Hill Soldiers.

"That's interesting," said Skey. "I've been delivering fruit here for many months, but never found out who the Hill Soldiers were or what they did. I have to head back to Elsis when I finish this delivery, but I'll drive by to see Blink and Baslin on the way. When I come north again, I'll plan to stay longer and spend time with all three of you."

As she watched him drive away, Akara smiled to herself. She was happy to see Skey again, and even happier to know that he would visit Blink and Baslin before he returned home. Blink and Akara had talked about Skey during their trip north to Midra, and Akara was aware that her friend had a special liking for the young man.

CHAPTER 17

A Fascinating Discovery

Akara's life at the House of the Hill Soldiers quickly settled into a pleasant pattern. She continued her practice of breathing through her trumpet at the beginning and end of each day. She liked her work in the garden and the library, and enjoyed the daily courtyard meetings. And she saw Blink frequently. Either Blink would ride one of the farm horses up to visit her or Akara would catch a ride on a Hill Soldiers' wagon that was heading toward the village and get off to spend an afternoon at the farm. Skey joined them whenever he came to Midra to deliver fruits and vegetables.

The paintings that hung in the Gold Hall continued to interest Akara, particularly the ones of the people in armor. She often went there to look at them. How long ago were they painted? Did mountain dwellers of the present day still wear armor and carry trumpets? She continued to read a little of the King's Book each day, though there were parts she did not understand. She also read the books that Oletta recommended, though she found them only moderately interesting. However, she remembered what Garis had said: "Listen to all points of view, then decide for yourself what to believe." This, she decided, was good advice!

Then one morning something happened that was to make another change in her life. When Akara entered the library, ready for work, Oletta pointed to a box on one of the tables. "Someone found these old parchments in a storeroom," she said. "They seem to be records dated seventy or eighty years ago. Before we throw them away, I want to make sure there is nothing here that might be worth keeping in the library. Would you look through them for me? Separate the material by subject, then we'll look at it together."

Akara was glad for a change from her usual duties. She put the box on the floor in a corner, sat cross-legged beside it, and pulled the pieces of parchment out one at a time. On most of them were lists of food products and financial accounts, but near the bottom she found a roll, tied with cord, that looked different. On the outside of this roll was written "The Letter of Lors".

Akara unrolled it and spread it out. It was certainly old, for the ink was faded and some of the words were hard to decipher, but she soon forgot these difficulties as she realized what the letter was about.

"Greetings, cousin," it began. "How I wish you were up here with me watching the sunset from our castle tower at the top of the Great Mountains. I miss you, but plan to travel down to the valley to see you soon. I hope then you may agree to come back with me for a visit."

Akara caught her breath. For the first time she was reading a message from someone who had actually lived on the mountaintop! She read on. "I've written you how I first climbed the mountain out of curiosity, and how when I reached the castle, I stayed to learn more about the King.

"Here in the clear mountain air I have read much of the King's Book. Cousin, it has the ring of truth! I now know that the Good Carpenter we heard about in our village was not just a great teacher. He is the true ruler of the valley, and he is alive today, though we do not see him with our human eyes.

"Yes, my friend, I have become a Soldier of the King, and I now wear the King's armor. I look forward to telling you more when I see you. Until we meet again, your cousin, Lors."

Akara read the letter over several times. Then she finished reading through the rest of the parchments, put them back in the box, and carried them to Oletta. After examining them, Oletta agreed that, while the other materials were of no use, the letter would be a valuable addition to the library.

To Akara, the letter was much more than that. Though the writer belonged to a previous generation, his words seemed to speak directly to her. She asked Oletta for permission to copy the letter, so that she could read it over in the quiet of her room, a request the librarian readily granted.

That evening, as she reread the message, Akara found that her interest in climbing the Great Mountains had become a strong determination to do so. She knew it would be foolish for her to go alone; she would have to find one or more companions.

On the following afternoon, as previously planned, she visited Blink at the farm. Skey was there, having come north on one of his regular trips. While she relaxed with Blink and Skey in the shade of a large oak tree, Akara took this opportunity to tell her friends about finding the letter written by Lors. Taking her copy from her blue bag, she read it aloud. When she finished, Skey, who was stretched out at full length on the grass, was the first to speak.

"That's interesting. How long ago was it written?"

"It isn't dated, but some of the other papers in the box are at least seventy or eighty years old."

"Hmmm," said Skey. "I guess the stories about people living up on the mountain are true."

"Seventy years is a long time," put in Blink. "I wonder if any of them are still there?"

"Zemla and Garis have both said so," responded Akara. "That's one reason why I was excited when I read the letter. It made me want to climb the mountain and see what those people are like."

"Why, Akara?" Blink was puzzled. "Aren't you happy at the House of the Hill Soldiers?"

"Yes, but...well, I want to find the truth about things for myself."

"What things?" Blink persisted.

"My trumpet, to begin with. You see, I have learned that the people who live on the mountain carry trumpets like mine, and this is important. You remember, Blink, how my trumpet helped when Trask and the miller's men had us trapped?"

Skey sat up. "So what do you plan to do?"

Akara took a deep breath. "Climb the Great Mountains."

"All alone?"

Akara hesitated, "I was hoping one or both of you might also be interested in coming."

Blink looked at her soberly for a long moment. Then she suddenly flashed her familiar grin. "Akara, I'm not entirely certain it was the trumpet that helped us when we met the peddler in Elsis. It may have been a coincidence that you saw the archway in the lane when you did. Also, I must tell you I can be content without climbing any mountains. But we've been through a lot together. If you want to go to the top, I'll go with you!"

Skey flopped down on the grass again and sighed in mock resignation. "Count me in, Akara. I'll go along too."

At that moment, Baslin and his two young cousins descended on the group, and the conversation about the letter ended. The subject was not raised during the rest of Akara's visit.   Back in her room at the House of the Hill Soldiers, Akara thought over that conversation. She was happy that Blink and Skey had volunteered to accompany her, but she realized that neither of them really wanted to go. They had agreed to do so only as a favor to her, and she decided that it would not be fair to accept the offer.

When she came down to breakfast the next morning, she found Tazen waiting for her. "I tried to find you yesterday," he said. "I heard you discovered an old letter, written by someone who lived in the Great Mountains. Can I read it?"

"Certainly. I have a copy I can loan you."

"Good. I want to learn more about the mountain folks."

Akara was curious. "Why?"

"I've always been interested in strange people. And I've heard stories about a tribe that lives in the mountains."

"I'll get the letter for you after breakfast."

Akara did so, and Tazen returned it that same afternoon. "Now I'm sure I want to climb the mountain," he told her. "No doubt this fellow Lors is dead by now, but I want to see the castle he talked about."

"The letter I have was written many years ago. Things may be different now."

Tazen waved off the objection, "If these are primitive people, their customs won't change quickly. I suspect the castle Lors wrote about is not much more than a stone house, but even so, there must be some sort of path that leads to it."

"But how can we find it?"

"I've been thinking about that. The old books say that the Hill Soldiers used to be part of that mountain bunch before they settled here. If they came straight down the mountain when they left, the path may start somewhere pretty close to us."

This idea was exciting to Akara. She did not particularly like Tazen, but she was glad that he too wanted to find a way up the mountain. "If you are going to look for the path, I'll be glad to help," she told him.

"Good! Maybe I can persuade some others to go with us."

CHAPTER 18

In Search
of the Path

Tazen's recruiting efforts were successful. The next day he reported to Akara that three other young people had agreed to go with them — another young woman, Ossa, and two young men, Broff and Redalus.

On the date chosen for the expedition, Akara was scheduled to work in the library, but Oletta readily agreed for her to be absent. The five of them left the House of the Hill Soldiers after breakfast and headed for the mountains. A half hour's walk brought them to the foot of the mountain slope, and there their hunt for the path began. This area was thickly grown with small trees and bushes, and by noon, they had found nothing. They stopped to rest and eat, then began searching again, but with less enthusiasm. Redalus and Ossa urged that they give up the search, then Tazen gave a shout. He had found the path!

Once the discovery was made, it seemed clear that this was the way up the mountain they were looking for. It was well worn, and it zigzagged upward through a low stand of bushes at the bottom of the mountain slope. Tazen looked up at the sun. "It's still early afternoon. We have time to follow the path partway up the mountain before we go back."

Akara agreed, but there were immediate objections. "If we plan to climb that," said Broff, "we should start early in the morning. There's no point in climbing now."

Ossa and Redalus agreed with him, and in the end, those three decided to head back to the House of the Hill Soldiers. Akara was tempted to return with them but decided against it. She was excited about having found the path, and hated to leave without going at least a little way up the mountain.

"I know those three," Tazen said to Akara in a low voice as the others prepared to leave. "Now that they've seen how steep this slope is, I won't be able to get them back out here. We'll have to find others. Maybe the two of us can climb a little way up before we go back." He stared up the slope. "See where the woods begin? It won't take long to climb that far. We'll get a great view of the valley from there, then we can come down."

After a moment's hesitation, Akara agreed. The plan seemed safe enough, and while she did not know Tazen well, Vidella had assured her he was trustworthy. So, as soon as the others left, they headed upward. The slope was steep, and they were soon panting freely. When they reached the edge of the woods that appeared to stretch unbroken above them, Tazen's face was deep red, and he was gasping for breath.

He threw himself down on the ground and closed his eyes. Akara, in better physical condition as a result of her days of travel, was less exhausted, but she too was glad to rest. She sat down on a nearby fallen tree trunk and looked out over the pattern of woods and fields in the valley below. In a few minutes, Tazen sat up. "That is a beautiful view, isn't it?" Then he suddenly pointed to his left. "I wonder where that goes."

Following his gaze, Akara noticed for the first time a narrow path that branched off from the one they were following and ran laterally along the side of the hill, disappearing into the bushes. "I don't know," she said. "It doesn't look as though it's been used for a while. Anyway, it's not going in the direction we want."

Tazen grinned. "You're right. But after all this climbing, it's nice to find something running horizontally. Let's see where it goes."

Akara shook her head. "No, we came as far as we said we would. I want to start back down."

"I'll only go a short distance." He got to his feet. "Are you coming?"

"No, I'll stay." And Akara turned back to her study of the valley. Suddenly she stiffened! Below on the mountainside, a figure appeared, moving up the path toward her. She could not tell whether it was a man or a woman, but she saw that it wore a dark traveling cloak, with a hood that covered its head. A sudden terrible thought seized Akara. There was no logical reason for this thought, but it instantly became a conviction in her mind. Somehow her enemy had found her! The person climbing the path toward her must be the Tall Woman!

Her usual courage deserted her and panic took its place! She had to hide, and quickly! Jumping to her feet, she raced down the horizontal path after Tazen, her only thought being to get away from the path up which the hooded figure was coming!

Running between tall bushes, she quickly overtook Tazen and raced past, leaving him staring after her in surprise. A little farther along, the path turned up the hill, ending suddenly at the base of a small cliff. Here Akara stopped. Then as Tazen came up behind her, she saw a narrow opening in the rock in front of her. Before he could speak, she dashed through this opening and into what seemed to be a large cave.

Tazen followed her in. "What's wrong, Akara?"

Akara was breathing heavily. "There's someone coming up the path I don't want to meet."

"Well, you should be safe enough here." He stepped into the entrance and peered out. "I can't see far, but there's no sign of anyone following us."

"Good!"

Tazen turned his attention to the cave entrance, then gave an exclamation. "Akara, this isn't just a natural cave. It has a door!"

It was true. Heavy metal hinges were fastened into one side of the entrance. These were connected to a stone slab within the cave that looked as though it would fit snugly into the entrance when swung shut. Tazen tugged at it, and it moved slightly.

"Don't close it," warned Akara, "we may not be able to get out again."

They turned toward the interior of the cave. "There's some sort of light farther in," said Tazen. "Perhaps there's another entrance. If there is, we can go out, turn downhill, and reach the valley without running into whoever it is you're worried about."

"I'd like that." Akara shivered. "But let's be careful not to get lost in here."

Ahead was a chamber with a high vaulted ceiling, illuminated by a soft light from some unknown source.

As they moved forward, Akara saw that on each side of the room there was a broad ledge and on these ledges were piled objects of various shapes.

Tazen darted to one of the ledges. "Look here, Akara! Pieces of armor!" He picked up something that looked like part of a breastplate.

Akara's panic had subsided somewhat, though she still threw glances over her shoulder. She followed Tazen. "Yes, and here are helmets and armored shoes."

They moved ahead, examining objects as they went. "Over here, Akara! Shields and old-fashioned swords!"

"Tazen, these weapons and armor are exactly like those in the pictures at the House of the Hill Soldiers. They are what the mountain soldiers wear!"

"I think you're right." Tazen picked up a sword, drew it from its scabbard, and swung it over his head.

Akara was becoming uneasy. "We shouldn't disturb these things, they don't belong to us."

"I'll put the sword back before we leave. I'm not sure what we'll run into, and I'd feel better with a little protection."

Akara, gave a sudden little cry. "Tazen! Look! There's light coming from the sword."

Tazen moved the blade of the sword closer to the ledge, and sure enough, the objects lying there were illuminated. "You're right, Akara! The sword doesn't glow, but the light certainly comes from it!"

Struck by a sudden thought, Akara looked upward, and in a moment the mystery of how the cave was illuminated became clear. High along the wall on each side was a row of swords, set in holders like candle sconces. She pointed them out to Tazen, and both agreed that it was from the blades of the swords that the soft light came.

By this time, Akara realized they had stumbled on a complete armory, and she was sure it belonged to the Soldiers of the King. Any lingering doubt was erased when she saw a stock of small silver trumpets stored neatly in rows. Akara slipped her own trumpet out of her blue bag for comparison. It was identical to those on the ledge!

Akara's uneasiness grew, and she was ready to turn back when Tazen pointed to a narrow tunnel that led upward. It looked as though it might be the way out they were looking for, but unfortunately, it led them only to a vertical slab of smooth rock.

"No opening here," said Tazen, groping over the surface.

Akara came beside him and ran her hands over the stone. "This feels like another stone door, Tazen, and here's something that feels like a handle." She tugged at the projection, there was a click and a grating of stone, and the barrier moved. Tazen joined her in pushing against it, and bit by bit, the slab swung back. A minute later they stepped out again into the open air.

They looked at each other, smiling with relief, then turned to scan their new surroundings. For a moment Akara thought the sun had set, for she was standing in near twilight. Then she realized that the dimness was caused by the thick canopy of leaves and tree branches under which they stood. They were on a narrow strip of clear ground that looked like a sunken wagon road and that stretched ahead of them up the mountain slope until it was lost in the trees. It was bounded on both sides by partly ruined stone walls. The higher ground behind each wall was densely forested.

As they stood staring at this scene, there was a sudden noise behind them. They spun around, and Akara gave a little cry! The heavy stone door was swinging shut!

Tazen leaped to stop it, but too late, as the slab clicked into place. He ran his hands over the surface. "There's no handle on the outside, only a little slot like a keyhole."

"It's good we weren't planning to go back through the cave," said Akara.

"But now I can't put this sword back." Tazen swung it through a small arc. "Oh well, I'll take it with me. There are a lot of them in there, so they won't miss one. What shall we do now?"

"That old road ahead goes upward, but we have to get back to the valley. Let's climb over one of these walls and then head downhill through the woods."

"All right. Let's go." Tazen raised the sword and swung it in a wide arc over his head.

At that moment something strange happened! A high-pitched wailing noise began, echoing through the trees and rising until it sounded for all the world like a high wind, although the tree branches around them were still. To Akara it seemed that the air became chill.

She looked around wildly, then seized her companion's arm. "Look, Tazen! Up the hill under the trees!"

Tazen followed her gaze. There, at the far end of the open track, stood three shadowy figures. He drew in his breath sharply. "I think I see someone there, I'm not sure. Maybe they are mountain soldiers. I'm going to call to them!"

In Akara's mind a warning bell sounded. "Don't do it!" she said quickly. "Let's just go!"

But Tazen had already stepped forward. "Greetings!" he called, once more swinging the sword overhead. "We are friends."

There was no answer. The figures stood motionless. Tazen called again. "Greetings!"

He took one more step forward, and then things happened with unexpected swiftness. The high-pitched wailing noise grew louder, one of the figures moved, and a flaming object came hurtling through the air toward Tazen. As it flashed close to his head, he leaped back, lost his balance and fell backward, striking the ground with a thud, and lay still.

Akara dropped to her knees at his side. His head had apparently struck a rock, and he was unconscious. The sword had flown from his grasp and lay some distance away. She scrambled to her feet again and looked fearfully up the slope. The dark figures seemed to be advancing slowly toward her. She wanted to run off into the woods and then down toward the valley, but she knew it would be wrong to leave Tazen.

She was preparing to make a desperate dash for the sword when she heard a creaking sound behind her. She spun around. The stone door was swinging slowly open. Out stepped the cloaked figure Akara had seen on the path. She saw the glint of eyes, but in the shadow cast by the hood, she could make out no features. Terror paralyzed her! There was no doubt in her mind. Facing her was the Tall Woman!

CHAPTER 19

A Fight in the Forest

Paralyzed with shock and fear, Akara faced the hooded figure, everything else for the moment forgotten. Her eyes met those beneath the hood, then the newcomer stepped quickly to one side and looked up the mountainside. A hand loosed the corded belt, then the cloak and its hood were flung off, and Akara found herself staring at a young woman in shining armor!

Even as she gasped in surprise, she recognized that the armor was of the style she had seen in the painting. While the young woman wore no helmet, the breastplate, belt, short armored skirt, all were there. A trumpet exactly like Akara's hung from a silver cord around her neck. Above the trumpet were a well-shaped face and a mop of brown curly hair.

The newcomer turned and smiled at her. "I'm sorry to have startled you," she said. "I wanted to get ready quickly in case the evil ones up there continued to come forward. They've stopped for the moment."

Akara found her voice. "It's all right. I was afraid you were...someone else." She glanced over her shoulder at the figures under the trees. They were no longer advancing. "You called them 'evil ones'?" she asked.

"That's right, there are three of them." The young woman unhooked a silver helmet from her belt. She put it on her head and buckled its strap underneath her chin. Then she swung to the front a shield that had hung behind her shoulder, and drew her sword. Still keeping an eye on the mountainside, she stepped forward to where the unconscious Tazen lay and dropped to one knee beside him.

"What happened to your friend?" she asked.

"He fell and hit his head. Something like fire came through the air..."

"Flaming dart," said the young woman in a matter-of-fact tone. She glanced again up the mountain. "A favorite weapon of our enemies! It's a good thing it missed him."

She put down her sword and lifted Tazen's head gently, passing her fingers behind it. "Quite a lump. All we can do is wait until he wakes up, that is, if the evil ones will give us enough time." She picked up her sword and rose to her feet. "Perhaps if you bathe his forehead with a little cool water, it will revive him. Meanwhile, I'll keep watch."

Her words stirred Akara to action. She dug into her bag for a handkerchief, moistened it from her water bottle, then knelt down and laid it gently across Tazen's forehead.

Without taking her eyes from the dark figures, the stranger spoke again, "Who did you think I was?"

"Because of your hood, I thought you were the Tall Woman, but now I see you are not much taller than I am."

The other was silent for a moment, then she said in a puzzled tone, "It is true I am sometimes called the Tall Woman but only by those who live in the southernmost villages. The people there are short in stature, and I look tall to them." She threw a sharp glance at Akara. "Where did you hear that name?"

"I heard it from Dame Dessit, in the orphan home where I was raised. She was planning..." Akara could not keep the bitterness from her voice. "She said she planned to get rid of me by turning me over to the Tall Woman."

The young woman spun around, her eyes wide with surprise. "Then you must be Akara, the orphan girl!"

Akara was now totally confused. "Yes I am! But...but if you're really the Tall Woman, you must know that! You followed me up the mountain, didn't you?"

"No," said the other, smiling. "I've heard nothing of you since you disappeared that night." She turned again to face the evil ones. "My name is Keila. I'm one of the King's Soldiers, and my home is on the mountaintop. I was on my way up the path today when I saw two people running toward the old armory, so I turned off to investigate. You see, the weapons in that cave belong to the King, and... But we've no more time for conversation, here come the evil ones!"

Akara jumped to her feet and looked up the hill. The high-pitched wailing sound had grown louder, and the three figures were striding toward them, looming larger as they came. As they drew nearer, she saw that they too were dressed in armor and carried shields and swords, but all of these were made of some dark metal. She caught a glimpse of strange, fierce faces under the dark helmets.

Even if Keila had not called them "evil ones," Akara would have known they were evil. Looking at them gave her the same uneasy feeling she had when she was near the miller, but much stronger. Without consciously deciding to do so, she slipped the blue bag off her shoulder, reached in, and drew out the little trumpet.

Her eyes came back to Keila. The King's Soldier had calmly sheathed her sword, then used her sword hand to raise her own silver trumpet to her lips. Without taking her eyes from the approaching figures, she blew through it. At first Akara heard nothing, but then she became conscious of a note, high and clear, that rode above and over the wailing sound that filled the air around them.

That scene engraved itself deeply on Akara's mind. Long afterward, she could close her eyes and see again the dark forms of the evil ones advancing down the hill, and facing them, the slender figure clad in gleaming armor, with silver trumpet upraised!

Her call finished, Keila again drew her sword. She gave Akara a quick glance, and her eyes widened in surprise. "You have a trumpet too!" she exclaimed. A sudden smile illuminated her face. "Send out a call for help, will you? It looks as though I'll be busy!" She turned again to face her enemies and then, sword in hand, began walking steadily toward them.

Terrified but obedient, Akara raised her own trumpet with trembling hands and blew. Would it too make a sound? No! She took a breath and blew again. At the same time, the King's Soldier gave a ringing shout, "For the King!" and with sword and shield held high, charged the enemy!

The shining figure and the dark ones came together under the shadows of the trees. The enemy warriors surged forward, their swords swinging in great blows against the King's Soldier. The figure in bright armor twisted and turned, leaping forward to lunge at one of her foes, then back again to catch the blow of another on her shield. Incredibly, at least for the moment, she had stopped the advance of the enemy trio!

Akara knew nothing of fighting, but she saw that Keila had timed her rush forward so that she met her enemies in a place where the stone walls were high enough to form a barrier on each side. There with her slashing, twisting style, she was able to keep all three of them in front of her. She seemed to be invincible!

As Akara continued to blow her trumpet, she realized suddenly that the vision she had seen long ago at the orphan home had come to life. While no music played, the lunges of the dark figures and the graceful leaps and turns of the bright one recreated the dance she had seen that night under the bush!

Akara watched, entranced, almost forgetting that she was seeing a deadly struggle. Then suddenly, an enemy thrust seemed to hit home, and the bright figure stumbled and almost fell! Her recovery was quick, but now she was forced to give ground. The vision of the dance was shattered! Step by step, and fighting all the way, Keila was forced backward!

Fear gripped Akara, and her silent trumpet calls for help became even more frantic. In only a few moments, the retreat would reach a point where the stone walls were low, and the evil ones could surround the King's Soldier. Then as a last desperate appeal left Akara's trumpet, the situation changed. A new shout rang through the forest! Two men in the armor of the King bounded over the wall near Akara, their cloaks streaming behind them, their swords in their hands. As they threw aside their cloaks and raced toward the fight, the evil ones fell back. Akara's defender stood panting and leaning on her sword as the newcomers rushed up to her.

"Keila, are you all right?" called out the taller of the two.

The girl in armor straightened up. "Greetings, Lanus and Henda. You come at a good time." She waved a hand toward the mountainside. "There are three enemies to deal with and two valley people behind us.

One is hurt."

The new soldiers glanced at Akara and Tazen, then up the slope to where the black-armored figures had stopped under the trees. The one called Lanus spoke again. "It's your fight, Keila. What do you want us to do?"

"First, let us three drive against the evil ones — you on my left side, Lanus, and you, Henda, on my right." She looked over her shoulder. "Akara, send another trumpet call when we meet the enemy."

She raised her sword. The shout, "For the King!" rang out in chorus, and the three soldiers charged up the slope, shoulder to shoulder. But there was to be no fight. Faced with equal numbers, the enemy soldiers turned and disappeared into the woods. The King's Soldiers made certain they had gone, but did not pursue them. Instead, they sheathed their swords and turned back to where Akara stood.

"It looks as though they weren't ready to fight on even terms," said Keila. "Now let's..." Suddenly her voice wavered and ceased. She stood swaying for a moment, then slumped to the ground!

CHAPTER 20

An Invitation to the Castle

Lanus dropped down beside her. "Keila! Keila!" he called, then looking up at Henda, "She's wounded, seriously I think. We must get her to the castle."

Keila's voice came, but weakly, "A thrust wound in my side, Lanus. I'll be all right. Lay the blade of your sword against it for healing, then I'll rest while you see what can be done for the valley people."

Lanus unbuckled Keila's belt and drew her tunic carefully away from the wound. Then he drew his sword and laid the flat of the blade gently against her side.

Henda noticed Akara's surprised expression. "The King's sword not only fights against the enemy, it also brings healing," he said quietly.

Lanus straightened up. "There! That has drawn the evil poison from the wound and stopped the bleeding," he said. "But, Keila, the thrust went deep. We must make a litter and carry you to the castle."

At that moment there was another crashing of underbrush, and four more Soldiers of the King, swords in hand, burst through the screen of trees.

Lanus stepped forward. "The fight's over, Robin, but it's good you came."

The leader of the newcomers answered, "We were on duty at the stone tower on the ridge when we heard the trumpet call and saw your sword light flaring. We came as quickly as we could."

"Henda and I were traveling on the path, so we got here first," Lanus said. "Keila is wounded. I see Tolsus is with you. He should check her wound since he knows more about healing than any of us. Then we must leave for the castle."

A soldier, evidently the one called Tolsus, came forward and dropped to his knees at Keila's side. Robin sent two others off with orders to scout the area to make sure no more of the enemy were around, then he and Henda began to cut down saplings with their swords to make a litter to carry Keila to the castle.

Lanus came across to where Akara was standing. "Thank you for being our trumpeter." He glanced down at the silver trumpet in Akara's hand, then touched the similar instrument suspended on a cord around his neck. "I see you have a trumpet like ours. My name is Lanus, and I heard Keila call you Akara." He paused and looked past her. "You, sir, are you all right?"

Akara turned. Caught up in the events in front of her, she had forgotten all about Tazen. Now she saw he was getting slowly to his feet. She put her trumpet back in her bag and ran to him. There was a dazed look in his eyes. At Lanus's question, he nodded his head slowly.

"Except for a headache, I'm all right," he mumbled. "I slipped on something and hit my head on a rock."

"You were nearly hit by a flaming dart," Akara told him.

Tazen's speech became a little clearer. "Nothing of the sort. I stumbled and fell!" He looked past her at Lanus. "You must be one of the people I saw up there in the shadows. I picked up a sword back in the cave and was waving it to attract your attention when I lost my footing. I didn't mean to steal your sword — it's there beside you on the ground."

Lanus bent to pick up the sword. "I'll take this back to our castle. But we were not the ones you saw. We came through the woods from the other direction. You saw three of the evil ones. They would have been invisible to both of you if you hadn't had the sword."

"Invisible? Are you talking about some sort of ghosts? In the valley we've done away with superstition, but perhaps you folks up here on the mountainside still believe in spirits. I'd like to talk to you about that."

"We are going to carry our comrade to our castle, and you are very welcome to come with us," replied Lanus courteously. "We can talk there.

It will be dangerous for you to stay here on the mountain by yourselves."

Akara noticed a flicker of uncertainty, and perhaps even a little fear in Tazen's eyes. "Thank you," he said. He raised his hand to feel the back of his head and winced as it touched the sore spot. "I think I had better go back to the valley. My head hurts."

Lanus nodded. "As you wish. One of us will guide you down the mountain." His eyes came to Akara. "And you, Akara, will you come and visit our castle?"

Akara's heart had leaped when she heard the invitation. But she felt she could not leave Tazen, who was still swaying unsteadily. "I want to come," she said earnestly, "but now I'd better stay with my friend."

Lanus nodded and turned back to join Tolsus who was still kneeling at Keila's side. Meanwhile, Robin and Henda, working swiftly, had lashed together two long saplings and two shorter branches to form a rectangular frame, using strips cut from one of the traveling cloaks. They left the ends of the saplings extended to serve as carrying handles. They then spread another cloak over the frame and tied it firmly in place.

As Lanus and Tolsus lifted Keila gently onto the litter, she said, "Wait, please! I must talk to Akara before we go."

"All right," said Tolsus, "but only for a minute. We must get you to the castle quickly."

Lanus beckoned to Akara, who ran quickly to stoop beside the litter. Keila smiled weakly and took her hand. "I'm weaker than I thought I was, Akara, but I must make sure you will come and visit me at the castle. I lost you once, I don't want it to happen again! Lanus or Robin can bring you."

Akara squeezed her hand gently. "I will try," she said. "I hope...I hope you'll be better soon." She rose and moved back to stand beside Tazen.

As Lanus and Tolsus picked up the litter, Robin came across to where Akara and Tazen stood. "Henda and I will go down with you to the valley," he said.

"Thank you, but that won't be necessary," said Tazen. "I'm one of the Hill Soldiers. If you take us to the path, Akara and I can find our way home."

Robin smiled, but said firmly, "We'll feel better if you let us go with you."

Tazen opened his mouth to protest, then apparently thought better of it. Lanus and Tolsus raised the litter and led the way up the bank and into the woods. A short walk brought the party to the path. Here Lanus and Tolsus turned up the mountain while Robin, Henda, Akara, and Tazen headed in the other direction. Robin led the way, helping Tazen over rough places since the Hill Soldier's footing was still not steady. Henda and Akara followed.

Henda turned to Akara with a shy smile. "I'm glad Keila urged you to visit our castle," he said. "It's a wonderful place!"

Akara returned his smile. "Have you always lived there?"

"No. I was raised on a farm in the valley near Midra. Three years ago, Lanus invited me to visit the castle. I stayed and became a Soldier of the King."

This revelation encouraged Akara. Apparently people from the valley were still joining the mountain folk as Lors had done in his day!

At the foot of the mountain, the little group headed toward the House of the Hill Soldiers. Robin dropped back to walk with Akara, while Henda moved up ahead with Tazen.

"I'm curious about your trumpet, Akara. It's unusual for a valley person to have one."

"It was given to me by a friend, and I use it often. But my trumpet is silent — it doesn't have a beautiful tone like Keila's."

Robin raised his eyebrows in surprise. "Our trumpets are silent when we want them to be. I often blow silent trumpet calls when I'm in the valley. But here on the mountain, I can let it ring out. I have never heard of a trumpet that was silent all the time."

Akara sighed. "I heard Keila's trumpet call. It was beautiful. I wish mine could be heard."

The conversation shifted to the possibility of having Akara visit the castle.

"I'd like to come soon," she said, "but I work for the Hill Soldiers and will have to talk to them about it."

"When the time comes, Henda and I will take you safely up the mountain."

The afternoon was drawing to a close as they approached the House of the Hill Soldiers. A dozen or so people were standing outside on the grassy lawn talking, among them Garis and Kevis. Garis saw them coming, Akara and Tazen in the lead, with Robin and Henda following. "Is anything wrong?" he called out.

When Tazen was silent, Akara answered. "Tazen was hurt on the mountainside. These two young men brought us back."

Tazen spoke gruffly, "I fell and hit my head! It's not serious."

Kevis stepped forward. "Come inside and I'll take a look at it." He took Tazen's arm and led him away toward the front entrance.

Akara said, "Garis, these are Robin and Henda, Soldiers of the King. They helped us."

Garis looked keenly at Robin. "I know you, Robin, though it's been a while since I've seen you. You worked at one time for my friend, Farmer Hanna, who lives just north of the village. I saw you when I visited him. He thought highly of you."

"He was very good to me, sir. I left his farm to become a Soldier of the King, but I visit him often. You may also know Henda's parents, Farmer Broadleaf and his wife. They also live near Midra."

"Of course! Greetings, Henda." He turned back to the girl. "Akara, can you tell me more about how Tazen was injured?"

Akara had assumed that Tazen had told Garis about their expedition. Now it appeared this was not the case. She decided to keep her answer simple. "Tazen and I found a path leading up the mountain and decided to explore it. We got off the path. Tazen fell and his head hit a rock. He was unconscious for a short time but seems to feel better now. Robin and Henda guided us back here."

"I see," said Garis. "I'm grateful to you both," he told the young soldiers.

"We're glad to have been of help," said Robin. "Also, sir, we've invited Akara to visit our castle on the mountain ridge. We will, of course, escort her there if she wants to come."

Garis raised his eyebrows and looked at Akara. After a pause, he asked, "Is that your wish, Akara?"

Akara drew a deep breath. "Yes, sir. It would be just for one or two days. You told me that the people on the mountaintop honor the Good Carpenter as you do but differ in some of their beliefs. I would very much like to visit their castle and learn more about them."

He shifted his gaze briefly to the mountain slopes above them, bathed by the afternoon sun, then down again. "Akara, my hope is that you eventually become one of the Hill Soldiers," he said. "However, I understand your desire to find out for yourself what others believe. Robin, I believe you are a responsible young man. If Akara goes with you to your castle, will you promise to see that she returns safely?"

"I will, sir," said Robin firmly.

Garis nodded. "When will you go back up the mountain?"

"Henda and I will take this opportunity to visit his parents at their farm and stay overnight and for the morning. We will return to the King's Castle early in the afternoon. Akara can come with us then if she wishes."

"Good. Go then, Akara, and learn what you can. I'm sure you can arrange with Kevis and Oletta to be absent from your duties."

After Robin and Henda left, Garis said, "Oletta told me about the old letter you found in the library. I suppose that is what gave you and Tazen the idea of climbing the mountain."

"That was part of it," Akara admitted, "though I wanted to go even before I found the letter. Have you read it, sir?"

Garis smiled. "I read it many years ago. You see, the cousin Lors wrote to was my grandfather!"

Akara stared at him in surprise. "Then you must know the rest of the story. Did your grandfather ever climb the mountain to the castle?"

"He made one visit there. Then he wisely returned to the valley and later became one of the Hill Soldiers. And that, Akara, is what I hope you will do!"

Akara's excitement at the prospect of visiting the King's Castle was tempered by her concern for Tazen. After Garis left her, she hurried to the small room at the back of the building that Kevis used as his office. There she found the gardener/physician standing at a counter mixing something in a small vial. He nodded a greeting, then turned to Tazen, who sat slumped in a chair nearby.

"Drink this, lad. It will dull the pain a bit. Then keep this wet towel against the lump on your head for the next hour or so. You'll be all right tomorrow."

He patted Tazen on the shoulder, gave Akara another nod, and left. Tazen drank the mixture Kevis had given him, shifted the towel to a more comfortable position, and glowered at Akara. There was a mixture of anger and fear in his gaze.

"One thing I can tell you right now," he said. "I've seen enough of those silly people in armor. I won't climb that path again!"

His head dropped for a moment, then came up again. "Also, I don't want you spreading stories about flaming darts. I know what happened. I was trying to talk to those mountain folks when I stepped on a loose stone and fell. While I was unconscious, they came down the hill and told you that wild story about evil spirits."

There was no use discussing the matter in Tazen's present mood. He obviously wanted to be left alone. Akara decided to say nothing about her own plans to return to the mountain. She simply expressed sympathy for his pain, then left him.

That evening she visited both Kevis and Oletta and told them of her intention to visit the King's Castle. Neither one objected to her absenting herself from work for that time. She also told Vidella about the day's adventure in more detail, as well as about her acceptance of Keila's invitation. Vidella enjoyed the story but thought Akara was foolish to visit the mountain castle and told her so. When she realized her friend was determined to go, she wished her well. The next day Akara packed her blue bag and prepared for her journey.

CHAPTER 21

The Hall of the Trumpets

A s Akara sat in the sun the next afternoon outside the House of the Hill Soldiers waiting for Robin and Henda, her feelings were mixed. The King's Soldiers were enthusiastic about serving their King, but Garis and the Hill Soldiers were equally committed to following the teachings of the Good Carpenter. Did it really make a difference which view she accepted? Her thoughts about this question were interrupted by the sight of two distant figures coming from the direction of Midra. Robin and Henda! She left her question unanswered and stood to wave a greeting.

When the two soldiers arrived, Akara had already slipped her arms through the straps of her backpack and was swinging it into position.

"I see you're ready to go with us," said Robin. "We're glad. How long will you be able to stay at the castle?"

"Garis said I could stay for two nights."

"Good. That will give you time to learn a lot about us."

They set off for the mountain immediately and were soon climbing the path. At the edge of the woods where Akara and Tazen had left the path the day before, the two soldiers put on their helmets, brought their shields forward, and drew their swords.

"Just a precaution," said Robin in response to Akara's questioning look. "The enemy is seldom bold enough to attack people who stay on the path, but when it does happen, it is either at night or under the dark shadows of the trees. So we must be prepared."

It was indeed dark beneath the trees, but the soft light that came from the swords illuminated the way ahead. No enemy appeared, and after a long climb, they came out of the woods again and into open sunlight. They had reached the summit. Akara caught her breath. There on the mountain ridge, its towers and battlements lit by the afternoon sun, stood a great castle.

Around it was a high stone wall and in the side facing them, an open gate. Robin and Henda sheathed their swords and led the way toward it As they passed through the gateway, Akara saw the words "Knock and it shall be opened unto you" cut into the stone arch above her.

"One of the sayings of our King," Henda told her. "It means that all are welcome here."

As they crossed toward the entrance to the castle itself, Robin pointed out a stocky, pleasant-faced man who stood at one side of the castle doorway talking with another soldier. "That is Jamin, one of the leaders of our fellowship. I'd like you to meet him."

Jamin ended his conversation as they approached, and Robin introduced Akara. The older man inclined his head courteously. "Are you the young woman who sent out the trumpet call for Keila during her fight yesterday?"

"Yes, sir," answered Akara, surprised at his knowledge.

"Lanus told me about you and said you might visit us. Welcome to the King's Castle!"

"Thank you, sir," she said, then asked anxiously, "How is Keila? It was my fault she got hurt, you know. I left the path and she followed to help me."

"Her wound is serious, but she is recovering. You'll be able to see her while you're here. In any case, you must not blame yourself. Part of our job as Soldiers of the King is to help people of the valley, and that's what Keila was doing." Smiling, he said, "You'll learn more about our mission during your visit here. But now, Robin will take you to Demars, who is the seneschal of the castle, and also my wife. She will, I'm sure, provide a room for you."

Robin and Henda led Akara to a room in the castle where a pretty, dark-haired woman sat writing at a desk. She wore an attractive light-colored gown and her armor and helmet lay on a table behind her. Her sword and traveling cloak hung from a hook in the wall nearby. She rose as they entered.

Introductions were made, then Robin and Henda left.

"Welcome to the castle," said Demars. "I heard you might visit us. I also heard you carry a trumpet. That is unusual for valley people. Is it like this one?" She touched the trumpet that hung at her own neck.

"Yes, it is. It's in my pack."

"I'd like to see it, but that can wait. Let me show you to your room."

Demars conducted Akara to the upstairs room where she would sleep. It was a pleasant room with a window overlooking the castle yard. "There is a room for bathing next door, and a pitcher of water and a basin for washing here on this table," she said. "I'll let you know when it's time for the evening meal."

Akara washed, changed her traveling clothes for others she had brought in her pack, and was ready when Demars knocked on her door. The dining hall was a large room with a high vaulted ceiling. Filling much of the space was a large, U-shaped oaken table, with seats around the outside. It was piled high with food of various kinds. Akara noted that many of those filing into the room wore armor. Others, like Demars, were dressed in clothing of a style similar to that worn by valley people. This clothing, she learned later, was woven from the fleece of mountain sheep. Robin and Henda waved to her from across the room, but she did not see Lanus in the group.

After all had taken their places, a tall, white-haired man stood and raised a trumpet to his lips. Low and sweet, the tones echoed through the chamber. They died away, then he sat down again, and the meal began.

The food was delicious, and Demars told her that it was all produced on the mountaintop, not carried up from the valley. As they ate, Akara said, "Jamin mentioned your title. It was a word I hadn't heard before. What was it?"

Demars laughed. "Like everyone else here, I am first of all a soldier, but I'm also called the seneschal. That means I'm responsible for the operation of the castle. This responsibility was my husband's until he moved to other duties. But titles mean little among the King's followers. They are not badges of honor but simply mark ways in which we serve each other. Each soldier has his or her own responsibility to fulfill for the King; some of these duties have titles, others do not."

Near the end of the meal, Jamin rose. "As many of you know," he said, "our fellow soldier, Keila, was seriously wounded yesterday in a fight against three of the evil ones. This evening, there will be a gathering in the Hall of the Trumpets for her. We will send a call to the King asking that she be healed. All who are free of other duties are invited to attend."

Akara turned to Demars. "I want so much for Keila to recover. Do you think they will let me attend that meeting?"

"Certainly. I plan to go, and I'll take you there."

When the meal was finished, all stood behind their chairs and sang together a song of praise to the King. Then everyone worked together to clear the great table and stack the dishes on a smaller one along the wall near the kitchen entrance. After they left the dining hall, Demars and Akara joined others who were making their way toward the Hall of the Trumpets. At the suggestion of Demars, they detoured past Akara's room to pick up her trumpet, then climbed several flights of stairs and entered a large rectangular room. A number of the King's Soldiers were already seated there, and Demars found seats for the two of them.

The walls of this room sloped outward from floor to ceiling and were painted a light blue. The center of the room was clear, but there were several rows of seats along each of the four sides. At the centers of the two longer walls were spaces in which there were no seats, and in each space was a large wooden wheel, mounted on a shaft that extended into the wall. Two young soldiers stood by each wheel, and when everyone was seated, they began turning the wheels slowly. As they did so, sections of the roof slid back until the whole room was open to the sky.

Akara caught her breath. Because of the outward slope of the walls, a great arc of the sky was visible. Dusk had fallen, and in the sweep of the heavens above, stars were beginning to gleam. She realized that they were brighter and more beautiful than they had ever appeared from the valley. The room had been lit by swords mounted on the walls, but now these were taken down. As darkness fell, the walls reflected the starlight so that those seated in the room could see each other clearly.

Akara saw that Lanus, Robin, and Henda were among those present. After a few moments of silence, Lanus rose and told in a few words the story of Keila's fight and how she had been wounded. When he finished, a trumpet at the far end of the room sent forth a rich, low tone. It was joined by another trumpet and another, until their music filled the room. While the trumpeters sounded different notes, they were in harmony, and all in the same low, resonant range.

As Demars raised her trumpet to her lips, she saw Akara's lying in her lap and motioned to her to join the trumpet chorus. Hesitantly Akara did so, even though, as she expected, it made no sound.

As the harmonies sounded out, Akara found that thoughts of the mysterious person called the King filled her mind. Then the trumpet tones moved upward into a new range. The melodies were different now, though still in harmony. These higher notes drew Akara's thoughts to Keila. She remembered Keila's gallant fight against the evil ones and how she had slumped to the ground, wounded. Tears came to Akara's eyes and a silent message went out through her trumpet. "Please heal Keila...make her well again!"

At last the trumpet notes died away. There was silence for a time. Then those present rose quietly and filed out of the chamber. Questions about what she had seen and heard crowded Akara's mind, but she did not know how to put them into words. In silence, she and Demars walked to the door of her room, where Demars bade her good night.

CHAPTER 22

Dame Prendil

The window in Akara's room faced eastward, and she awakened the following morning as the sun came up over the mountain ridges to the east. She reached for her trumpet and breathed through it quietly, thinking over the events of the day before. Then she rose and dressed.

Yielding to a sudden desire to look again at the Hall of the Trumpets, she put the silver trumpet into her blue bag, empty now of clothing, picked up the bag, and set off. She met no one on the way and soon reached the hall. The roof panels were still open and the bright arc of morning sky stretched above, lighting the seats that had been filled the night before by Soldiers of the King.

As she stood looking at this unusual room, a voice spoke behind her. "Last night was a memorable experience, wasn't it, Akara?"

She turned quickly. There a few feet away, with a smile on his face, stood Robin. He was clad in armor. With him was an elderly man with white hair and a lined face who was wearing a white, knee-length tunic. Akara remembered him as the one who sounded a trumpet at the evening meal the night before. Robin turned to the older man. "This is Akara, sir, the young woman who came to the castle yesterday. Akara, this is Latta, one of the leaders of our fellowship."

Latta said, "I understand you were with Keila during her fight on the mountainside."

"Yes, I was."

"Then you'll be glad to hear that her condition improved last night."

"I'm so glad!"

"Robin and I are meeting with a few others to give thanks to the King. Would you like to join us?"

"Oh yes!"

"Come along then."

A little farther along the corridor was a heavy oak door. Robin pushed it open, and they stepped out into the open air. A flight of stone stairs took them to the top of a tower where several other men and women were waiting.

Robin introduced Akara, then Latta told the group about the improvement in Keila's condition. When he finished, a woman across the circle raised her trumpet. "Wonderful! Let us send a call of thanks to the King."

As the others also raised their trumpets, Jamin came quietly up the stairs and joined them. The notes were low and vibrant, like those that had begun the previous evening's session. As Akara breathed through her own silent trumpet, she found it easy to lift her thoughts to the King.

When the last sound had died away, the circle broke up. Some of the people left, others stood in small groups talking. Akara walked to the battlement and stood looking out over the wooded slopes and the valley beyond.

Directly below her was the castle yard bounded by a high wall. Outside this wall, the mountaintop area around the castle was clear of trees. At the edge of this cleared area, she could see the opening to the path up which they had come the night before. A short distance to the right of the path, a ridge jutted out toward the valley. Near the end of this ridge stood a circular stone tower around which Akara could see figures moving. The glint of the morning sun on their armor showed that they were Soldiers of the King.

Robin, who had come to stand beside her, pointed downward. "That fortress overlooks the path and helps us to keep the way open to the valley," he said. "My unit was on duty there yesterday when we heard a trumpet call and saw through the trees below us the light of Keila's sword flaring high. We knew then that she was in battle with the enemy and rushed to her rescue. Lanus and Henda were closer and reached you first."

"What do you mean about the light of Keila's sword flaring?"

"Whenever the enemy is near, the light from the sword is much brighter than usual. This increased light warns the soldier of danger even before the enemy comes into view, and in this case it also alerted us. With all the excitement, you may not have noticed this change, but we saw it clearly."

Jamin joined them in time to hear part of this explanation. "That's true, Akara," he said. "Each of the six pieces of the King's armor — the belt, breastplate, shoes, shield, helmet, and sword — was designed by the King for our use, and each has its own special quality. He has also given us his trumpet. While not a piece of armor, it is a wonderful resource.

He paused, then continued "Akara, I understand you are especially interested in the silver trumpet. After you have breakfasted this morning, I'd like to take you to someone who knows more about the trumpet than anyone else in the castle does. She is old now, but over the years her wisdom has encouraged many of us to use our trumpets more intelligently."

Akara and Robin sat together at breakfast. During the meal he told her how he had left the valley a few years before to explore the Great Mountains, and as a result, had become a Soldier of the King. As they finished their meal, Jamin appeared in the doorway and beckoned to Akara.

Their destination this time was a room on the ground floor of the castle. Jamin stopped before a door, tapped on it lightly, then in response to a quiet voice within, opened it. Akara found herself in a large airy room whose only occupant was an old woman sitting in a chair near the open window. She wore a light gray robe and had a blanket across her knees.

"Come in, child, and you too, Jamin," she said cheerfully. "I've been waiting for you."

"This is Akara, Dame Prendil," said Jamin. "She's the visitor from the valley I told you about earlier. She has a trumpet and would like to learn more about it. I have not yet heard her story, and I thought perhaps we could listen to it together."

While Jamin was speaking, Akara had become aware of the sound of children's voices coming from somewhere outside the room. She glanced at the open window. Dame Prendil chuckled. "What you hear is the noise made by my young friends. I love to listen to them. Go to the window and look."

Akara did so. There she saw a number of children sitting in groups on the grass of the castle yard, talking and laughing together. With each group was a young man or woman who apparently served as a leader or teacher. Unlike the children at Dame Dessit's orphan home, these boys and girls looked well and happy.

"We have many families in the castle," said Dame Prendil. "What you see is part of our school where their children are taught."

"Will they grow up to be Soldiers of the King?"

"We hope so. They are learning about the King, but later they must decide for themselves where they wish to live. I am sorry to say, some have turned their backs on the castle when they were grown and chose instead to become valley dwellers."

She shook her head sadly, then gave Akara a smile. "Now, my dear, I want to hear about you. I understand you met Keila on the mountainside. Sit down and tell us how you came to be there and why you, a valley person, carry a trumpet."

Akara once again told her story, this time in detail, for she felt these two could answer some of the questions that troubled her. As she finished, she took the silver trumpet from her bag. "This little trumpet is the only thing I ever owned, so it has become very precious to me. I feel that someone, somewhere listens to my trumpet calls. But I am sad because it makes no sound."

Jamin leaned forward to take the trumpet from her. He looked at it, then passed it back to her. "It is certainly a genuine trumpet. You were able to hear our trumpets last night, were you not?"

"Yes, I heard Keila's on the mountainside and those in the Hall of the Trumpets last night."

Dame Prendil was silent for a moment, then she said, "I'm not sure why your trumpet is silent. I suspect it may be because you are not a Soldier of the King. But be assured that the King hears you, for he hears everyone who calls to him."

Dame Prendil's words made sense to Akara. She nodded. "I also have a question about the trumpet calls I heard last night. The notes were low at first, and higher later on. Can you tell me why that was?"

"I was not able to be at that assembly," said Dame Prendil. "What ranges were sounded, Jamin?"

"The deep level and the next one higher."

"Ah, yes," Dame Prendil nodded. "Well, Akara, within the King's Book are the writings of a great soldier named Paul. He wrote of four types of notes that the trumpet sounds. These tones help us express our concerns to the King. The deepest, most resonant tones, we use to honor and praise him for who he is, and thank him for his goodness to us. With the next higher range, we send a call to him for others — for those who we believe may need his help."

"On the tower this morning," Jamin put in, "we met to praise and thank the King, so we used only the deep range."

Dame Prendil went on, "Still higher come the tones through which we pour out to the King our personal thoughts, hopes, dreams, and fears. We know he wants us to share these things with him, for his Book tells us so.

"Finally, at the top of the register are the high, clear tones. These call on the King for help. If Keila sounded her trumpet before the enemy attacked her on the mountainside, I'm sure you heard a high call. Whenever a soldier asks for help, the King hears, and he has promised to answer."

Jamin nodded in agreement. "Keila's call for help was heard by the King. As Dame Prendil said, your call was heard as well, though you are not one of us. The King sent help through his soldiers."

Akara looked down at her own trumpet in her lap. "I guess I have much to learn."

Jamin smiled. "That's true, Akara, but you already know a great deal more than most valley people. The King taught you some of the wonders of the trumpet by the way he answered your calls in the valley, and he also used it to bring you here."

"You have also learned something else," said Dame Prendil. "You told us how, one night when you blew your trumpet under a bush, you heard wonderful music and saw bright and dark figures moving in a dance. A few of the King's Soldiers also have glimpsed that great dance, in which both good and evil play a part, and have written of it. It teaches an important truth — that while the King does not bring evil upon us, he allows it to play a part in our lives. But always, Akara, he is in control, and the outcome of the dance is our good!"

"Thank you. I use my trumpet every day and want to keep on doing so."

"There is much to be learned about the silver trumpet. I was taught about it many years ago by a dedicated old soldier named Lors."

Akara's eyebrows shot up. "Did you know Lors?"

"Yes, he was one to whom the King gave a special power in using the silver trumpet. He was quite old when I knew him and has long since died. How did you know of him?"

"In an old box in the Hill Soldiers' library, I found a letter he had written. It told about the King's Castle, and this encouraged me to try to find it."

"It would please Lors to know that after so many years his words were used to bring someone to the castle." The old woman leaned forward and took both of Akara's hands in her own. "My child, the King gives each member of our fellowship a special way of serving him. I believe that, if you choose to become a Soldier of the King, perhaps he will lead you to devote much of your time to the silver trumpet, as Lors and I have done."

Jamin and Akara had just left Dame Prendil's room when a young soldier hailed Jamin, a scrap of parchment in his hand. "I have a note for you from Lanus, sir," he said.

Jamin read the parchment, then turned to Akara, smiling. "It seems there is someone else who wants to see you."

He led the way up several flights of stairs, then stopped and pushed open a door. Akara stepped through and found herself in the open air on top of a castle tower. Here a small group of people were gathered. Lanus and Robin were seated on chairs while Henda perched on the battlement at the edge of the tower. All three were in full armor. But it was the fourth person whose presence caused Akara to give a little cry of joy. Reclining on a couch, covered with a blanket but looking very much alive, was Keila!

CHAPTER 23

A Visit with Keila

The three soldiers jumped up, and Lanus and Robin made their chairs available to the new arrivals. However, Jamin declined to stay. He crossed the tower to press Keila's hand, accepted Akara's thanks for the time he had spent with her, and departed. Lanus escorted Akara to the chair he had occupied beside Keila, then sat down on the foot of her couch.

When all were seated, Keila said, "It's good to see you again, Akara. I was afraid you might return to the valley before I was well enough to talk with you."

"Thank you. It is wonderful to see you looking so well!"

"I am feeling better. With the rest and the care I'm getting, I should be ready for duty soon."

"Though maybe not as soon as she thinks," Lanus put in, smiling at her. "When do you have to go back to the valley, Akara?"

"Tomorrow. I have jobs to do at the House of the Hill Soldiers."

"Then Henda and I will escort you down tomorrow morning," said Robin.

"I'd like to go too," said Lanus, "but I'm on duty here at the castle."

Keila said, "Now that that's settled, I want to learn more about you, Akara. I've thought about you often since the night I went to Dame Dessit's orphan home only to find you had gone. Will you tell us what happened then, and how you came to be on the mountain two days ago?"

"Gladly," said Akara, and once again she told her story.

"You've had some real adventures," said Henda when she finished.

"Yes," said Keila, "and we're glad that through the trumpet, the King brought you to us at last."

"I want to know more about you too, Keila. Why did you come to the orphan home to get me?"

"It came about in this way. Demars and I were in the valley on the King's service. I was introduced to one of the elders of the village of Palloweth who had traveled north on business. He told me there was an orphan in Palloweth who needed a home and asked me if I knew someone who could help. I decided to go to Palloweth and bring you here to the castle."

Robin leaned forward from his place on the other side of Lanus. "You see, Akara, our mission is to help people, and also to tell them about our King and invite them to visit his castle."

"Yes," said Lanus. "All of us are involved in that mission. Robin was the one who told me about the King and brought me here."

"And later, Lanus brought me," added Henda.

Akara smiled ruefully. "So if I hadn't run away, I would have been here much sooner and had a lot less trouble on the way!"

"That's right," said Keila. "But the important thing is that you are here now."

"And now that you are here, we hope you will enjoy it and perhaps want to come back," added Lanus.

Akara stared thoughtfully out across the mountaintop. "I'll certainly think about that. I've heard many things lately, and I need time to sort them all out. I would also like to find out who my parents were and where I came from."

"Do you have any clues about that?" asked Robin.

"Only this blue bag, which had my baby clothes in it. I've been told the style is unusual, but no one I've met so far knows where it might have come from."

Keila put out a hand. "May I look at your bag?"

Akara handed the bag to Keila, who looked at it closely. "This is exceptionally fine needlework," she said, "and these handles of red and blue woven cord are unusual. I've never seen anything quite like it."

She passed it to Lanus, who also examined it carefully, turning it over in his hands. He said nothing but handed it to Robin, who looked at it and said, "I've never seen a bag like this either." Henda came across, took the bag from Robin, looked, shook his head, and gave it back to Akara.

"It's a slender clue," said Keila, "but I understand why you want to continue to search."

Robin glanced up at the sun. "It is almost noon. I must leave you to go on duty."

"Where is your duty?" asked Akara.

"I'll be in the castle yard, right below us. I'm to help Gayne, the sword master, train young soldiers in the use of arms."

Henda stood up. "I must leave too. It's outpost duty for me."

Lanus also rose, and turned to Akara. "My duty comes later. Keila is not yet strong enough to go to the dining room to eat, so we plan to lunch here on the tower. If you'll stay here and talk with Keila, I'll go down and get food for the three of us."

He left and Akara said, "Now that I've met you, Keila, I'm truly sorry I ran away that night when you came to the orphan home."

"Perhaps our enemies, the evil ones, helped to influence your decision."

"How could that be? I was alone under the bush! Besides, the evil ones are up here on the mountainside, not down in the valley."

"The evil ones are in the valley too. Valley people don't realize this because the evil ones are invisible to them."

"But Tazen and I are valley people, and we saw the evil ones yesterday on the mountainside. They sent a flaming dart at Tazen!"

"That was because your friend was waving a sword from the cave. The sword-light made them visible. When they saw Tazen with the sword, they probably thought he was one of our soldiers."

A short time later, Lanus reappeared carrying a large tray loaded with fruit, bread, cheese, butter, and honey, and also a large pitcher of water. He brought over the second chair to serve as a table and set the tray down on it. Then, before they ate, he lifted his trumpet and sounded a note of thanks to the King.

He picked up the pitcher. "This water comes from the spring beneath the castle," he said, pouring a cup and passing it to Akara. "Some say it has special powers." Akara tasted the water and found it cool and refreshing.

While they ate, Keila told Lanus what she and Akara had talked about. Lanus said, "The evil ones do not usually hurl their flaming darts at valley people. As Keila suggested, it must have been the waving of the King's sword that brought the dart." He gestured toward the valley. "I remember the night that Robin brought me up the mountain to the King's Castle for the first time. We were attacked by two of the evil ones. Because I was not yet a Soldier of the King, they ignored me entirely and turned their weapons against Robin."

"I see," said Akara, "but it's hard to believe that the evil ones are also around me when I am down in the valley. And I certainly don't understand how they can influence my thinking."

Keila swallowed a bite of bread and cheese. "Let me tell you what I've learned from the King's Book. The miller was right when he told you there are two invisible powers. One of them is the King, whom we follow and who is the rightful ruler of the valley. The other is the Evil One, also known as the Dark Power, who with his followers is at war with the King."

"So the creatures you fought against on the mountainside, which you called the evil ones, are the followers of this second power?"

"Yes. The King's Book tells us that long ago the valley people revolted against the King. Then evil ones came invisibly into the valley in force, bringing with them hate and wickedness and warfare. While they cannot actually control people of the valley, they can whisper their thoughts into their ears. Their purpose is to keep any of these people from turning to the King."

Akara nodded. "And that's why you said the evil ones may have influenced my decision to run away from the orphan home."

Lanus reached for a piece of fruit. "The evil ones are powerful and clever, Akara," he said. "When the King came to the valley long ago as the Good Carpenter, they certainly influenced the thinking of the valley people. Though he did nothing but good, they arrested him and put him to death."

"I suppose you know that many of the Hill Soldiers don't believe the Good Carpenter and the King are the same person," said Akara. She sighed. "I wish I knew just what to believe."

Keila put down her fork and leaned back against her pillow. "I believe that the King is drawing you to himself and that he will make it clear to you what you should do. Call on him through your trumpet, Akara."

CHAPTER 24

A Tour
of the Castle

Soon after their lunch was finished, the door to the tower opened and a young girl of about Akara's age came out. Keila introduced her as Tril. "Tril takes care of me," she told Akara, "and I'm afraid she's come to tell me I must go back to my room."

Tril gave her a saucy smile. "Don't complain. You've already been up longer than Tolsus recommended."

Lanus helped Keila to her feet. At Keila's request, Akara followed them as they made their way back to Keila's room.

At the door she turned. "Now that you know where my room is, Akara, I'd like it if you could come here after the evening meal tonight and sit with me for a while. I don't know how wide awake I'll be, but perhaps we can talk a little more."

"I will," Akara promised.

After they left Keila's room, Lanus turned to Akara. "And now, would you like a tour of our castle?"

Akara's eyes sparkled. "Very much. I'd especially like to visit the garden and the library, since those are the places where I work at the House of the Hill Soldiers. Oh, and could I see where that special drinking water comes from?"

Lanus chuckled. "Sounds as though you've already got the tour planned. All right, let's go!"

Their first stop was the library, where a number of soldiers sat at tables. Some were reading the King's Book, and some, other volumes. Unlike the Hill Soldiers' library, which was visited mainly by scholars and teachers, the readers seemed to be soldiers of all ages. "We have a few copies of the King's Book in the Hill Soldiers' library," Akara said, "but they are not often read."

"I know little about the Hill Soldiers," Lanus answered, "but all of our soldiers are encouraged to study the King's Book for themselves."

From the library, they passed through the kitchen where men and women were already preparing for the evening meal, then out through the castle yard and the gardens where still others were working. Near the gardens was a grassy area where Robin and another soldier were guiding younger members of the King's army in practice with sword and shield. Robin was too busy to stop and talk, but he gave them a friendly wave as they passed.

"The King's followers serve in many ways, don't they?" asked Akara thoughtfully as they re-entered the castle.

"We all serve," said Lanus. "We hire no servants here."

"What are your special duties?"

"I stand watches at the outposts that guard the castle from attack. I also assist Demars in her duties as seneschal. The idea is that each King's Soldier serve in the areas in which he or she is especially qualified."

"What does Keila do?"

"As you have seen, she is very skilled with the sword, but battling the enemy is not her major role. She spends much time in the valley, telling the story of the King, particularly to young people. She has brought many to the castle." Lanus pulled open a door and they re-entered the castle. "And now, Akara, I'll show you the source of that water you found so refreshing."

Down a flight of stairs they went. Since this took them below ground, there were no windows. A row of swords set in sconces high on the wall lit their way. Partway down, the stairway changed to a tunnel that sloped downward through the rock, but here, too, steps had been cut in the floor, so the descent was easy. At the bottom, Akara found herself in a large, high-ceilinged cave, illuminated by swords mounted on the walls. The walls themselves also sparkled with many colors so that the cave seemed ablaze with light.

"How beautiful!" Akara exclaimed. "What makes these bright colors?"

"The light is reflected from precious stones of all kinds embedded in the walls. They've been here since the mountains were created and are part of the King's treasure."

Akara saw that in the center of the cave was a pool into which water flowed from a crack in one wall. On the other side of the pool, the water disappeared through another fissure. Gems also sparkled beneath the water in the sides and bottom of the pool. Over the center of the pool, a shaft cut in the rock led upward.

"The water we drink comes from this spring," said Lanus. "We also collect rainwater into cisterns and use it for washing and other general purposes, but the water from this pool has a special quality. Drinking it helps to keep our bodies well and our minds clear. Pails of water are pulled up the shaft each day with ropes, and our soldiers also carry larger casks of it up through the tunnel."

Akara scooped up some of the water in her hand and drank, then stood staring at the pool.

"Is something troubling you?" asked Lanus.

"I was thinking about the water that flows out of the gorge behind the mill at Arn. That water also comes out of the Great Mountains, yet the peddler warned me against drinking it."

Lanus nodded soberly. "There is a deep valley in the mountains south of here in which a castle of the evil ones lies. Everything about that castle is evil, including the dark lake that surrounds it. I know this water flows out into the valley somewhere. Perhaps it is at Arn. If so, it no doubt contaminates the wells in that area. Some say this water can cloud the minds of those who drink it, making it hard for them to understand and believe the King's truth."

When they had climbed back up the stairs and were again aboveground, Lanus stopped beside a window and looked up to check the position of the sun. "I have only a few more minutes before I must go on duty," he said. "I'm sorry, for there's more of the castle I'd like to show you. I must be on watch at the stone tower above the path to the valley tonight and tomorrow, so I won't see you before you go."

"I'm sorry too. I wish I could stay longer."

"I'm glad you're going to sit with Keila tonight. She's been badly wounded, but your visit has already helped her a great deal." He paused for a moment, then continued. "You see, when Keila went to Palloweth she was anxious to find you because she knew you were someone who needed help. Since then, she has made many trumpet calls to the King asking him to help you, even though she didn't know where you were."

Akara felt tears springing to her eyes. She blinked them away. "I'm sorry. I had no idea she, or anyone, cared about me."

"She does indeed care about you. You are important to her and to all of us. I hope you will visit again soon."

Akara promised to do so. Lanus walked with her to the door of her room where he said good-bye. She rested there until the chiming of the bell signaled the dinner hour, then washed her face and went to the dining hall. Demars was waiting for her at the entrance and they ate together. Afterward, as she had promised, Akara made her way to Keila's room, where she found her in bed. Tril was sitting nearby.

"I'm so glad you came," said Keila. "Tril, Akara will stay with me for a while, so you are free to go if you wish."

Tril left, and Akara slipped into a chair beside the bed. She took Keila's hand. "I'm so glad you asked me to come."

"After our talk this afternoon, I feel I know you much better. Are there more things you'd like to ask about?"

Akara thought for a moment. "I've been thinking about that night when you came to Dame Dessit's. If I had stayed, you would have brought me from Palloweth straight to the castle. I've been wondering why the King didn't do something to stop me from running away. Wasn't his power strong enough?"

"The King's power is truly stronger than the power of evil, Akara, but he chooses how to use it. Sometimes he allows things to happen that we don't understand. Perhaps in your case there were things he wanted you to learn from your experiences with Trask and the miller."

"I don't understand."

Keila was silent for a moment, her eyes fixed on the far wall. Then she said, "Akara, you were there the other day when one of the evil ones wounded me badly. The King didn't prevent that. He could have, but I believe that he knows what is best for me."

"How can being badly hurt be good for you?"

"I don't know yet," Keila smiled, "but when I sounded my trumpet before the fight, I put the outcome in the King's hands. I'm willing to trust his judgment."

This was a new thought to Akara, and she pondered it as the conversation shifted to talk of Keila's wound and her recovery. Soon afterward, Keila said softly, "I'm becoming very tired. I'm going to rest now, but don't leave right away. Hold my hand for a while."

She closed her eyes, and in a few minutes her regular breathing showed that she was asleep. Akara sat contentedly holding her hand until Tril reappeared. She tiptoed to the bed and felt Keila's forehead.

"She probably won't wake again tonight," Tril whispered. "I'll sleep on the couch in the corner to be available in case she needs me."

Akara nodded, gently disengaged her hand, and left the room.

CHAPTER 25

History of the Hill Soldiers

It rained during the night, but the morning dawned cool and clear. After breakfast, Akara, Robin, and Henda left the castle and headed toward the woodland path.

As they reached the edge of the clearing, Akara paused to look back at the castle. Its towers were outlined sharply against the morning sky. She smiled at her companions. "It has been an exciting time for me, and I'm sorry to leave. I also feel badly that you two must travel to the valley on my account."

"It's no trouble," said Robin. "I have business in Midra, so I'd be going down anyway."

"As for me," chimed in Henda, "I'll welcome the opportunity to visit my parents and brothers in the valley."

When the three reached the point on the downward path where the thick woods ended, and the valley was spread out before them, Robin turned to Akara. "This is where you and your friend left the path two days ago, isn't it?"

"Yes. Tazen started to explore that crossing path. Then I saw Keila coming up from the valley. Her head was hooded. I knew her then only as the Tall Woman, and I was afraid. I ran after Tazen, and we hid in the cave where the armor is."

"I'm surprised you found the entrance open," said Henda.

"That is unusual," said Robin. "I'm sure Keila locked it when she followed you in, but I'd like to check it again."

He led the way along the lateral path. When they reached the cave, Akara saw that where the entrance had been, there was now only a slab of smooth rock.

Henda turned to Robin. "How can the door be opened?"

"With the King's sword." Robin held up his sword for inspection. "I'm sure you've noticed the five grooves that run the length of the blade, Henda. Each sword is also a key that opens doors. Let me show you." Robin inserted his sword tip into a small slot in the rock, pushed it in to the hilt, and turned it gently. There was a click and the stone slab swung inward.

He pulled the door shut again, removed his sword, and then turned to Akara. "I don't know how it was that you found it open."

Henda frowned. "It was careless of someone."

"Maybe so. It's also possible that the King himself arranged for it to be open."

Akara stared at him. "Why would he do that?"

"Had the door been shut you might have kept running into the woods. The open door brought you to where Keila and the rest of us found you. Because of this, you came at last to the castle!" He smiled at Akara. "That's just a guess, of course, but I've learned not to be surprised at the way circumstances work out to accomplish the King's purposes."

As they turned away from the armory, Henda said, "I've never heard why this cave is here and why it contains pieces of the King's armor."

Robin sheathed his sword. "I have heard the story. It has to do with the Hill Soldiers. I'll tell you about it as we go."

Once back on the main path, he began. "Long before any of us were born, some of the King's Soldiers became dissatisfied with the castle on the mountain ridge. They knew that learned men of the valley were studying the life of the Good Carpenter. (That's the name by which our King was known when he lived in the valley.) They thought they might learn more about this part of the King's life if they lived down here on the slope nearer to these valley scholars."

Henda, who was walking in front of Robin and Akara, turned his head. "Couldn't others of the King's Soldiers have stopped them?"

"They tried. The leaders of our fellowship knew their move was not wise. They pointed out that the King himself had chosen the mountaintop site for his castle, and that the clear mountain air and the pure water from the castle spring help us to understand his truth. But it is not the King's way to force people to stay at his castle. The discontented ones left. They found this cave, built doors to protect it, and began to construct a castle above it. The ruins of their walls can still be found in the woods."

Henda turned again. "Why did they stop building? Did the evil ones attack them?"

Robin shook his head. "No. Our enemies gave them no trouble. I suspect they were happy to see the King's Soldiers divided. And since there were no attacks, they found no use for swords and armor. Eventually, they stored them in the cave."

"But what stopped them from finishing their castle?" asked Akara.

Robin shrugged. "More dissatisfaction. As they spent more and more time with the valley people, they decided they were still too far up the mountain. So they moved down to the foothills. With the help of the valley folk, they built what is now called the House of the Hill Soldiers. Since they feared no attack, they did not fortify it. They left their armor here and, I'm sure, have forgotten it entirely. The King's Soldiers keep an eye on these weapons, but since the weapons were issued to those who are now Hill Soldiers, everything has been left here."

Henda said, "Now that the Hill Soldiers live down in the valley and no longer have the light of their swords, the evil ones must be invisible to them, as they are to the other valley folk."

"I suspect you're right, Henda. They may well have robbed themselves of the ability to see evil for what it is."

The three travelers left the mountain slope and headed across the rolling foothills toward the House of the Hill Soldiers. Suddenly Akara noticed a figure on horseback, riding parallel to them and in the same direction. She stopped, shaded her eyes, and looked at this rider. It was Blink! At the same moment, Blink evidently saw them, for she turned her horse's head and galloped toward them. Reining to a stop, she slid to the ground.

"I was coming to find you, Akara," she said breathlessly. "Kelidon just arrived home from the village with news. I thought you should hear it so I climbed on Browny's back and came over."

"What news?"

"A messenger came to Zemla from the miller of Arn. I don't know how the miller found out you're here, but his message claims that your real home is in Arn. He says you have a relative who lives in Arn, and he demands that we send you back there!"

Akara stared at her friend in shocked surprise. "That's awful! I thought he would stop chasing me when we escaped from him at Elsis. What did Zemla do?"

"He has sent a message back rejecting the miller's claim but thought you should hear about it right away anyway."

"Thank you." Akara turned toward the King's Soldiers who were standing quietly by. "Blink, these are Robin and Henda, Soldiers of the King. I've been at their castle on the mountaintop, and they've been kind enough to escort me back down the mountain."

The two young men acknowledged the introduction. Then Robin asked, "Is there any chance this miller has evidence to support his claim, Akara?"

"I'm certain that what he says is not true, but I am concerned. As I told you at the castle, I have no real information about where I was born." Her face took on a stubborn set. "I'm sure I didn't come from Arn, and I won't let him take me back there."

The group set off again toward the House of the Hill Soldiers, Blink walking with Akara and leading her horse.

"Something occurs to me," said Robin. "Yesterday you showed us your blue bag that was with you when you were found as a baby. Did the miller ever examine it?"

Akara shook her head. "He saw it, but he had no chance to look at it closely."

"Good. That may be important. Anyone who claims to be a family member should be able to describe it in detail."

"Thank you, I'll remember that," answered Akara.

As they came within sight of the building, a carriage whirled up the drive and stopped at the front door. Zemla stepped out. When he caught sight of the approaching party, he stood waiting for them.

"Now you'll hear the story firsthand," said Blink.

Zemla greeted them, and Akara introduced the two soldiers. Zemla said, "I remember you, Robin. You grew up in our village. I also know Henda's father, Farmer Broadleaf. It's good to see both of you." He turned back to Akara. "Since Linka is with you, I assume you've heard about the message I received earlier this morning."

Akara nodded. "She told me you refused the miller's request."

"That's right. I hope that will be the end of it. However, it is important that I discuss it with you."

"Thank you. I'd also like my friends to hear what you have to say. Is that all right?"

"Certainly, if you wish it." Zemla turned toward the building. "We can sit on those chairs under the portico."

CHAPTER 26

Disturbing News

Robin and Henda arranged chairs in a circle, while Blink fastened Browny's reins to a nearby hitching post. When all were seated, Zemla said, "As I'm sure Linka has told you, Akara, the miller of Arn says that you were born in his village, and he wants you to be sent back there. He also says that one of your relatives, an aunt, lives in Arn."

Akara took a deep breath. "He's lying! I'm sure he did not know who I was when I came to the mill with Trask. Then, just a few days later, he told the people at Elsis that he was my grandfather. Now he's made up a new story!"

"I believe you, Akara. I'm sure the miller can't prove his case. But if he insists, we'll have to hold an official hearing."

Blink had been controlling herself with difficulty. Now she burst out, "Why is a hearing needed? If Akara doesn't want to go to Arn, that should settle the matter."

Zemla's face was grave. "I wish we could let Akara decide, but we must abide by the law of the valley."

"What does the law say about it?" pursued Blink.

"It's part of the new treaty that all the villages have signed. Remember I told you about it when you first came to Midra. The treaty says that all young people below the age of eighteen should stay under the control of their families. If they run away to another village, they must be returned."

His eyes came back to Akara. "You're an unusually mature young woman, Akara, You're certainly capable of making your own decisions, but in the eyes of the law you are still a child. That's why we must hear the miller's claim. But since it is untrue, you should have nothing to fear."

Robin, who had been listening intently, leaned forward. "One question, sir. May I ask when the miller's village signed this treaty?"

"They were the last to sign. As the Reeve of Arn, the miller signed just three days ago."

"Then right after that he sent a message demanding that Akara be sent to Arn?"

"Yes."

"Isn't it possible that he agreed to the treaty only so he might use it against Akara?"

Zemla hesitated. "That thought crossed my mind. Some people do try to twist the law for their own ends. This is a good treaty, but of course it can be misused. I'll do my best to make sure justice is done."

"When will the hearing be?" asked Akara.

"If the miller pursues the matter, we'll act as soon as he comes to Midra to present his claim."

Akara looked at her friends. There seemed to be nothing more to say. Then Blink ventured a last question. "If a hearing is held, who will judge the case?"

"Since the matter involves Midra, and I'm the Reeve of Midra, I cannot preside. There will be two judges, Syden and Karnethal, both from nearby villages, to do so." He rose to his feet. "I must leave now, Akara, but you and I must meet soon to discuss this matter again. You must be prepared, and since I will not be a judge, I'll be free to represent you."

After Zemla's carriage had disappeared down the drive, Robin turned to Akara. "Henda and I must leave now, but we will certainly use our trumpets to call to the King for you."

Blink spoke up in her usual blunt manner. "Trumpets are well and good, but other kinds of help may be better. I don't expect the judges to rule against Akara, but if they do, are you soldiers prepared to defend her?"

"We will help in every way we can," answered Robin, "but we may not use the King's sword against valley folk."

Blink made no immediate response, but after the two soldiers left, she said, "Well, Akara, if things go wrong, I don't think you can count on much help from your mountaintop friends. I'd hide you at Kelidon and Delsa's place, but I'm sure you'd be discovered there. I can't leave Baslin, otherwise you and I could run away together."

Akara gave her friend a warm hug. "I understand, Blink, but I don't want to run or hide unless I have to. Zemla thinks the truth will win out, and I'll have to trust him."

For a few days nothing happened. Akara returned to her duties at the House of the Hill Soldiers. When her friends there heard of her problem, they expressed their sympathy. Garis pledged his support and encouraged her to believe that all would be well.

Robin and Henda came again to see her. "Keila wanted to come when she heard of your new problem," reported Robin. "She's doing well but is still not strong enough to make the trip to the valley."

"How is Lanus?" asked Akara.

"Lanus has gone on a journey. I don't know where. Maybe on a special mission. He left the day after we brought you back to the valley.

"A special mission for the King?"

"Very likely. He didn't say, but Lanus is often called on for such things."

The next day Akara had another conference with Zemla. He told her the miller had sent another message requesting a hearing, and he assured her he would do his best to defeat the miller.

In spite of Zemla's optimism, Akara worried about the outcome of the hearing. She discussed her fears with Blink. "If the judges try to send me to Arn, I'll run away," she said.

Blink, ever practical, answered, "Then let's plan for that." And plan they did. They decided that Akara's best escape route would be north on the old valley road. If she went that way, she would pass near the grassy knoll. They made up a package of food and other items she would need for traveling, wrapped it in a waterproof cloth, and hid it under the bushes on the slope of the knoll.

The day of the hearing came, dawning gray and windy. Heavy dark clouds hung over the western mountains. "Storm brewing," the wise old farmers said to one another. "It will reach Midra before nightfall!"

The proceedings were to begin early in the afternoon in Midra's village hall, a large barn-like structure. News of the unusual event had spread, and by midday, the hall was crowded with spectators.

Akara came in a carriage with Garis and others from the House of the Hill Soldiers. Following Zemla's instructions, she brought her blue bag, hidden inside a larger cloth bag. Zemla hoped to produce the blue bag to contradict the miller's witnesses. What Zemla didn't know was that the blue bag also contained a change of clothing and the silver trumpet. If the case went against her, Akara was ready to run!

Zemla was there when the carriage stopped. He took Akara's arm. "We'll go in the side door, then we won't have to go through the crowd to get to our seats."

Into that door they went, then across a small storeroom and through another door into the main part of the building. Akara found herself in an open area at the front of the hall. Immediately in front of her was a table and two chairs, and here they took their seats. This table was placed diagonally so that they faced the low platform centered at the front of the hall, but could also look across to a similarly placed table at the other side of the room. Beside Akara stood a flagstaff from which hung the flag of Midra. On a similar staff across the room hung a different flag. This, Akara decided, must be the banner of Arn.

On the platform at the front of the hall stood the judges' table. From its front hung two flags that Akara assumed were those of Syden's and Karnethal's villages. On the table lay a polished wood staff. The rest of the hall was filled with benches, which were crowded with spectators.

Akara and Zemla had been seated only a few minutes when a rush of carriage wheels came from outside the building. The front door flew open, and the miller entered. He walked swiftly up the center aisle, looking neither right nor left. Behind him trailed two women, neither of whom Akara had ever seen. The miller and the two women took their positions at the table across from Zemla and Akara. Two men had entered with the miller but remained at the back of the hall.

A few moments later, there came a call to rise. Everyone stood, and the two judges made their way down the aisle, mounted the platform, and took their places behind the table there. Syden, who led the way, was frail and white-haired. Karnethal was a younger, barrel-chested man with grizzled gray hair. Syden picked up the staff that lay on the table and thumped it three times on the floor. "I call you to order," he said in a high, reedy voice. "My name is Syden from the village of Kerth. My colleague is Karnethal from Bellis. We are here to preside at the first hearing to be held under the new treaty. Please be seated."

The hearing had begun.

CHAPTER 27

The Hearing

When all were seated and the spectators were quiet, Syden gave a brief statement about the reason for the hearing. Then he said, "We will hear first from the miller, the honorable Reeve of Arn and his witnesses."

The miller rose to his feet, his face bland. He spoke in a soft, clear voice. "Sirs, I am known simply as 'the miller of Arn'. I am proud to serve those who live in that village by grinding their grain. I had no interest in this girl, Akara, until she was brought to my mill by Trask the peddler. She had earlier run away from an orphan home in Palloweth. I became interested in her history and wrote to that village seeking information."

"Before I received an answer, Akara ran away again. However, I now have a written statement from Dame Dessit, who operates the Palloweth orphan home. It is signed and witnessed." He held up a paper. "When I read it, I realized immediately that Akara was the baby who had been stolen from our village fifteen years ago and whose relatives still live in Arn." After receiving Syden's permission to do so, he read Dame Dessit's statement aloud. It described how Akara was found as a baby and brought to the orphan home.

The miller put down the paper and continued. "The witnesses I have brought with me will tell you that..."

Syden thumped the end of his staff on the floor. "I must interrupt, good miller," he said mildly. "Your witnesses should speak for themselves. Have you any more of your own testimony to give?"

"No, sir."

"Then before we proceed, I will ask Akara and Zemla if they have any questions about what the miller has said."

Zemla looked at Akara, who shook her head. Then Zemla rose to his feet. "I have a question, sir," he said. "Are you yourself one of Akara's relatives?"

"No, I am not."

"Then may I ask, sir, why you recently told the people at Elsis that she was your granddaughter? I have statements here from residents of that village testifying that this was the case."

Akara gave Zemla an appreciative look. But the miller replied in the same calm voice. "That was not an untruth. It is a tradition in Arn for villagers to call me 'grandfather'. When I came north to Elsis, I already believed she was rightly a member of our village. It was natural for me to speak of her as my granddaughter." He turned to Syden. "I'm truly sorry if this has led to a misunderstanding."

Akara clenched her fists until the nails bit into her palms. The assurance in the miller's manner and his smooth answers made him seem invincible. There was movement behind her. Skey had left his seat, tiptoed down the aisle, and dropped to one knee behind Zemla and Akara, his head between them.

"He's lying," he whispered. "I've carried fruits and vegetables to the village of Arn and know people there. They fear the miller, but none call him 'grandfather'!"

"Thank you," Zemla whispered in return. "I'll call you to testify when we present our case."

The two witnesses at the miller's table then gave their testimony. The first, a short, heavy-set woman, gave her name as Dame Lasdell. She testified in a harsh, expressionless voice, as though she was reciting something she had learned by heart. According to her story, Akara's mother was her sister. Akara's father had been killed in an accident before she was born, and her mother died shortly after giving birth. A cousin, an elderly woman, had disappeared with the family's wagon soon afterward, taking the baby with her. Neither she nor the baby was heard from again.

Not surprisingly, Dame Lasdell's description of the missing horse and wagon agreed with what Dame Dessit said in her written statement.

Akara's heart beat faster when Zemla asked Dame Lasdell to describe the bag in which the baby's clothing was kept, and that the woman would have taken with her. The woman seemed confused, shot a glance at the miller, then finally said she knew nothing about any such bag.

Her testimony was supported by the second witness, a small, frightened-looking woman named Purvie. She claimed that she had lived next door to Dame Lasdell for many years and remembered being told about the baby's disappearance when it occurred. Zemla asked her no questions.

This completed the presentation from the miller's party. Syden then called on Zemla, who introduced himself, then asked Akara to give her testimony. Akara's legs shook and her throat was dry as she rose to speak. Her voice trembled at first, but grew stronger as she went along. "Sirs, I grew up in the orphanage at Palloweth, as the miller stated. I lived there until just a few months ago. Then I foolishly ran away by hiding in the wagon of Trask the peddler. When he discovered me, he agreed to allow me to travel north with him. I paid for my food by working at farmhouses along the way.

"When we reached the village of Arn, the miller tried to get me to agree to stay there with him. I was afraid of him and did not want to stay. Late that night I heard the two men arguing. The miller offered Trask money to leave me at the mill. He said that unless the peddler agreed to leave me, he would take me captive by force. I ran away again and made my way north. At the village of Elsis, men hired by the miller tried to capture me, but with the help of friends, I escaped and came here. I am now living and working at the House of the Hill Soldiers. I do not want to go back to Arn."

She paused, took a deep breath, and then went on. "When I was in Arn, the miller said nothing about suspecting that I had been born there. He told me he wanted me to stay because I could help him in his worship of what he called the Dark Power. I believe he has made up this story about my birth and gotten others to tell that story."

When she sat down, Zemla called on Skey, who stated that the miller was feared in his own village and not known by the honorary title of "grandfather." The two judges listened impassively, and the miller did not bother to refute this testimony. Garis was Zemla's final witness. He painted a picture of the good life available for Akara at the House of the Hill Soldiers and asked that she be allowed to remain there.

Then Robin stood and asked for permission to speak. When it was granted, he said, "I am a Soldier of the King and come from the King's Castle on the mountain ridge, which Akara has visited. I have with me a paper signed by the leaders of our fellowship stating that they will be happy to welcome her if she chooses to come there. I ask that the judges allow her to choose for herself where to live, either at our castle or at the House of the Hill Soldiers."

As Robin sat down, a heavy roll of thunder shook the hall. Akara suddenly realized that for the last hour it had grown steadily darker. The hall was now deeply shadowed, though it was only mid-afternoon.

Karnethal spoke for the first time. "It seems the storm has come," he said in a booming voice. "Perhaps we should have light."

Several men rushed to light the oil lamps that hung along the side walls of the hall. Others who had horses tethered outside slipped out to see to them.

Syden called for closing statements from both sides. Zemla gave a vigorous argument. While he stopped short of accusing the miller and his witnesses of lying, he held up Akara's bag with its brightly colored handles and expressed surprise that neither woman could remember it. He suggested that Skey's testimony cast doubt on the miller's motives. He finished by calling on the judges to allow Akara to decide where she wanted to live.

Syden spoke. "Since the weather is getting worse, we will not take a recess. Karnethal and I will take a few moments to consider our verdict." As the two judges put their heads together, the thunder became louder and almost continuous. The windows rattled as the rising wind shook them. There was a patter of rain on the roof.

Zemla spoke to Akara over the noise. "We have done our best," he said. He did not look hopeful.

Before long, Syden's staff again struck the floor. "We have agreed on a verdict," he said, shouting to make himself heard. "This is not a difficult case. I will ask my colleague Karnethal to review the evidence, and then I will announce our conclusion."

Karnethal stood. His voice boomed out. "The principal question in this case is whether or not the girl Akara is indeed related to the woman who claims to be her aunt. We have testimony which states that she is. There is no evidence to the contrary. The girl herself does not know where she was born.

"We have considered Akara's testimony, which contradicts the miller's story about events at the mill. Skey's testimony supports her view of the miller. The honorable Zemla also states he believes Akara is telling the truth. We are also moved by the pleas of Garis and the young man from the King's Castle. Personally, both Syden and I would like to rule that Akara be allowed to make her own decision. However, we are bound to follow the clear words of our newly signed treaty. It states that children must remain with their relatives until they reach the age of eighteen. Syden will announce our verdict."

Akara slouched in her seat. There was no doubt in her mind what the verdict would be. Syden, steadying himself with his staff, stood erect beside Karnethal. There was another crash of thunder as he opened his mouth to speak, but before words were spoken, something else happened!

The door to the hall flew open. Two people entered and started down the center aisle toward the front. Heads turned, some people stood to see what was happening, and a buzz of conversation swept through the room. Syden thumped for order. "This hearing is still in session," he said. "The newcomers will stop where they are, and others must be quiet."

"Excuse me, sir," came the clear voice of Lanus. "I have brought a witness whose testimony must be heard!"

Akara had heard the door bang open, but it was not until Lanus spoke that she knew who had entered. She watched with renewed hope as the King's Soldier made his way slowly to the front of the hall. An old woman hobbled beside him, clinging to his arm with one hand, and supporting herself with a cane clutched in the other.

The room was in turmoil. In vain, Syden thumped his staff and called for order. When the newcomers reached the open area below the platform, Robin bounded up the aisle bringing a chair, which Lanus placed near the judges' table and facing the audience. He guided the old woman to the chair and took his stand beside it.

When quiet was finally restored, Syden looked at Lanus severely. "We have heard the testimony of both sides, young man. As judges we are ready to render our verdict."

Lanus met his gaze steadily. "Sir, we could not arrive sooner. The witness I have brought is vital to the just settlement of this hearing. If you do not allow her to speak, an injustice may be done!"

Syden shook his head. "Under the rules of our treaty, the judges decide when to close the testimony. After that decision, the opportunity for testimony is past. We have made and announced that decision. If you indeed have new evidence, you must request a new hearing, to be held at a later date!"

CHAPTER 28

The Testimony of Lanus

A moment of silence followed Syden's words. However, what he said did not please the good villagers of Midra, and a noise of grumbling was heard from the audience. They had come to hear the truth, not a discussion of legal regulations.

Zemla rose and addressed the judges. "Sirs, the purpose of this hearing is to learn the truth. I believe judges have the authority to grant exceptions under unusual circumstances. I ask that you do so now and hear this witness."

Syden again shook his head and opened his mouth to speak. A shout came from somewhere in the back rows. "Forget the rules. Let's hear the evidence!"

Cheers rose and Syden thumped his staff on the floor to no avail. A chant of "Hear the witness! Hear the witness!" began. The room was in an uproar. The judges conferred; then they turned and signaled for silence. Gradually the noise died down until Syden could again be heard.

"It is most irregular to hear evidence after the time for testimony is past. However, every rule must have exceptions, and this situation is indeed unusual. We will therefore delay the verdict long enough to hear what this witness has to say. We will then decide whether or not the testimony is important enough to be admitted."

The hall erupted in cheers, but the miller was on his feet, his voice raised in anger. "We of the village of Arn object!"

Syden struck his staff on the floor. "Your objection is noted, sir." He turned to Lanus. "Present your evidence, young man."

Lanus spoke. "Thank you, sirs. I will speak first, then I will call on this lady, whose name is Dame Paragenna. My name is Lanus. I am a Soldier of the King and live at the King's Castle on the mountain ridge. However, I was born and raised here in Midra."

His eyes traveled across the audience, stopped briefly on Akara, then returned to the judges. "A short time ago, the young woman Akara visited the King's Castle. While there, she showed us a blue bag that she stated was her only clue to where she was born or who her parents were. I recognized the bag. I had seen it before, when I was a small child.

"I said nothing of this to anyone at that time. However, I knew that Dame Paragenna, who formerly lived in Midra, but had moved to a village in the north, would also remember this bag. So when I learned that this hearing was to be held, I traveled in search of her. I ask you now to listen to her testimony."

Though the rain was now beating heavily on the roof, Dame Paragenna's voice came with surprising clearness. "My name is Paragenna, and I lived for many years in this area. I served as a nurse and midwife for many families in Midra. My testimony concerns an event that happened fifteen years ago.

"A young couple named Tallessus and Clea lived near Midra. Their farm was on an island in the river that flows through the valley. Many of you will remember them. They were close friends of mine. An elderly aunt of Clea's, named Dessa, lived with them. When Clea was about to have a child, I was called to come from Midra to help. A healthy baby girl was born. I have always been fond of needlework, so some weeks before the baby came, I made and gave to Clea a blue bag, like the one Lanus has described to me."

The room was quiet except for the noise of the rain as Dame Paragenna continued. "Tallessus rowed me back to Midra. However, that very night, tragedy occurred. The season was rainy, and a sudden flood swept down from the north part of the valley covering the island where Tallessus and Clea lived. Floating trees smashed their small house. When the waters abated, the bodies of Tallessus and Clea were found but not those of Dessa and the newborn infant. We thought they too had died, and their bodies had been swept away. But when Lanus told me this girl's story, I realized she could be the missing baby.

"Dessa was a resourceful woman, though old and easily confused. If she and the infant had managed to get into a boat, they could have survived, but they would have been swept far down the stream. Dessa had money of her own and could have purchased a horse and wagon. In her confusion, she might have driven south instead of north."

Karnethal's voice boomed out. "Excuse me, Dame Paragenna, but if all you have to go on is your recollection of the color of Akara's bag, your case is not a strong one."

Dame Paragenna put out a hand toward Lanus, who handed her a paper-wrapped parcel. With fumbling hands she undid it and pulled something from it. Across the room, Akara caught her breath. What Dame Paragenna held up was a bag exactly like the one she herself carried!

The old woman turned toward Karnethal. "You are right, sir," she said. "Unless the bag the girl carries is identical to this one, my testimony is useless. You see," she went on, "when I made the blue bag I gave Clea, I made a duplicate for myself at the same time. Both were the finest needlework I have done."

Like everyone else in the hall, Akara had sat motionless, mesmerized by Dame Paragenna's story. Now she was suddenly spurred to action! After Zemla had held up Akara's bag for the judges to see, he had given it back to her. It was now on the floor beside her. She snatched it up and handed it to Zemla. He carried it across the room, took the other bag from Dame Paragenna, and held up both of them. The room again erupted in cheers, and Syden had to bang for order.

When quiet was restored, he asked Dame Paragenna if she had more testimony to give. "No, sir," she said.

Zemla showed both bags to the miller, then to Syden and Karnethal, before giving them back to their owners. The miller rose to his feet. His voice was again smooth. "May I speak?"

"Of course," answered Syden.

The miller turned toward the audience. "Let us consider this supposed testimony a moment! For reasons of his own, this young man is determined to keep Akara here. He brings to us a woman from another village who shows us a bag similar to the one the girl carries. Is this evidence?"

"Five days is plenty of time for a clever seamstress to make a bag that looks like the one Akara has. Once that was done, all Lanus had to do was invent a story for this woman to tell." He turned to Lanus and Dame Paragenna. "Is it not true, you two, that your story is an invention, a clever attempt to deceive the judges?"

Before he went further, another voice rang out that Akara recognized immediately. Akara turned. Dame Leck, Zemla's wife, had been seated several rows behind her. Now she was standing, looking over the audience, her eyes flashing.

"The citizens of Midra can lay the miller's doubts to rest very quickly," she said. "How many of you remember Tallessus and Clea?" A number of hands were raised. "Dame Paragenna lived for years among us. How many of you know her?" This time a forest of hands shot skyward. "Do any of you who know her believe for a moment that she would testify to a false story, as the miller suggests?"

"No!" thundered a chorus of many voices.

Dame Leck sat down. Syden thumped his staff angrily. "This is a hearing, not a demonstration!" He turned back to the miller. "I apologize for the interruption, sir. We will consider your doubts. Do you have further questions?"

"Yes," said the miller. "There is another reason to doubt this testimony. The young man, Lanus, cannot be more than a few years older than Akara. Yet he tells us he had such a clear memory of a bag that he had seen as a small child that it drove him to seek out the woman who made it. We need a better explanation if we are to believe him."

All eyes turned to Lanus. For some reason his face had flushed a deep red, but his voice was steady as he answered the miller. "I remember that bag well." He paused for a long moment, then went on. "You see, Clea and Tallessus had an older child, a son who often stayed with Dame Paragenna. He had watched her sew on the blue bag that she later presented to his mother. That boy was sent to stay with friends at Midra when it was time for the baby to be born, so he escaped the flood." He turned and looked at Akara. "I am that son. I am Akara's brother!"

Akara clapped her hand to her mouth, stifling a small scream. She looked wildly across the room. The miller glanced at her, the familiar small smile playing over his lips.

"That in turn raises another question," he said to Lanus. "You told us you saw the bag when Akara brought it to your castle, and you recognized it at that time. You therefore knew she was your sister. Yet you said nothing to her! Can you explain this?"

For the first time, Lanus seemed to lose his poise. He took a deep breath, then opened his mouth. But before he could speak, the thump of Syden's staff was heard, and his thin voice was raised.

"We will indulge your questions, sir miller, as long as they bear on our decisions. However, the verdict in this case rests upon the testimony of Dame Paragenna and the evidence of the two bags, not on what this young man said or did not say to Akara. If he desires to explain, he can do so later. My colleague and I are now ready to rule on whether or not to accept this new evidence."

As if on signal, there was another tremendous thunderclap, the loudest of all. The wind rose, and the rain increased to a deluge. The two judges rose to their feet, but this time Syden nodded to Karnethal, and it was Karnethal's voice at its loudest pitch that sounded out over the noise of the storm.

"This new testimony is important enough to be accepted, even though it came late. The blue bag is convincing evidence that Akara was born in Midra, not Arn. We rule that she is free to remain here. This hearing is now adjourned."

The final thump from Syden's staff was intended to end the discussion, but one more thing was to come. The miller's voice rang through the hall in a tone of cold rage that none had heard before.

"Hear this, judges, and all those gathered here. We came to participate in what was supposed to be a fair hearing under terms of our new treaty. These terms have been violated by the very judges who are supposed to uphold them. The testimony of this old woman came late and should not have been permitted. The village of Arn does not accept this verdict. We withdraw from the treaty! From henceforth, look you to the interests of your own villages and defend them. We will look to ours!"

He turned and strode toward the door, followed by his two witnesses. Zemla stared after him in dismay, then belatedly turned to congratulate Akara. But the seat beside his was empty! Akara was gone! Sometime after Lanus had identified himself as her brother, and while all eyes were elsewhere, she had picked up her blue bag, risen quietly, and gone out through the side door into the storm!

CHAPTER 29

Kidnapped!

Zemla was not the only one to notice that Akara had vanished. Lanus also saw and acted. He scooped up his traveling cloak and dashed across the room, past Zemla to the side door through which she must have left. The little storage room was empty, and he stopped there only long enough to put on his cloak and pull the hood over his head. Then he too plunged out into the storm.

He soon returned to the hall, dripping wet. "I saw no sign of Akara," he said to Zemla, who was still standing by the Midra table. "I didn't see her. It's raining so hard, I can't see far in any direction."

"She may have gone to my home," said Zemla. "It's near and she knows we leave the door unlocked."

"In any case, there's not much use in searching until the rain stops," said Dame Leck, who came up to them at that point. Others of Akara's friends soon joined them, including Blink and Skey, Garis and Vidella, and Robin and Henda.

"I hope she's all right," said Vidella.

"We'll try to make sure of that," said Zemla. He sent his eyes around the circle. "Suppose all of us who are concerned about Akara meet at my house as soon the rain slackens. If she is not there, a search can be made elsewhere. In the meantime, I must confer with Syden and Karnethal about what the miller's last statement means for our villages."

After Zemla, and the others left, Lanus signaled to Robin and Henda, and the three soldiers made their way down the aisle to the main entrance and outside to a covered porch where several villagers stood talking in low tones and looking out at the pouring rain.

Lanus led the way to an unoccupied corner of the porch. "It may be my fault that Akara left so suddenly," he said. "I should have told her I was her brother that day on the castle tower. Learning about it this way may have hurt her badly. I'd like you both to join me in a trumpet call for her."

Robin nodded. "All right. Let's make it a silent call so as not to disturb the others."

The three soldiers raised their trumpets and blew noiselessly through them, committing Akara to the care of the King.

At the same time, far above the valley in the King's Castle, other trumpets were calling to the King. Keila had recovered enough to be able to walk by herself, and that afternoon she had wrapped herself tightly in a cloak and made her way out to one of the castle towers. The castle was above the valley rain, but winds were gusting and a thick layer of dark clouds covered the valley below. The castle seemed to float like a giant ship on a sea of cloud. As Keila stood gazing out over the battlement, the door behind her opened and Dame Prendil emerged, leaning on Jamin's arm. Both were also well wrapped in cloaks.

The older woman looked at Keila in surprise. "I didn't expect to see you outside in this weather," she said. "Are you sure you feel well enough?"

"I'm fine. I felt I had to come out. I've been thinking about Akara. As you know, she faces a hearing today in Midra."

"I, too, have been restless all afternoon," said Dame Prendil. "When Jamin came by, I asked him to come here to the tower with me." She paused thoughtfully. "Perhaps the King has brought the three of us here so that we can lift our trumpets asking Him to help her."

"An excellent idea," said Jamin, and a moment later the three trumpets sounded.

Meanwhile, where was Akara? She had left the hall deeply troubled. She had stayed long enough to hear the judges' ruling and their decision had been a great relief to her. She was free! She had also learned that Lanus was her brother, a discovery that under other circumstances would have been a joyous surprise. However, it was also evident that Lanus had not wanted to disclose that fact. He had known she was his sister that day on the castle tower when he examined her blue bag, but he had admitted it only now when forced to do so by the miller.

The thought devastated her. He was willing to help her prove who she was, but he did not want her to know of their relationship. Why? It must be because he didn't want to be bothered with a sister. It was this conclusion that had driven Akara out into the storm, and once she was outside, had urged her onward. She had stopped at Zemla's house but only long enough to scribble a note and leave it on the small table in the front hall. It read, "I'm sorry I must leave. Thank you all for everything you have done. Please don't look for me. Akara." Then she headed westward through the village. Her cloak provided little protection from the pelting rain, and she was soon soaked to the skin. But she pressed on. Her plan was simple. She would go first to the spot where she and Blink had hidden her supplies. Then she would head north on the old valley road, find a spot to camp, and huddle under the waterproof cloth until morning. Then she would travel on to the north villages. It would be hard to leave her friends, but she felt she had no choice. She could not stay near a brother who did not want her. She would make a new life for herself elsewhere.

Dame Leck found the note and read it aloud. "She's probably gone north up the valley," said Blink. Then she told about the supplies for travel that she and Akara had hidden on the slope of the grassy knoll.

When she finished, Garis spoke. "Let me drive you out in my carriage to where you hid them. Perhaps we'll see Akara on the road and can persuade her to return."

This seemed like a good idea, and Garis, Blink, and Skey went off in the carriage to carry it out, while the rest waited.

A short time later, the rain slackened, and the group of Akara's friends met at Zemla's house. The carriage returned with more puzzling news. The supplies had not been disturbed, nor was Akara on the road. A further search that day and the next morning showed that she was neither in Midra nor at the House of the Hill Soldiers. She had vanished! Where had she gone?

After leaving Zemla's house, Akara had pushed on to the western edge of the village. Here she paused before turning northward toward the grassy knoll. At that point a new thought struck her. In leaving the area of Midra, she was also going farther from the King's Castle. Would the King still hear her when she called to him with the silver trumpet? Perhaps this was the time to find out. What was it Robin had said? "The trumpet is as powerful in the valley as it is on the mountaintop."

Standing there beside the road in the pouring rain, she dug the silver trumpet from her bag and blew through it. As usual, it made no sound, but it brought a sense of comfort to her. She had no way of knowing that at that precise moment, six other trumpets were calling to the King on her behalf, three from the porch of the village hall and three from those on the tower of the King's Castle.

The King heard all of those calls. His answer was already on the way, though it was not the answer that any of the seven trumpeters would have chosen.

Akara lowered her trumpet, but before she had time to slip it back into her blue bag, something happened. In the rain and the howling wind, she had failed to hear the sound of approaching carriage wheels. Now a dark shape loomed out of the mist beside her. An alarm bell clanged in her mind. Though she could not see the shape clearly, she somehow knew it was the miller's carriage. She turned to run, but too late. Two figures swung down from the front of the carriage and ran toward her! On a sudden impulse, before they could reach her, she flung her bag as far as she could over the bushes beside her into the field beyond. Then hands seized her roughly, the carriage door opened, and she was pushed into the dark interior.

She fell into a seat, facing the rear of the carriage. There was a large bulk in front of her. The miller! Two other forms, one beside her and the other diagonally across were, of course, the two women witnesses.

The miller spoke. "Was that her trumpet she threw away?"

"No, sir," said a voice through the still-open door. "She is still holding her trumpet; I felt it when I grabbed her."

"Good! It was probably that bag of hers. Find it, Ruddle! We want to leave no clues."

He closed the door and the men stumbled off through the wet bushes, cursing as they went. After a time, they returned empty-handed. The miller curtly ordered them to mount to the box and drive on. As the carriage rolled, Akara felt a tiny thrill of hope. If her blue bag was discovered, her friends would surely realize that she had been kidnapped and perhaps guess where she had been taken. Whether they could do anything to rescue her was another matter.

The carriage had swung southward onto the valley road before the miller spoke again. "Well, Akara, your friends did their best to defeat me, but as you can see, I have won. The Dark Power I serve brought us together."

From somewhere, Akara found the spirit to answer him. "The judges ruled against you, sir. They said I can live where I choose. I don't want to go to Arn."

"That ruling was illegal, and anyway, it no longer matters. If the people of Midra want you back, they can take up arms, march to Arn, and try to rescue you."

This answer quenched Akara's last shred of hope. She did not reply, and the conversation ceased. She expected a long night's drive, but only a short time later the carriage turned again, passed through some sort of gate, and soon afterward stopped in front of a lighted house. By this time the rain had almost ended. The door of the house flew open, and a small, plump man bustled out. He opened the carriage door and bowed.

"Greetings, sir and ladies."

"Greetings, Skudd," said the miller, leading the way from the carriage. The miller's two men walked on either side of Akara as the group made their way to the door of the house and into the lighted front hall. The miller turned to her. "Squire Skudd and Dame Lasdell will take you to your room, Akara. We'll travel on in the morning."

The squire led Akara to an upstairs room, Dame Lasdell following behind. "I'll have a serving girl bring you a robe and a tray of food, Akara," said the man. "You can give Dame Lasdell your wet clothes, and we'll dry them for you."

He bowed again and left. Dame Lasdell's lips curled in a tight little smile. "There are shutters on the windows, so there's no way out. Skudd will be back to lock the door. Then I'll leave and go to dinner myself."

Something drove Akara to challenge the woman. "You know I am not really your niece, don't you?" she said.

Dame Lasdell gave a short laugh. "When you live in Arn, you believe what the miller says."

Akara looked at her wonderingly. "If life in Arn is like that, why don't people leave and live elsewhere?"

"Humph! Easier said than done." The woman's expression changed suddenly. "Don't try to trick me. I didn't say anything about wanting to leave." She crossed to the door, then turned again. "Remember this, young lady, from now on, you are who the miller says you are!"

CHAPTER 30

The Trumpet
and a Dream

Akara was able to eat only a little food, and her sleep was restless. In the morning, her dried clothes were waiting for her. She ate a few bites of the breakfast brought by the servant girl, then the carriage again headed south. Stops were made for food, or to change horses, but at each stop she was guarded by Dame Lasdell or one of the men, so there was no chance for escape. There was little conversation in the carriage. Neither of the women spoke unless the miller addressed them, and he was mostly silent. At last, as the sun was setting, the drab houses of the village of Arn came into view, and soon afterward, the carriage turned into the mill yard.

Akara was surprised to see Trask's ramshackle wagon standing near the flat rock. The peddler was backing his horse into the wagon shafts, apparently preparing to depart. He looked up as the carriage stopped and the travelers emerged from it. He nodded briefly to the miller and then returned to his task.

Amusement flickered in the miller's eyes. "Let's go and greet your old friend," he said, taking Akara's arm.

As they reached the wagon, Trask finished with the horse's harness and was fussing at something at the side of the wagon. He straightened up as they drew near, and nodded again, his face impassive.

"You're leaving, peddler?" asked the miller.

"Yes, I came last night. Now I'm on my way north." He jerked his head toward Akara. "I see you brought the girl back with you."

At that instant, there came a thud from the direction of the carriage where baggage was being unloaded. Something had fallen. The miller turned, while keeping tight hold on Akara's arm, and called a sharp command to the workers. As he did so, the peddler took a quick step forward, brought a hand from behind his back, and thrust a leather water bottle into the girl's free hand.

Akara knew at once the reason for this gift. On her first visit to the mill, Trask had warned her against drinking the miller's water. Now he was giving her a bottle from his water supply in the wagon. She gave him a grateful look and slipped the bottle under her cloak.

When the miller swung back to face him, Trask was standing as before, his face once again expressionless. The miller had apparently noticed nothing for he said only, "I'll see you when you come south again, peddler," and led Akara off toward the mill.

Dame Dreng met them at the door. "The girl's room is ready," she said. "Greetings, Akara."

Akara could not bring herself to answer. Numbly, she followed the miller up the stairs to the milling room. In one wall of this room was a doorway that, Akara remembered, led to a small storeroom. She was surprised to see that a metal grill had been mounted across the entrance to this room. The miller took a key from a peg on the wall, opened a padlock, and swung the grill open. "Here is where you will stay," he said.

He ushered Akara inside. The furnishings included a bed, a chair, and a small table on which was a pitcher and basin. The miller crossed the room and pulled open another door that, Akara remembered, led to the grassy area behind the mill. As the miller stepped outside, Akara was able, unobserved, to take the bottle of water from beneath her cloak and slide it under the bed. Then she followed him.

"We must keep the metal grill locked," said the man, "but this door to the back will be open. The fences on each side of this yard will keep you from escaping."

During her earlier time at the mill, Akara had paid little attention to the fences that ran from each rear corner of the mill building across to the cliffs. As they walked to the edge of the millpond, Akara's eye was caught by a small rowboat moored to the stone coping. She dimly remembered having seen it there on her previous visit to the mill. Noting her interest in it now, the miller said, "It may occur to you to try to get away in this boat. As you see, there is no lock on its mooring, and there are oars lying in the bottom. However, the only place it can take you is back into the gorge and through the dark fog. That leads to the Dark Power, and I don't think you want to go there!" He gave her a mocking smile. "In fact, you may have the boat if you want to try to escape that way!"

Akara did not reply. She had never rowed a boat in her life, and the evil fog terrified her so much that she had no wish to escape in that direction. She followed the miller back into the little room, where he left her, locking the metal grill behind him.

A short time later, the man called Ruddle appeared with a tray of food. He did not enter the room but opened a small door in the center of the grill. The door swung down to form a shelf on which he set the tray. He grinned at Akara who was sitting despondently on her chair.

"Our caged bird isn't singing," he said. "Well, Akara, we'll feed you anyway."

Dame Dreng appeared behind him. "That's enough, Ruddle," she said. The man departed, chuckling, and Dame Dreng instructed, "Put the tray back on the shelf when you've finished, Akara. There's water outside in the well if you need it."

Left alone, Akara ate a little of the food. She took a few sips from the water bottle the peddler had given her, then hid it under the bed again. After putting her tray back on the shelf, she took her trumpet and went outside. There she breathed through it, asking for the King's help.

The sun had set, and the cliffs were dark and forbidding. Above them, she knew, was the mountain ridge, and somewhere to the north on that ridge was the King's Castle. She thought about the last cry for help she had sent through the trumpet, in the pouring rain just outside Midra.

A strange whisper sounded in her mind. "That call didn't do much good, did it?"

Akara knew the voice belonged to no real person, but she also realized the words were true. She had called for help and immediately afterward had been captured by the miller. As a result, she was a prisoner, caged like an animal!

She sighed. Could it be that the trumpet didn't work...that the good things that had happened when she blew her trumpet in the past were coincidences? A feeling of despair gripped her. Then her common sense took over. There was no proof that blowing the trumpet had helped her, but deep inside she believed that it had. Anyway, the trumpet was her only resource. She would push her doubts aside and trust in it and the invisible King.

She remembered how, in the Hall of the Trumpets, the King's Soldiers had begun with the deep tones — those that praised the King. She would begin the same way. Again she breathed through her trumpet, and as she did so, concentrated on what she had heard about the greatness, goodness, and love of the King.

She stopped for breath, and in her mind, shifted upward to the next range of tones. These, she remembered, allowed her to seek help for others. In spite of the fact that she was in more need of help than were her friends, she forced herself to think of each of them in turn, and to wish good things for them. This was particularly hard to do when it came to Lanus, for the hurt she felt at his failure to acknowledge her as his sister was still strong. However, she reminded herself that it was he who had brought Dame Paragenna to help at her hearing, so she included his name with the others.

On to the third level, the one where she could pour out her own feelings and thoughts to the King. She did so, and thoughts of despair, frustration, and fear surged out through the trumpet. She realized that she was angry with the King for letting the miller capture her, and those thoughts came tumbling out too! She was frightened at her own boldness but also felt a great sense of release. Something inside her assured her that the King understood!

A sense of calmness followed, and in this spirit of peace she took the last step and breathed out a plea for herself. Surprisingly, this call was the shortest of all. The King had allowed her to be captured. He knew where she was and what she needed. All that was necessary, Akara felt, was to ask for his help.

When the trumpet call was finished, she turned from the cliffs and the dark water and went back inside. Her tray had been collected from the shelf while she was gone, and all was quiet. She blew out the candle, went to bed, and almost immediately fell asleep.

A dream came. She was floating in cloudy space while shadowy forms drifted in and out of her vision. Some of them she recognized as children from the orphan home at Palloweth. Then two adult forms appeared. One was Dame Dessit looking prim and proper; beside her was old Fendilla.

Akara heard Dame Dessit's voice, "She was certainly a rebellious girl."

"She was that," Fendilla cackled, "but she's gone now."

"Akara thought life should be all roses. You and I know it's a grim and unhappy business. She'll learn that too, sooner or later."

The two women drifted away, and their place was taken by Trask the peddler. He was standing beside his wagon, a jug in his hand. His lips did not move, but Akara found that she could hear his thoughts. "I'd help Akara if I could, and I'm sorry the miller captured her," he was thinking. "But there's nothing I can do. After all, nobody helps me. I have to make my own way."

As Trask's image faded, Wenk's face appeared. She also heard his voice. "I wish I could have answered Akara's questions, but I have no guidance to give her. I hope she makes more of her life than I have made of mine."

The Wanderer disappeared and for a moment there was darkness. Then Akara saw a sunlit meadow and a stone wall. Into this scene strolled Blink and Skey. Blink perched on the wall, and Skey leaned against it beside her.

"A beautiful day!" he said. "Every day should be like this. Sunny and warm and with no work to do."

Blink laughed. "That would be nice. But work is important too; we can't just sit around all the time."

"You're beginning to sound like Akara. She's a nice person but a little too serious about things. Life should be fun!"

"Akara is more of a thinker than you or I. She wants to find out the truth about life, and I admire her for that, don't you Skey?"

Her companion shrugged. "Hey, I'm no philosopher. I leave the big questions to other people. Let's walk some more."

Blink slid down from the wall and the two strolled off. The scene faded and other faces slipped past her. Zemla appeared briefly and his voice spoke. "Akara's freedom is important, and so is peace among the villages. I hope we can arrange for both."

His face dissolved into that of Garis, whose message was different. "Wherever Akara is, I hope she will keep in mind the teachings of the Good Carpenter."

Dame Leck's face appeared, and her voice was strong and clear. "Whatever happens, Akara, be true to your best instincts."

There was darkness again, and Akara felt herself sinking deeper into sleep. There were no more images, but the miller's voice cut suddenly through the darkness. "All of what you have heard is nonsense!" he said. "There can be no peace, no future for life until the valley people submit to the Dark Power."

The miller's voice died away, and sleep came. But in her last conscious moments, Akara heard a distant sound. It was no human voice, but a single clear note, high and triumphant: the sound of a silver trumpet!

CHAPTER 31

A Second Prisoner

After breakfast the next morning, Akara went outdoors where she was joined by Dame Dreng. "Did you find your room comfortable, Akara?" was her greeting.

"I'm comfortable enough, but I won't be content until I'm free."

There was no change in Dame Dreng's voice. "You are being held because it is important to keep you here. No harm will come to you. When you learn what the Dark Power has to teach you, it will no longer be necessary to lock you up."

"But why was I selected? I have no interest in serving your Dark Power."

"My brother will have to tell you that. But there is much you can learn here. We have books that you will not find in the library of the Hill Soldiers where you have been living." Noting Akara's surprised look, she added, "Yes, I know about the Hill Soldiers and their library. As a girl, I lived there for a time. They have knowledge, but I learned that their beliefs are without power."

She left Akara and disappeared inside the mill through one of the other entrances. Akara stared after her, puzzled. Why was she thought to be important to the Dark Power? She determined to find out.

Her opportunity came that same afternoon. Akara was again outside when the miller came up to her, moving noiselessly as usual.

"You talked with my sister this morning."

Akara turned to face him. "Yes, I asked her why I had been brought here. She said only you could tell me."

The miller seated himself on the bench behind the stone table and motioned for her to join him. She sat down as far away from him as possible. "You're here, Akara, because of your silver trumpet."

This didn't make sense to Akara. "If it was the trumpet you wanted, why did you not take it and leave me in Midra?"

"Trumpets by themselves are useless. But you and your trumpet together have power. When you were here with Trask, you blew your trumpet while I was walking across the yard. Do you remember that?"

"Yes."

"When that happened, I felt the power of the trumpet stop me for just a moment. That never happened before. I knew then that I must keep you and the trumpet here."

"But, sir, I know very little about the trumpet. There are many people in the King's Castle on the mountain ridge who can tell you more about it than I can."

The miller shook his head. "I have no desire to talk to the mountain people. They are committed to serving their King. I am their enemy, for I serve the Dark Power. You use a trumpet, but you are not one of them. You live in the valley. I believe you can be taught to use your trumpet in the service of the Dark Power."

Akara took a deep breath while she tried to sort out this twisted reasoning. "But as I understand it, the trumpet is only a way to call upon the King. It was the King's power you felt that day."

"That cannot be true. There is power hidden in the trumpet, and you unlock that power in some way, though you may not know how." He rose to his feet. "When you submit to my master, then your trumpet and mine can work together to advance the cause of the Dark Power!"

That night, as she lay on her cot, Akara went over and over that conversation. How could she convince the miller that the trumpet was not a source of magic power? And what would happen to her if he remained unconvinced? She dreaded their next conversation.

However, it seemed the miller considered the subject closed. On the next day, and the ones that followed, he greeted her when they met but said nothing about the trumpet. For the rest of the time, he left her alone.

The following days saw a repeat of this pattern. On some days the mill was busy grinding grain, and then the miller did not speak to her at all. On these days she watched through the metal grill as sad-faced men and women brought sacks of grain into the large room. There they were weighed and the weight recorded in Dame Dreng's book before the grain was ground by Ruddle and his helper. On other days, there was no activity. During these times Akara had a great deal of time to think. It began to dawn on her that her flight into the storm after the hearing had been the act of a disappointed child. She had run away from friends who loved and supported her simply because she was angry at Lanus.

Faced with this new view of herself, Akara wept. How selfish she had been, how foolish. If only she could tell her friends how sorry she was! Then the thought came. She could begin by confessing these faults to the King. After all, if the King was really guiding her, it was he who had given her these friends. This kind of confessing would be a special way to use that range of trumpet call that poured out her thoughts to him.

She came to this conclusion one day while walking by the pool. With no further hesitation, she raised her trumpet to her lips and breathed a full confession. This time she did not even finish with a plea for help. If the King chose to forgive her, he would help her. When that call was completed, she felt a great weight lifted from her heart.

But there was another more practical problem. The peddler's water supply had run out, and she was forced to drink from the well behind the mill. At first she noticed no change, then she discovered that, little by little, her memories of the King's Castle became fuzzy though her mind was clear when she thought of other things. What was worse, it became harder to focus her thoughts on the King.

One morning, when the sky was particularly gray and gloomy, the miller joined Akara as she walked in the mill yard. He carried a small metal pot in which coals smoldered. There was a glint of excitement in his eyes. "You must return to your room at once," he said. "The Dark Power is speaking!"

Akara realized that indeed something strange was happening. The roar of the water as it went over the dam had dwindled to a murmur. As she listened, it stopped entirely, and the mill wheel creaked to a stop. The water level in the millpond had dropped, and water seemed to be flowing back into the gorge.

"What is happening?" she gasped.

"The backward flowing of the water," said the miller. "Go to your room!"

Akara went, but left her door open a crack so she could watch. She saw the miller open the door beneath the stone table and take out a gray robe that he put on over his clothing. He also brought out a box and a small pair of metal tongs. He dipped his hand into the box, took out a handful of powder, and piled it on the table. With the tongs he picked a live coal from the pot and placed it on the powder. A blue flame leaped up. Then the miller took his stand beside the table, facing the gorge with both arms raised.

It was a strange scene with the dark clouds overhead, the blue flame flickering on the altar, and the motionless figure of the miller beside it. After a time, the flame died away and the miller lowered his arms. He took off the robe, swept the top of the table clear with a small brush, and put away the items he had used.

Akara waited until she thought it safe, then went out again to where the man still stood, the pot of coals in his hand. The level of the pond was very low. "The water flows again," he said without turning his head. "The millpond will be filled soon."

"What does the backward flowing mean, sir?" Akara ventured.

"No other river in the valley flows backward. This stream does. It is a sign from the Dark Power." He wheeled abruptly to face Akara. His eyes bored into hers. "I believe it means you must begin your service, Akara! Tomorrow the mill will be working, but the next day we will begin your training as a Priestess of the Dark Power."

He turned abruptly and walked toward the mill, leaving Akara to stare after him in dismay.

She slept badly that night, and sleep when it did come was troubled. The next morning, after breakfast, she sat listlessly on her bed looking out through the grill. In the milling room, the villagers were gathering with their bags of grain as usual, while the miller's men were preparing the mill wheel for use. Suddenly there was an interruption! The miller entered, walked to the center of the room, called his men to him, and spoke to them briefly in a low voice. Several of the men then began herding the villagers toward one side of the room. Ruddle headed for Akara's prison. He took the key from the hook, unlocked the door, and entered.

He stuffed the key in his pocket, leaving the door unlocked. Then, with an unpleasant grin, he seized Akara by the arm and pulled her to her feet. "We're having visitors," he said. "The miller doesn't want you interfering, so you and I will wait in the alcove until they leave."

He pushed her around the foot of the bed and into a small recessed area in the far corner, the only place in the room that was out of sight from the door. He wedged himself in after her. Akara did not resist, for she knew it was no use to do so. She was only mildly interested in who the visitors were.

There was a brief period of silence, then she heard the murmur of voices on the mill floor. The visiting party had arrived. At first she could distinguish nothing, then she heard the miller's voice, "This is where we grind the grain. As you can see, it is an open area with no place to hide anyone."

The next voice shook Akara abruptly out of her lethargy. "What's in that room over there, the one with the barred metal door?" The speaker was Zemla! Akara made a sudden move, and instantly Ruddle pressed her against the wall of the alcove and clapped a rough hand over her mouth. "Be quiet!" he hissed in her ear.

From the larger room came the miller's answer. "One of my men sleeps there to guard the mill at night. Come, let me show you the rest of the mill."

Akara struggled with all her strength to break free, but Ruddle was too strong. Pressed against the alcove wall, she could not move.

"May I look inside that room?" Akara's heart leaped with excitement. The voice was Keila's!

"I've told you its purpose, and you can see that there is no one in there," the miller said smoothly.

Akara realized she must act, and quickly. In a last desperate attempt, she let her body suddenly go limp. Ruddle shifted his weight to hold her up. As he did so, the pressure of his hand against her mouth eased momentarily. She forced her mouth open so that her teeth were pressed against his palm. Then she bit down on it as hard as she could!

With an oath, the miller's man wrenched his hand away, and Akara, her mouth free, screamed as loud as she could. "Keila! Zemla! In here!"

There was a flurry of action outside the grill, and a clang as the metal door was flung open. Ruddle turned toward it, and Akara pushed her way out of the alcove. There, her dark eyes blazing, the hood of her traveling cloak thrown back, and her brown hair falling free, was Keila! The two girls rushed together, and Keila threw her arms around Akara.

For a moment, Akara was conscious of nothing but Keila and Keila's arms around her. She had been found and all was well! Then she heard the metal grill again slam shut. Keila released her, and both girls turned. Ruddle had slipped outside, and the miller had closed the grill. With a grim smile, he clicked the lock!

Akara's initial joy turned to dismay. Instead of one prisoner, there were now two!

CHAPTER 32

A Watery Escape

Once again, it seemed the miller had won. Not only was Akara still a prisoner, but the attempt to save her had resulted in the capture of Keila, the person she admired most. Looking out into the larger room, Akara caught a glimpse of the visiting party — Zemla, Wahler, and several others. Then the miller's men lined up shoulder to shoulder with their backs against the iron grill, blocking her view. She and Keila were cut off!

From beyond the barrier came Zemla's voice, harsh with anger. "Open that door, miller! Keila is an officially appointed delegate of Midra, and Akara has been declared free to live where she wishes. You must release them both immediately!"

"I'll let your mountain woman go shortly," came the miller's answer. "She should not have rushed in where she doesn't belong. As for Akara, she will stay."

"You brought Akara here against her will!"

"You have no proof of that. And you haven't enough men with you to take her back by force. But we of the village of Arn are reasonable. Bring down your witnesses and we'll have a hearing, as we had in Midra."

Zemla's voice was still firm. "The official hearing has already been held. Your claims were rejected."

The miller laughed softly. "That was in your village. Here we make the rules." His voice took on a hard edge. "Listen well, Zemla. Your valley treaty is finished. Arn has withdrawn, and other villages will join us. The woman Keila is free to go, but Akara must stay."

Akara listened with growing despair. Then she felt Keila's hand on her shoulder. "There's nothing Zemla can do," the King's Soldier whispered. "Is that other door unlocked?"

"Yes, but it only leads to the yard and the millpond."

"Is that where the boat is kept?"

"Yes, but there's nowhere we can go in the boat."

"Let's try," said Keila, turning quickly toward the door.

Outside the metal grill, the voices of Zemla and the miller were still locked in debate. Keila lifted the latch quietly, pushed the door open, and slipped through. Akara scooped up the silver trumpet and her cloak and followed. Then the two raced across to the water's edge where the boat was moored. It was floating free, fastened by two lines, one from the bow and one from the stern. Each ended in a brass ring that fitted over a post on the bank.

Keila seized the stern line and pulled the boat in against the wall. "Get in quickly!" she said.

Obediently, Akara tumbled into the stern. Keila lifted the two rings off their posts and tossed them into the boat, then she too jumped in. She took the center seat, pushed the little craft away from the wall, fitted the oars into the oarlocks, and began rowing.

Their escape was none too soon, for from the mill behind them came a shout. A door was flung open, and the miller's men poured out. Behind came the miller and Dame Dreng, followed by Zemla and the party from Midra. All of the pursuers stopped at the water's edge, except Ruddle. He paused there only long enough to kick off his shoes. He left the wall in a long flat dive into the water and swam with powerful strokes after the boat.

Akara realized that, in spite of Keila's vigorous efforts with the oars, he would soon reach them. She looked around desperately for a weapon. Her gaze lighted on the brass mooring ring lying near her feet, and she snatched it up. Holding it in both hands, she knelt facing their pursuer. As his brawny hand came out of the water and reached for the stern board, she raised the ring over her head and brought it down sharply.

With a curse, Ruddle jerked his hand away just in time to avoid the ring, which thudded into the wood. He stopped swimming and, treading water, eyed her warily. Akara's fighting spirit was up, and she met his eyes squarely, holding the ring over her head, ready for another blow. Meanwhile, Keila's steady, strong strokes were taking the little boat ever farther from shore. Ruddle glared at her for a moment, then with a muttered curse, turned and swam back toward the mill.

"Good work, Akara!" came Keila's voice.

The crisis over, Akara turned and slumped weakly into her seat. Keila pointed the boat toward the mouth of the gorge. Akara put down the mooring ring. "The miller says there is no escape this way," she said. "He says the cliffs are too steep to climb, and humans cannot pass through the dark fog. He also says the Dark Power lies behind the fog."

"He's only partly right. I need my breath for rowing now, but I'll explain later."

After they had left the pond and traveled a little distance into the gorge, Keila shipped the oars. Akara looked back over her shoulder. The miller and his people were grouped near the stone table, watching, Ruddle was with them. A short distance away stood the Midra delegation.

"We'll stop here for a few minutes," said Keila as Akara turned to face her again. She reached inside her traveling cloak, brought out a leather water bottle, and passed it to Akara. "This is water from the spring beneath the castle. I suspect the water here hasn't been good for you."

The water was as refreshing as Akara remembered it. Keila continued. "Since the miller has refused Zemla's demand to release you, we must try to escape this way. This river does indeed lead to the castle of the evil ones but we won't go that far. Once we've passed through the black fog, I'll look for a place where we can land and climb to the ridge. Somewhere in that area, I hope to meet Lanus, Robin, and Henda. I'll explain that part later.

"Now about the fog. It was created by the evil ones to guard their territory. It contains a poison that causes those who breathe it to lose their strength."

"But we can't go through it without breathing!"

"We won't have to. Our soldiers have learned that breathing against the blade of the King's sword purifies the air and neutralizes the poison. Since I have my sword with me, we should be all right."

Akara looked at the dark fog looming ahead of them. "Are you sure that will work?"

"Yes. Lanus and Robin have both penetrated the fog in the past using that method. Anyway, our only path of escape is through the fog. That's why we had to steal the miller's boat."

Akara grinned. "We didn't really steal it, you know. The miller was so sure I couldn't escape by boat that he told me to take it if I wished!"

Keila smiled too. "He may be wishing he hadn't made the suggestion." She raised her trumpet. "And now, before I start rowing again, let's ask the King to help us."

Akara was still sipping the water Keila had brought her. She felt her mind becoming clearer. She too reached for her trumpet. The sound of Keila's instrument rang out, first in the deep vibrant range of praise and thanks, and then in the high tones that called on the King for help. Akara followed her lead, though her trumpet was, of course, silent.

When the trumpet call was finished, Keila reached into a pocket in her cloak and brought out a silver cord. She handed it to Akara. "This is the kind of cord we soldiers wear around our necks on which we hang our trumpets. I brought this one for you. It will let you keep both hands free, and that may be important."

Akara thanked her, then threaded the cord through the tiny ring on her trumpet and fastened it around her neck. Meanwhile, Keila reached for the oars and began rowing. Akara watched for a few moments, then asked, "How is it that you know so much about boats?"

Keila smiled. "I grew up beside the river that runs down the center of Broad Valley. I learned to row a boat almost as soon as I could walk." Suddenly she stopped rowing and a puzzled look appeared on her face. "What's happening?" asked Akara.

"I don't know. For some reason we are beginning to move upstream without my rowing!"

Akara gasped. "It must be the time of 'back flowing'!" Then, in response to Keila's puzzled look, she explained. "The stream sometimes flows backward for about an hour. It has happened once since I've been here. The miller says it is caused by the Dark Power."

Keila frowned. "I've never heard of a stream flowing backward." She shrugged, "Well, at least it's carrying us in the direction we want to go. Let's take advantage of it." She laid one oar in the bottom of the boat, then made her way back to sit beside Akara, bringing the other oar with her. In the center of the stern board was a semicircular notch, and into this she fitted the oar so that the blade trailed in the water behind and the handle extended forward between the girls.

"Most rowboats have a stern notch like this," she said. "As long as the current flows in this direction, I can use this oar for steering and let the stream carry us."

During this time the boat was moving forward, slowly at first, then with increasing speed. Soon they were near the fog. Seen close up, the fog was not all of one color. It was a mixture of gray mist and black strips that moved continuously and melted into each other. Suddenly, as they watched, it began to swirl and boil vigorously. Akara threw a frightened look over her shoulder. She could no longer distinguish the miller among the now-distant group at the mill, but the faint tones of his trumpet reached her ears.

She turned back. "That's the miller's trumpet!"

Keila nodded. She was using the steering oar to keep the boat halfway between the two rock walls and pointed directly upstream. "Time to use the sword." Without letting go of the oar, she drew the weapon and held it horizontally so that its blade was just a few inches in front of Akara's face and her own. "Take hold of the blade near its tip to help support it," she said. "It won't cut you."

Akara did so, and a moment later the bow of the boat sliced into darkness. Then the fog rolled over them, and they were in a silent world, cut off from sight and sound of everything outside the boat. The light from the sword made a small circle of brightness around them, but all beyond that circle was darkness. The only sound that reached their ears was the ripple of water against the boat. Akara kept her face close to the sword, breathing against it, and found that the air she breathed remained fresh.

After a few moments, Akara said, "I wonder if we're still in the middle of the channel. If not, we could smash into one of the cliffs."

"We're all right," said Keila. "I'm listening to the sound of the water lapping the rock on each side. When it grows louder on one side than the other, I know we're closer to the cliffs on that side and steer away."

The trip through the fog seemed endless. Then, at last, they broke out into the gray light of the gorge. Akara blinked and looked around. Sure enough, they were in midstream. Ahead was a straight stretch of water down which they were moving swiftly. The sun had disappeared, and there were dark clouds overhead.

They raced past a break in the cliff to their right, out of which poured a torrent of water. Under normal conditions, this added water would have joined the mainstream in its flow toward the mill. Now it swelled the backward-flowing current, carrying the little boat along at even greater speed. Looking ahead, Akara saw that the sheer cliff walls gave way to slopes, steep but climbable.

Keila reclaimed her sword and slid it into her scabbard. "So far, so good!" she said cheerily. "Now we must look for a landing place."

She scanned the valley ahead, then gave a little cry of pleasure. "Look, Akara! Ahead and to your left." Akara looked where Keila was pointing and saw, standing on a rock high on the hillside, a figure in armor.

"It's one of the King's Soldiers!" she said.

"It's Lanus!" said Keila.

At the same instant, Lanus (for indeed it was he) caught sight of them. He waved both hands over his head and then pointed downward at something in the stream, then swung an arm horizontally.

"He's trying to tell us something," said Keila. Shading her eyes, she stared ahead, then lifted the oar from the steering notch and scrambled forward to her original seat, carrying the oar with her. "Something is wrong," she said, fitting both oars into the oarlocks. "We must get to shore!"

She turned the boat's prow toward the shore, where Lanus was standing. But though she pulled strongly, it soon became clear that the current would carry them past the spot where Lanus stood before they reached shore.

Meanwhile, Lanus had left his rock and was leaping and sliding down the steep slope toward the water. Farther up the hill, another soldier, whom Akara recognized as Henda, was also racing downward. She did not see Robin.

Lanus stopped at the water's edge, cupped his hands, and shouted something that Akara could not quite understand. However, Keila got the message and a look of dismay crossed her face.

"We must get ashore quickly! There's a big whirlpool ahead!"

CHAPTER 33

Into the Whirlpool

Whirlpool! Akara had heard of whirlpools. There was a tiny one in the river near the orphan home at Palloweth where she had grown up. The village children used to throw sticks into it and watch the water whirl them around and pull them down into the hole in the center. But how big was the whirlpool their boat was headed for?

Akara became conscious of a low roar that seemed to come from the gorge ahead. Keila had heard it too, for she had swung the nose of the boat toward the bank where Lanus stood and was rowing as hard as she could. However, they were making little progress, and at last Keila swung the oars into the boat.

"There's no use rowing," she called above the noise. "The current is too swift." She leaned forward, urgency in her voice. "Listen, Akara. If this is a big whirlpool, it may swing us in a circle. We may come close enough to the bank so that I can throw a line to Lanus. If that doesn't work, maybe we can jump out. But hold on tight until I give the word!"

Akara nodded and gripped the seat with both hands. Keila coiled the mooring line that was attached to the bow of the boat, and laid it down near her.

Looking past Keila, Akara caught just a glimpse of turbulent water before the boat surged into it. Then the bow of the little craft twisted to the right, away from the bank where Lanus stood. Keila swung out the oars again, holding the blades high until the bow was pointed toward the shore. Then she dipped them in a single powerful stroke, and shipped them again.

For the first time, Akara was able to see the danger they faced. In company with tree limbs and other debris, their boat was skimming around in a giant funnel that sloped inward toward a dark hole. Keila's timely stroke with the oars had kept the boat on the outer rim of this funnel! Akara looked down into it and saw a tree limb almost as long as their boat plunge into the hole and disappear!

As their boat neared the bank in its wild ride, it headed toward a huge flat rock that extended out from the shore. A scraggly tree grew out of its center. Akara was certain they were going to smash into the rock, but at the last minute, their craft veered to the left, scraping the rock as it passed. Then away from the shore they went as the whirlpool carried them across the stream toward the north bank!

Henda and Robin had joined Lanus, and the three had linked hands to form a rescue chain. Lanus had waded out into the water, Robin had followed to form the middle link, and Henda, nearest the shore, served as anchor for the chain. Lanus stood shoulder deep in foaming water at the very rim of the whirlpool. The current buffeted him, and he kept his footing only with difficulty. As the boat swept toward Lanus, Keila rose precariously to her feet and threw the coiled line as hard as she could toward him. Her throw was accurate, but to Akara's dismay, the ring at the end fell just short of his outstretched hand and they whirled on by!

Away went the boat again toward the opposite shore. Their second circuit of the whirlpool had begun! This time, Akara realized, they were lower down. The boat was now tilted so that she could look directly down into the center of the whirlpool, but because of their speed, she was held firmly in her seat.

Meanwhile, Keila had pulled the line back into the boat and dropped to her knees, working hard at something. An instant later she held up a small three-pronged anchor. Keila had used the short piece of line that was attached to this anchor to lash it to the brass mooring ring.

"I'll try for the tree," she called above the roar of the water. She pointed to the twisted trunk on the flat rock that was now ahead of them. "Hold tight! If the anchor catches, it will jerk our bow toward the shore."

They sped toward the rock, but farther away from it than before.

Again Keila stood and braced herself. She swung the anchor once around her head, then let it go. As it sailed through the air, over the rock, and past the tree, Keila dropped back onto the seat. As the boat's forward surge dragged the anchor back, one of its points caught the tree trunk and held.

Then everything happened at once. Akara felt a terrific jolt as the bow of the boat swung toward the rock, and the stern, where she sat, was flung terrifyingly out toward the center of the whirlpool. She hung on desperately as the stern swung through a giant arc until the boat was facing in the opposite direction. As Keila had foreseen, the momentum of that swing carried the stern up and out of the whirlpool until the boat grated on the bottom! At that moment she heard Keila's voice, "Now, Akara. Jump!"

Akara leaped blindly out toward the shore. She landed in swirling, hip-deep water, that swept her off balance, but as she began to fall, Keila, who had made the longer jump from the center of the boat, caught her arm. Together the two friends struggled ashore, dragged themselves out of the water, and collapsed at full length on the ground.

After a few moments, Akara raised herself on an elbow. Keila was still on her back, her eyes closed and face white, breathing heavily. "Are you all right?" Akara asked anxiously.

"Yes." Keila opened her eyes. "It's just that I haven't entirely recovered from my wound. It's left me a little weak." She sat up. "I'll be all right in a minute. Help me up. We must let the others know we are all right." With Akara's help she stood up, and together they waved to their comrades across the stream. The three soldiers returned their waves. Then, almost immediately, Robin left the other two and headed upstream.

"He's gone to watch for the evil ones," said Keila. "We're not far from their castle."

At that instant, there was a sudden ripping sound as the anchor of the boat tore loose from the tree. Stern first, the little craft spun away into the whirlpool. Keila and Akara watched in silence as it circled, getting lower with each passage. It reached the center and plunged into the hole with an explosive sound. Instantly, splintered pieces of wood were tossed upward to splash in the water and circle for a few minutes before disappearing again.

"That finishes the miller's boat," said Keila, "But we're safe. We're on the south side of the stream, the side away from the King's Castle, but if the whirlpool stops when the stream flow changes direction again, we should be able to get across."

Akara stared at the whirlpool. "I think it's slowing now."

It was true. The hole at the center of the funnel was becoming smaller. As they watched, it disappeared, and the roar of the water subsided. While the surface continued to swirl, it was clear that its force was gone.

Akara said, "If the Dark Power is responsible for the backward flow, I wonder if it also causes the whirlpool."

"Perhaps," said Keila. "But it is more likely that there is a natural cause. Perhaps there is a fissure in the stream bottom that opens and closes periodically. Whatever the reason, the water is flowing toward the mill again. Let's see if we can get across."

Before they could make the attempt, a trumpet call rang out. It came from Robin who, Akara saw, was standing some distance upstream, his sword drawn. Across the water, Lanus and Henda drew their own swords and raced away toward him.

Looking into the gloom beyond Robin, Akara saw shadowy figures advancing toward him along the shore. She heard the high, eerie wail that, she remembered, signaled the presence of the evil ones. She shivered. Beside her, a grim-faced Keila buckled on her helmet, swung her shield into position, and drew her sword. The light that came from its blade flared high. She turned to Akara.

"It seems our enemies have found us."

"How did they know we were here?"

"They probably didn't. This may be only a routine patrol. Anyway, they know now that our three friends are here!"

Across the stream, Henda had reached Robin's side. Lanus had stopped short of that point. He scanned the area ahead, then turned to face Keila and Akara. Since the noise of the whirlpool had died, he was able to keep his voice low as he called across the water.

"There are evil ones on your side of the stream too!"

CHAPTER 34

Toward the Summit

Akara's heart jumped. She looked up the gorge, but from where she and Keila stood, the bank on their side of the stream was not visible. Lanus called again.

"You can't see them, and I'm sure they haven't seen you. If you start up the slope right away, you may get out of the valley without being seen. And Keila, once you reach the top, try for the high bridge across the gorge; then if you don't find us, head for the castle."

Without waiting for a reply, he waved farewell, then ran to join the others. Keila watched him go, then turned to Akara. "I wish we were across the stream so I could help in the battle. Now we'll only create another battle by staying here. The sooner we go, the better it will be for our comrades. Come."

She turned and with sword still in hand, began climbing the slope, angling diagonally upward on a course that took them in a downstream direction away from the battle. As Akara followed, she heard from the riverbank behind her, the shout, "For the King!" followed by the clash of swords. The battle had begun. She glanced back. There she could see the King's Soldiers standing shoulder to shoulder and the dark forms of the enemy beyond them. She heard the high-pitched wailing noise of the evil ones and saw bright and dark swords flash in the gloom.

She turned again and scrambled after Keila. "What will happen to them?" she asked anxiously. "They're outnumbered, and they have no way to escape."

Without slowing her pace, Keila replied, "I'm concerned too. But

Lanus and Robin are experienced mountain fighters. I'm sure they have a plan for retreating."

This explanation did not reassure Akara, but she said no more. After a short climb, they reached a ravine. Keila slid down into it, and Akara followed.

"We're out of sight here, Keila said. "We can rest for a few moments and give our comrades some trumpet support."

"Won't the sound of your trumpet tell the evil ones where we are?"

"No, they can't hear our trumpets, just as they can't see the light given off by our swords."

Akara joined in the trumpet call, after which she and Keila raised their heads cautiously above the edge of the ravine and peered down the slope. They were farther from the battle now and could not see the action in detail, but they could tell the fight was still going on. Following Keila's pointing finger, Akara saw a group of the evil ones clustered on the side of the stream closest to them.

"They are watching the battle across the river, not looking for us," said Keila, "but to be safe, we'll climb in this ravine. It seems to lead toward the summit."

The slope grew steeper as they neared the summit, and they had to climb on all fours. The sounds of battle became fainter as they climbed, then ceased entirely. As the afternoon drew to a close and dusk made the gloom even darker, they emerged from the ravine onto level ground. Here they threw themselves down to rest.

"What shall we do now?" asked Akara when she had caught her breath.

Keila sat up. "We can't travel far in the dark. We must find a place close by where we can camp for the night."

Wearily they got to their feet and turned away from the gorge, Keila holding her sword high to light the way. To their right, the ground sloped downward in the direction of Broad Valley. On their left, a line of cliffs jutted upward. Keila led the way along the base of these cliffs until she found a small, sheltered hollow whose floor was covered with dry leaves.

She propped her sword upright against the rock wall so that the hollow was flooded with its gentle light. "This will be much more pleasant than sitting in darkness," she said. "Also, its light will flare higher if any evil ones come near, so our enemies can't surprise us."

The travelers sat down, their backs against the rock wall, and Keila opened her pack. "I have some bread and cheese. We'll eat some now, and save the rest for tomorrow."

As they were eating, Akara said, "You haven't yet told me how Lanus, Robin, and Henda came to be down in the enemy valley."

"So I haven't. Well, Akara, when you disappeared, your friends searched for you. Blink and Skey checked the supplies you had hidden by the grassy knoll and found they were undisturbed. So we knew you hadn't traveled north as you had planned. When your blue bag was found near the valley road, it was easy to guess that you had been seized by the miller. The four of us — Lanus, Robin, Henda, and I — asked our castle's leadership if we could try to find you and free you if possible. They not only gave us permission but encouraged us to do so."

"I had no idea the King's Soldiers were so concerned for me."

"The King loves you, and we do too. We wanted to help. Lanus and Robin had been to the valley where the enemy castle stands. Among the King's Soldiers, it is known as the 'Valley of Despair'. Both Lanus and Robin thought that the river which flows through this valley is probably the one that enters Broad Valley behind the mill at Arn. We thought that if we traveled down the mountain ridge to the Valley of Despair, we could then work our way down along the stream to the mill. If you were held prisoner there, we hoped to find a way to free you.

"Your valley friends were also concerned. Zemla decided to lead an official delegation from Midra to Arn to find you and demand your release. Since I had once visited that village, he invited me to travel with his party. I had little hope Zemla could free you, but I hoped that by traveling with him, I could see you and learn how you were.

"So Lanus, Robin, and Henda followed our original plan without me. But before they had time to travel down the valley to the mill, you and I escaped in the miller's boat."

"I'm so grateful that all of these people wanted to help me," said Akara. Then, after a short silence, she added, "One thing still puzzles me. How did you know there was a boat at the mill that might help us escape?"

"I'm sure the King helped me to learn about that. On the way down the valley, our delegation met Trask the peddler. I had never seen him but recognized him from your description. I hailed him and asked if he knew where you were. At first he would say nothing, but when I convinced him that I was your friend, he told me where you were. He described the mill in detail and in doing so, mentioned the boat. So you see, it all worked out!"

It was now fully night, and both girls were ready for sleep. But Akara had one more question to ask. "We're on the opposite side of the gorge from the King's Castle, aren't we? How can we get across? Didn't Lanus say something about a bridge?"

"Yes, there is a natural stone bridge that spans the gorge. I've never seen it, but it's high, somewhere near the top of the mountain ridge."

Akara's face wore an anxious frown. "A natural bridge? How wide is it? I'm terribly afraid of high places, Keila."

"So am I. It's one reason why I have never been interested in even hearing people talk about the high bridge. When they do, I get a shaky feeling in my stomach and quickly walk away."

"There must be another way to cross."

"I wish I could think of one. With the enemy alert and patrolling the river, it would be foolhardy to go back down into their valley. But all that is tomorrow's problem. Right now, you should get some sleep."

Akara nodded agreement and prepared to roll herself in her cloak and find a spot to lie down on her bed of leaves. Then she noticed that Keila was making no move to do likewise. "What are you going to do?"

"I'm going to stay awake on watch. The sword will tell us if any enemy comes near, but I must be awake to see it."

Akara protested. "It's not fair for me to sleep all night while you stay awake. You must let me stand guard for part of the time."

"All right, I will, but you must let me take the major part of the watch. As a Soldier of the King, I've been trained for this kind of duty. You sleep now, and I'll wake you before dawn, then I'll sleep for a time while you watch."

While this arrangement placed a heavy burden on Keila, Akara felt that she must yield to her friend's judgment. She wrapped herself in her cloak, dropped back on her bed of leaves, and was almost instantly asleep. Keila seated herself against the rock with her sword beside her and stared into the darkness. Her face now bore a look of greater concern than she had allowed Akara to see.

CHAPTER 35

A Running Battle

After his call across the water to Keila and Akara, Lanus turned and raced upstream to join his companions. As he ran, his mind focused on the battle ahead. He and Robin had hoped to avoid conflict with the enemy while they searched for Akara. Now they were forced into a fight. It was good, Lanus thought, that when they first arrived at the valley they had scouted it thoroughly. He and Robin had agreed on the best escape routes up the steep slopes, and the places on those routes where they could turn and fight.

However, Lanus felt a nagging concern for Henda, who had little combat experience. The young soldier had begged hard to come along, and Lanus and Robin had reluctantly agreed. How would Henda fare now against the enemy?

Running hard, Lanus reached the battle site. Robin had chosen the spot well. Ages ago, a huge boulder had tumbled down the slope and come to rest at the bottom, leaving only a narrow passage between it and the water's edge. There the three soldiers could fight shoulder to shoulder. And no matter how many of the evil ones came against them, only three could attack at a time.

When Lanus arrived, about a dozen of the evil ones were advancing cautiously toward Robin. The King's Soldiers had just enough time to align themselves, with Henda between the two more experienced fighters, when the enemy charged!

In the past, Lanus and Robin had fought the best of the evil ones here in this valley. Now, after his first few sword strokes, Lanus realized that these were not the enemy's first-line soldiers. This was evidently a routine patrol, not a battle-hardened group. Robin and Lanus were able to defend themselves easily, and Henda held his own. While their opponents kept changing places, no skilled swordsman came forward, though both Lanus and Robin knew reinforcements might appear at any moment.

Lanus exchanged a quick glance with Robin and Henda. No words were needed, for the maneuver was one they had practiced. With a nod to his two comrades, Robin turned and darted down the path to the rear. At the same instant, Lanus and Henda raised the King's battle cry and charged forward together, forcing the enemy to give ground. Then they turned and raced after Robin, the fleet-footed Henda first, with Lanus right behind him.

By the time their enemies realized what was happening, the King's Soldiers had opened a substantial lead. As the evil ones streamed after them, it quickly became a foot race.

Ahead was another boulder that rested a little farther from the water. Henda and Lanus raced past this rock without stopping. But as the first of the enemy approached it, Robin leaped out, swinging a great overhand blow that smashed into the shield of the leading enemy, knocking him into the water and out of the fight.

Simultaneously, Lanus and Henda turned and came racing back. Robin shouted, "For the King!" and all three charged the remaining enemy. The evil ones were thrown into confusion. Those in the lead struggled to get into defensive position. Those behind, who were still running, collided with them, knocking them off balance. The charge of the King's Soldiers struck down the leaders and sent the rest tumbling backward.

A narrow path led up the slope at this point, a path that the King's Soldiers knew led to the summit. Before the evil ones could recover from their confusion, Henda turned and scrambled up this path. Robin followed, and Lanus, after a final sweeping blow at the enemy, turned and raced upward as well.

Already bewildered, the evil ones hesitated. On this path they would have to pursue in single file. The King's Soldiers would be above them, and in a position to turn and attack at any time. They hesitated, then the bolder ones started climbing after the King's Soldiers. Others followed more reluctantly. A few remained at the bottom and began hurling flaming darts over the heads of their climbing comrades. Henda saw the first of the darts and shouted a warning. Robin and Lanus turned and began backing up the slope, keeping their shields ready to ward off these missiles. They were poorly thrown, however, and only one came close enough for Lanus to catch on his shield.

Then came another shout from Henda. His quick eyes had seen a column of enemy reinforcements coming on the run along the river from the direction of the evil ones' castle. This group reached the path and immediately began climbing, pushing their way past the original pursuers.

Lanus realized that these newcomers were some of the enemy's more experienced fighters. But they arrived too late to catch the King's Soldiers before they reached the valley rim. The last several yards of the climb were almost vertical. Lanus and Robin boosted the lighter Henda to the top, where he threw himself down on his stomach and reached his hands down for Lanus to grasp.

With his help, Lanus pulled himself over the edge. Then, as he stood up, his sword light flared high. He turned. There, emerging from the trees only a short distance away, were three more of the evil ones. This was apparently another patrol returning to the castle, and when they saw Lanus, they halted in surprise. Lanus realized there was only one thing to do. He shouted to Henda to pull Robin to the top quickly. Then, raising the King's battle cry, he charged straight at the enemy!

The evil ones were unprepared for battle. Their swords had been sheathed and their shields slung on their backs. When the charging Lanus reached them, they were still trying to get their weapons into position. With a great swing of his sword, he knocked down the foremost enemy. However, at the same instant, one of the others swung a heavy club against Lanus's knee.

Lanus staggered and almost fell. At this moment Henda and Robin raced up with a shout and drove the two remaining evil ones into the woods. Then Robin put his arm around Lanus on one side, while Henda supported him on the other. With Lanus hobbling painfully between them, they hurried off into another patch of woodland.

There Robin halted. "Our pursuers will reach the top of the gorge in a moment," he whispered. "With your leg in this condition, Lanus, we can't outrun them. We must hide. Wait here for a minute." He darted farther into the woods, and as quickly returned. "There's a fallen tree a little distance away, with room under it for all three of us," he said. "We can pile brush over ourselves to hide us. The enemy won't expect us to hide this close to the gorge."

The three made their way to the tree. By the time Lanus and Henda burrowed their way beneath it, sounds behind them indicated that some of their enemies had reached the edge of the woods. Working quickly, Robin covered the other two, first with their traveling cloaks, then with brush. Then he crawled under the tree and covered himself in the same way.

"We must lie still for the next few hours," he whispered. "When the area is clear, we'll head for our supply base."

CHAPTER 36

Akara's Revelation

True to her promise, Keila woke Akara while it was still dark. "All is quiet," she reported. "If you will watch, I'll sleep for an hour." She handed Akara the water bottle. "A sip of this will help you wake up. If the sword light flares, wake me at once."

She pulled her traveling cloak around her and quickly fell asleep. Akara sat down with her back against the rock and Keila's sword propped up beside her. To her own surprise, she was not afraid, but with her friend asleep she felt very much alone. Her thoughts went to Lanus, Robin, and Henda. Their fight against the evil ones was long since over, but how had it ended? What had happened to those three brave soldiers?

With an effort, she wrenched her mind away from these thoughts. She and Keila were in danger too. They were on the wrong side of the gorge, low on food and water, and with the scary prospect of the high bridge in front of them. She raised her silver trumpet and sent out a silent call for help. This was a time when they surely needed the King's assistance. But could even the King get them out of this situation?

Akara sighed. How much did she know about the King anyway? His book said he was the same person as the Good Carpenter, though Garis and the Hill Soldiers doubted this. If the King was the Good Carpenter, why had he come to the valley? That part of the story seemed somehow pointless. He had come, and died, and then, according to the King's Book, had come back to life again. But then things in the valley had gone on just as before. Why had he come at all?

"I came for you, Akara!"

No human voice spoke those words, but Akara heard them clearly in her mind. Had she drifted into a doze and dreamed the words? She gave her head a shake. She had to stay awake! The words came again. "I came for you, Akara! It is written in my book. I was dead, but I am alive for ever and ever. By my death I destroyed the one that had the power of death."

Akara remembered reading statements like that, but they had made no impression. Now, suddenly, they began to make sense. Could it be that the King's coming to the valley was part of some bigger plan — a plan that affected everyone?

In her mind, thoughts began to fall into place like pieces of a jigsaw puzzle. If those words were true, the King was even more wise and good than she had imagined. She struggled to understand. If the King had a plan, what did his plan have to do with her?

For the third time, the words came into her mind, "I came for you, Akara. Will you come to me now?"

Deep inside her, something crumbled. The hard, rebellious little girl who had fought against Dame Dessit, who loved being independent, was disappearing. A new Akara was being born. There was much she did not understand, but certainty was growing in her. The King's Book was true! She did not yet understand the King's plan, but she wanted to be part of it. The King had come for her!

From somewhere deep inside herself, she answered. "Yes, Lord, I will come to you!"

A short time later, the sun rose. Keila opened her eyes, yawned, and sat up. Akara's immediate impulse was to tell her friend about what had happened to her. She scrambled to her feet, but while she was deciding how to begin, Keila said, "I'll sound out a trumpet call for us, then let's waste no time getting started. We must find the bridge today!" Akara decided to keep her news for a later time.

"There is just enough bread and cheese for a mouthful apiece," said Keila. "We'll eat that and find another source of food today."

Keila shouldered her pack and they left their overnight hollow. Keila again set out along the base of the cliffs. "We must go south, away from the valley, until we find a path up to the mountain ridge," she told Akara. "Once on the ridge, we can head north again and look for the high bridge." They traveled for almost an hour, with the cliff on their left before they found a path that slanted upward. The first part of the climb was through woodland, then they broke into an open area where they paused to catch their breath. There, diagonally downward to their right, they had a clear view of the valley far below. Akara saw green fields bathed in sunlight, and roads running between them.

She stood motionless drinking in the sight. Then an idea flashed into her mind. "Keila! We won't have to climb the mountain or cross the horrible high bridge! The valley is right down there! There is no path leading down to it, but if we follow this opening through the trees it will take us down there. We'll be south of the miller's village, but we can make a wide circle around Arn and travel up the old valley road to Midra. The miller won't look for us in the valley, and if we stay away from his village, we'll be safe."

There was no answer, and Akara turned toward Keila. Her friend was standing a few paces away and looking at her thoughtfully. "We can go that way if you wish," she said.

Something in Keila's manner puzzled Akara. "What's wrong? Don't you think we can get to Midra that way?"

"I'm sure we can."

"You sound as though you don't want to do it. Yet you told me you are afraid of the high bridge."

Keila smiled gently. "I must be honest with you, Akara. I am deathly afraid of that bridge. Nevertheless, if I were making this journey alone, I would cross it. But I will not tell you what your choice should be."

Akara was puzzled. "Does that mean that if I choose to go down to the valley you won't go with me?"

"I'll go with you if that's the way you decide to go. You're my friend, Akara. I've helped get you away from the miller, and I intend to see you safely to Midra."

Akara threw up her hands in exasperation. "I don't understand you, Keila. You're as terrified of going across the high bridge as I am. But you don't want to take the sure way of getting to Midra through the valley."

Keila unbuckled her pack, put it down, and sat down on a patch of grass. "Sit with me for a moment," she said, "and I'll try to explain it." When Akara was seated, she continued. "You remember what the

King's Book said about the rightful ownership of the valley and these mountains?"

"Yes, both valley and mountains belong to the King, who created them. I believe that now."

"That's right. And you remember hearing that the valley is under the control of the evil ones?"

"Yes. The valley folk turned against the King. That's why he built his castle on the mountaintop. Wait a minute! Are you saying that you don't want to go home through the valley because it is enemy territory?"

"That's right. When the King visited the valley as the Good Carpenter, people rejected him and put him to death."

Akara frowned. "I still don't understand. You travel in the valley. That's how you came to my village. Apparently the enemy soldiers won't attack us there. So why don't you want to go there now?"

"Here is my reason, Akara. As I told you, I grew up in the valley, but when I gave my life to the King, the mountain became my home. True, I travel to the valley, but I do so under his orders and to carry his message. I don't go there for my own benefit or to help solve my problems."

She gave Akara a warm smile. "That's my decision as a Soldier of the King. But my job now is to stay with you and help you. If you want to go down to the valley, I'll go with you. You are free to decide for yourself. I have made the choice to serve the King. You have not done so."

Akara jumped to her feet. "But I have!"

It was Keila's turn to look surprised. "What do you mean?"

"I have decided to follow the King. I came to that decision when you were sleeping this morning. I just hadn't told you yet."

Keila also scrambled to her feet, her eyes wide with surprise. "That's wonderful, Akara. Are you sure of your decision?"

"Yes. You see, I did a lot of thinking during the time I was locked up in the miller's cell. I realized that I had made a mess of things. I ran away from my friends who were trying to help me, and I caused you and the other King's Soldiers to risk your lives. I think I knew, deep down, that the King cares for me, but I wasn't sure what to do about it."

She paused for breath. "Early this morning while you were sleeping, the King spoke to me. I knew then that I had to decide whether to follow him or to go on doing things my own way. I told him I wanted to be his follower."

Keila threw her arms around Akara, then held her at arm's length. There were tears of joy on both faces. "I'm so glad, Akara!" she said. "I've been hoping you would make this decision."

After they sat down again, Akara described her morning's experience in more detail. When she finished, they were silent for a few moments. Then Keila said, "Akara, you can still choose which route you want to take to Midra. The King will not force you to do something you choose not to do. So if you decide to go back through the valley, I'll go with you!"

CHAPTER 37

Crossing the Bridge

Akara's immediate impulse was to accept Keila's offer to take the valley route back to Midra. It would certainly solve the problem of the high bridge! For a long moment she thought about it, while Keila sat quietly waiting. Then she sighed. "I guess you have cleared that up for me," she said. "It would be foolish to make my first decision as a follower of the King a bad one. If my home is to be in the mountains, I better get used to traveling there. I'll follow you up the mountain. But Keila, I'm...I'm really scared of the high bridge!"

Keila looked at her soberly. "I'm afraid too, Akara. The closer we get to it, the more terrified I am." She raised her trumpet. "I don't know how either of us can cross it, but let's tell the King about our fears."

A short time later, the two travelers took up their belongings. Akara resolutely turned her eyes from the sunlit vista of Broad Valley and followed Keila upward. Her feelings were mixed, but her heart was light. However, her knees grew weak whenever she allowed her thoughts to stray to the ordeal that lay ahead.

Up they went on a long climb, first through a growth of small scraggly trees and then across areas of bare rock. Finally they reached the summit. There, after a short rest and a drink from Keila's water bottle, they turned northward along the ridge toward the Valley of Despair and the high bridge.

On this part of the Great Mountains, the crest was bleak and bare. There was no clear path, and they traveled single file. Huge rocky spurs towered upward, and boulders barred their way, requiring them to detour down one slope or the other. But always, Keila led the way back to the ridge. There was no sunlight here on the mountain crest. Thick dark clouds stretched overhead. To Akara, the journey seemed endless. Finally Keila stopped, waited for Akara to come up beside her, then pointed with her sword. There just ahead was the edge of the gorge!

On hands and knees they crawled to the edge and peered over. Beneath them the ground fell away in a steep precipice. Far below, they could see the dark river. There was no sign of life anywhere. The gorge, like the mountaintop, was misty, but as Akara looked to her left, she thought she could pick out the spot where the whirlpool had been. To her right, she could see the black lake that fed the stream. This lake filled the floor of the valley. Rising from its center was a dark castle, the fortress of the evil ones!

As she stared at it, fascinated, Keila stood up. A moment later she said, "Look Akara, there's the bridge!"

Scrambling to her feet, Akara looked in the direction Keila was pointing. There, some distance from the castle and on the other side of it from Broad Valley, was one of those wonders of nature that people call "a natural bridge." From the side of the gorge on which they stood, a slender span of rock arched across to the opposite side. The river, which in ages past had carved out the valley, had left the rock bridge standing. Akara would have found the sight beautiful if it were not so terrifying. As it was, her heart sank. Was it on this slender piece of rock that they were expected to cross the gorge?

Backing carefully away from the edge, the two rose to their feet and made their way to the bridge. They stood looking at it in silence. The top of the arch was almost level, rising only a little bit in the center of the span. But what paralyzed Akara with fear was its narrowness! She turned a pale face to her friend. "I can't do it, Keila," she said. "It's too high and too narrow. I'll have to go back!"

Though the breeze was cool on the ridge, there were small beads of perspiration on Keila's forehead. Her face was pale and when she spoke, her voice was low.

"I'm afraid too, Akara. This is," her voice wavered for a moment, "worse than I thought it would be." She gave Akara a steady look. "I know it was hard for you, Akara, back there when you turned your back on the valley and chose to follow the King. I, too, am truly terrified of this crossing, but I would like us to go forward." She took a deep breath. "As we were climbing to the ridge, a saying from the King's Book came to my mind. One of the King's ancient warriors wrote of him, 'When I said, my foot is slipping, your love supported me.' " She put her hand on Akara's shoulder. "We can still turn back. But before you make a decision, let us call upon the King for help."

She reached for the trumpet hanging from its silver cord around her neck and put it to her lips; in a moment its call sounded out. Akara hesitated. What good would the blowing of trumpets do now? What Keila was asking, she simply could not do. Still, out of loyalty to Keila, she took her own instrument and breathed through it.

Then something happened.

Her silver trumpet, silent for so long, gave forth its own call as clear and sweet as Keila's own! Out across the dark gorge, the two high notes sounded — supporting, entwining, and harmonizing with each other! For a few moments, Akara forgot about the perilous path in front of her. A great sense of delight welled up within her. Without her willing it, the high note of her trumpet dropped to the low resonant notes of thanks. Keila's trumpet followed hers down, and both trumpets harmonized on a song of praise to the King.

As the trumpet calls died away, Keila turned and threw her arms around Akara. "Whatever happens now, there is no question you're fully one of us!" she said.

The mist in the gorge had grown and spread to become a thick gray blanket hiding everything below. This was not the black fog of the evil ones but a soft pearl gray mist that rose until it filled the valley. It seemed solid, as though the bridge itself were resting upon it. Then Akara became aware of something else. The bridge seemed to be growing wider. Its rock surface appeared to expand outward on each side until it was broad enough for three to walk comfortably abreast.

Akara's eyes were wide with astonishment! "Is the bridge really wider, or does it just seem so?" she whispered.

"I don't know," answered Keila. She gave a shaky laugh. "I'm not sure it makes any difference. We'll walk single file on that path in the middle anyway. Her voice took on its normal firm tone. "But, Akara, that extra width, real or not, gives me confidence. Now I'm sure the King is going to get us across safely. Will you come?"

Akara swallowed hard. "Yes," she whispered at last. And as Keila stepped forward, holding the King's sword in front of her, Akara followed, her hand gripping Keila's shoulder. Just below the now wide rock walkway stretched the thick pearl gray mist. Step by step they went forward. And as they crossed the crown of the arch and headed down the gentle far slope, the dark clouds above parted briefly and a ray of sunshine lit their way!

Safe on the other side of the gorge they stopped to look back. Akara shivered. The span on which they had crossed was already beginning to shrink in width. Also, the gray mist beneath was thinning. Once again they were looking at the slender rock span that had so terrified them when they first saw it.

They turned from the high bridge and looked around them. "Now that we're on the north side of the gorge, we must move quickly and speak quietly," said Keila. "It's more likely that there are enemy patrols here."

She was about to say more, when Akara suddenly clutched her arm. "Look, Keila!" she whispered. "There's something moving in the trees ahead." Then, as a figure stepped into the open, "It's Robin!"

It was indeed Robin, and he ran toward them, a broad smile on his face. He didn't speak until he reached them, then said, also in low tones, "Greetings, I'm glad I found you."

"It's wonderful to see you, Robin," Keila responded. "Are Lanus and Henda with you?"

"At our supply base. We hoped to be here earlier, but Lanus was hurt in the fighting. Not seriously," he added quickly, seeing the concern on their faces. "He and Henda are at the base. Come, we mustn't stay out in the open."

As they turned to leave, Robin caught sight of the rock bridge for the first time. His eyebrows shot up as he stared at it. "I've heard of the high bridge, but I've never seen it. Did you cross the gorge on that?"

Keila's eyes twinkled as she glanced at Akara. "Yes, thanks to the King's help. We'll tell you about it when we reach camp."

The mountain ridge here was heavily wooded, and the tree foliage deepened the gloom of the gray skies. A short walk brought them into an area where giant rocks jutted upward among the trees. Robin stopped and gave a low whistle. An answering whistle came, and Henda stepped out from behind a boulder and greeted them. Then Robin led the way through a narrow passage into a small grassy area that was surrounded on all sides by rocks. Here they found Lanus, leg bandaged and lying on a bed of leaves, but otherwise looking well.

Chapter 38

Reunion

When Lanus saw Keila and Akara, his face broke into a huge grin. "You're safe! Wonderful! Help me up, Robin."

"Stay where you are, comrade," Robin said severely. "That leg of yours needs rest."

"Yes, we'll come to you," said Keila. She crossed to where Lanus was lying, his bandaged leg propped up on a log. She dropped to her knees beside him. "How is your leg?"

"Painful, but not serious. It was a blow from a club, not a sword cut. Robin laid the flat of his blade on it. The healing has begun, but slowly."

"He'll need more rest before he travels," put in Robin.

"We'll see," said Lanus. "Akara, it's good to see you. Give me your hand."

Akara did so. Tears filled her eyes as she looked around the group. "Thank you all so much for rescuing me," she said. "I can't tell you how sorry I am to have run away after the hearing and so caused all this trouble."

"Some of what happened was my fault," said Lanus. "I, too, must apologize."

"Hold on, Lanus," said Robin with a grin. "Before these apologies go further, we must feed our new arrivals. I suspect they didn't have much food with them when they jumped out of their boat."

Keila smiled. "You're right. We've been rationing mouthfuls of bread and cheese."

Robin pulled a package and bottles of water from behind a boulder.

On a flat rock, he spread out bread, dried meat, cheese, and fruit, and Keila and Akara eagerly dropped down on the ground, cross-legged, to eat.

When they had finished, Lanus said, "Now for my apology. When you ran away, back there at Midra, I realized immediately that it was my fault. I'm sure you felt that I didn't want to admit you were my sister. That must have hurt you a great deal. Actually, I have wanted to tell you that I'm your brother ever since the moment when I saw your blue bag that day on the castle battlement. I should have done so then."

"Why didn't you?"

"I had a reason, but it wasn't a good one. You see, I wanted very much for you to stay at the castle and become a follower of the King. I was afraid that if you learned that I'm your brother, you might join our fellowship simply because you knew I wanted you to. I was wrong. You had a right to know who you are. I hope you will forgive me."

Akara's answer was to jump up and run to him. With Robin's help, Lanus struggled to his feet, and then brother and sister were in each other's arms, with tears running down the cheeks of both.

Sometime later, after Akara had returned to her place, Lanus said, "We're not safe here. The enemy is still hunting for us. One of their patrols might stumble on this place at any time, and once we were discovered, we'd have the whole evil pack here in no time!"

"I agree," said Robin, "but we can't go until you're fit for travel."

"How soon do you think that will be, Lanus?" asked Keila.

"I could hobble along using a stick Robin cut for me, but I'd hold you back if we left now. Then, if we were sighted, the enemy would send a force after us. Traveling at my speed, we would be caught. A faster-moving party could get away."

He pushed himself up to a sitting position and looked around the group. "I have a better plan. Henda and I discussed it while you were gone, Robin. We decided that, when Keila and Akara came, the three of you should head north. Henda has volunteered to stay with me until I'm ready to move at full speed, then we'll follow you."

Robin shook his head. "We won't leave you, Lanus."

"I agree," Keila chimed in. "We are all in this together."

"You're forgetting our mission," argued Lanus. "We came to rescue

Akara from the miller and to take her back to Midra. We mustn't let my leg stand in the way of finishing the job. Akara is not a follower of the King, and we must not put her at additional risk while my leg is healing."

Akara opened her mouth to protest, but Keila spoke first. "You're wrong about one thing, Lanus."

"What is that?"

Keila smiled at Akara but said nothing. Akara spoke. Her voice trembled, but her tone was sure. "You are wrong about me, Lanus. I am a follower of the King!" She took a deep breath and went on. "This morning, I realized I had to decide whether my future lay in the valley or with those who serve the King. I chose the King, and I want to be one of his soldiers."

With Akara's announcement, Lanus's proposal was temporarily forgotten. Robin leaped to his feet and congratulated Akara on her choice. Lanus insisted on giving her another hug.

When they settled down once more, Akara flashed a mischievous grin at Lanus. "If my new status gives me a vote, I agree with Keila and Robin. I don't want to leave you, Lanus, whatever the danger. After all," her voice quavered again, "I've just found you!"

Before Lanus could answer, Robin said mildly, "I don't think we need to make a decision right now. Keila and Akara should have some sleep before they start anywhere, and another night's rest won't hurt your leg, Lanus."

Everyone agreed with Robin's view, and the subject was dropped. Then, in response to a request from Lanus, Keila and Akara told of their adventures since they left the gorge. Later, Robin relieved Henda on watch, and Lanus and Henda recounted the story of their own battle and escape from the enemy.

The next morning Lanus, Robin, Keila, and Akara had just finished breakfast when Henda, whose turn it was to stand watch, came bounding in through the entrance. "The enemy has started a new search," he said, "and they're headed this way!"

His report was short and clear. Just before dawn, he had made a wide circle around their hiding place. At one point his sword light had flared, and he had crept quietly in that direction. He had discovered about fifty of the enemy soldiers spread out in a line, searching the entire area near the enemy's valley. At their present rate of advance, he guessed they would reach the spot where the King's Soldiers were hidden before midday.

There was no need for discussion. While it was possible that the evil ones might miss the narrow entrance to the hiding place, that was too great a chance to take. Lanus spoke for all. "We must leave as quickly as possible."

The group sprang into action. Keila picked up her weapons and went out to take Henda's post on guard. Henda and Robin quickly packed the remaining food and water, then erased all signs of their occupancy of the area. Meanwhile, Akara helped Lanus to his feet. Robin had made him a crutch, a stout oak staff with a crosspiece lashed to the top, and Lanus stumped back and forth across the area to test it. "I think I can keep up with the group at march pace," he told them, "though I can't go faster."

Robin nodded soberly. "March pace it is. Henda and I will be available if you need help over the rough places."

When all were ready, Robin sounded a trumpet call, and they filed out through the narrow entrance then headed north along the mountain ridge. Keila went first, holding her sword in front of her, alert for the flare of light that would indicate enemies ahead. Robin, Lanus, and Akara came next, with Robin lending Lanus a strong arm to help him over rough spots. Henda served as rear guard, keeping an eye out for pursuit. He also carried with him a leafy tree branch with which to brush out any footprints the party made when they crossed soft spots.

Lanus explained the plan to Akara. "Our first goal will be to reach a place we call the 'Cleft of the Rock'. My leg is bound to make our marching speed slower than normal, but if we travel today and through the night with as few stops as possible, we should reach the cleft tomorrow morning. There we can sleep and recuperate before trying the final day's march to the castle."

"Might the enemy catch up with us at this Cleft of the Rock and attack us there?"

Lanus shook his head. "We'll be entirely safe there. The evil ones fear the Cleft of the Rock and never go near it. We won't even have to post a guard."

And so the march began. All that day they traveled, stopping occasionally, but only for the shortest of rests. Early in the afternoon, Henda, bringing up the rear, reported that his sword light showed the presence of evil ones behind them, though the signal was faint, indicating that they were some distance away.

CHAPTER 39

The Trumpet's Plea

Throughout the afternoon, Henda's sword light continued to show the presence of enemy forces behind them, but these indications grew no stronger.

"If the evil ones are following us, I'm surprised they are coming so slowly," said Lanus during one of their brief stops. "I should think they would send fast runners to catch us as soon as possible."

The five comrades had thrown themselves down on a grassy area beside the path. Without lifting his head, Henda said, "Maybe they've stopped looking for us. We covered our tracks well. Perhaps this is just a routine patrol heading north."

Keila propped herself on one elbow. "That's possible, but our enemies don't usually give up this quickly."

"There may be another answer," said Robin thoughtfully, sitting up. "Suppose the evil ones sent a party north thinking we had raced toward our castle when we left the valley. If so, the group behind us could be a follow-up force, moving slowly and searching the ridge on each side as they come."

Lanus said, "If you're right, we could be caught between two enemy forces." He struggled to his feet and picked up his crutch. "In any case, all we can do now is keep moving."

Keila got up too. "I'd better range farther ahead to pick up any signs of an enemy in front."

They moved out again, this time with Keila well in front of the group, watching carefully for the slightest flicker of the sword light. But as the hours passed, she saw no sign that any of the enemy were in front of them.

On the other hand, Henda soon reported that the enemy force behind them was drawing nearer. The King's Soldiers paused for a brief council of war. "My leg is holding up well," said Lanus. "I think I can move at a faster pace."

"Good!" said Robin. "If we also cut down on the number of rest stops, we should be able to keep in front of the enemy until we reach the Cleft of the Rock."

On they went at a faster clip. This was more difficult for Lanus, Akara could see, but he pegged along without complaint.

Near sundown, they reached a place where the forest through which they had been traveling gave way to a stretch of open mountainside. Their path had followed the mountaintop northward, sometimes running along the ridge, at other times a little ways down the slope on one side or the other. To their left, the ground sloped down toward the valley for a short distance before dropping away in steep cliffs. Uphill to their right was another set of cliffs above which towered the mountain ridge. The path in front of them ran across an open area cut by a series of deep, rain-washed gullies.

"I'll have to rely on Robin and Henda to help me across this rough ground," said Lanus to Akara. "We certainly don't want the enemy to catch us in this open stretch!"

Robin and Henda were already swinging into action, and Akara was amazed at how efficiently they half-supported, half-carried Lanus across each successive gully. Even so, it was slow going. They were only halfway across this open space when Keila, who had advanced into the woods ahead, came racing back.

"Enemy ahead!" she said as she came near. "I went only a short distance into the woods when my sword light began flaring. I crept forward carefully and was able to get a look at them without being seen. There are about twenty evil ones, and they are coming in this direction!"

Robin's eyes turned back in the direction they had come. "If we turn back into the other woods, we'll run straight into the arms of the other force."

"And without ropes we can't climb down the cliffs below us," added

Lanus. "I think our best choice is the upper cliffs. Perhaps we can find an opening there where we can keep out of sight until both groups of evil ones have left."

Robin and Keila both nodded agreement.

"What if there's no opening?" asked Henda.

"Then we'll have to fight!" Lanus tucked the crutch under his arm and began climbing.

Robin and Henda rushed to help him, and Keila and Akara followed them up the slope. As they neared the cliff, it became evident that its face was smooth and sheer. Robin looked up grimly at the rock. "There goes our last hope! There is no way we can get through these cliffs or climb them."

"If it would hurry and get dark, perhaps the enemy wouldn't see us," said Akara.

Robin smiled sadly. "Unfortunately, they are creatures of darkness and can see at night as well as we can in the daytime."

Lanus gave Akara a hug. "I wanted so much to be able to bring you back safely to our castle," he said, "but it looks as though that may not happen."

"It's all right," Akara whispered.

The travelers exchanged embraces all around, then raised their trumpets together and sent out a call for help to the King. Then, with no further words, the four soldiers slipped off their packs, buckled the chin straps of their helmets, and shifted their shields and swords into position. They stood shoulder to shoulder, facing down the slope with Akara behind their line. They had not long to wait. Out of the woods to the north came the enemy force. They would surely have seen the King's followers immediately but for the fact that the second band of evil ones, also about twenty strong, came into view from the south at the same time. The two groups met at a point directly in front of the King's Soldiers.

Akara, who had never seen the enemy close up, looked down in awe and fear. She knew that at any moment one of the evil ones would glance up the slope and see them. Then would come the hopeless fight, four against forty. She wondered what it would be like to die, or perhaps even worse, to be captured. A feeling of despair engulfed her.

Then, suddenly, a quiet voice spoke inside her, "Your trumpet, Akara." It was the voice she had heard before, at Elsis when she faced the miller's men, and more recently, when she had made her choice to follow the King.

She hesitated. All five trumpets had sent a call for help only a few moments ago. What good could another call do, especially one from the newest of the King's followers? And what could she ask for in this desperate situation?

Instantly the voice came again, "Ask that they not see you."

Trembling, Akara raised her trumpet to her lips. Even though she knew that the evil ones could not hear its tones, she could not bring herself to blow it audibly. Instead, she breathed gently through it the noiseless message, "Please, don't let them see us."

She lowered her trumpet. Of the four soldiers in front of her, only Keila had caught Akara's movement from the corner of her eye. The rest were staring at the evil ones. Lanus muttered under his breath, "They surely must see us soon."

Akara, her hopes beginning to rise, whispered to herself, "Perhaps they won't." Keila's sharp ears heard, and she gave Akara a quick, wondering look.

Amazingly, the evil ones did not see them. The enemy soldiers stood in groups talking while the leaders of the two bands conferred. Not once did they glance up to where the King's soldiers stood motionless as statues, but in plain view. Then the two bands formed into one and marched away southward.

The King's followers watched incredulously until the last of the enemy disappeared into the woods. Then swords were sheathed, and there was another round of hugs, this time joyful ones. Robin shook his head. "I don't understand it. They couldn't have missed seeing us, but they did!"

"They looked everywhere but up the hill where we were." said Henda.

"That's right," said Lanus, lifting his trumpet. "It was a miracle, and we need to thank the King for it." Akara said nothing, but her heart was full as she blew her trumpet with the rest.   As the travelers took up their packs again, Lanus said, "You were right, Robin! The first group the enemy sent out was probably the band that came here from the north. They may have gone almost up to the King's Castle and then turned back."

Henda was puzzled. "If the evil ones thought we had gone north, why were they searching the area around the valley this morning?"

"They were covering all the possibilities," said Robin. "I think that's also why they sent a second group north. If the first group missed us, we could be caught between the first and second parties."

"And we were," said Keila. "Anyway, now the way should be clear for us to travel north to the Cleft of the Rock."

"Just the same," said Robin, "I think we should press on through the night and try to get there as soon as possible."

Lanus nodded. "Let's go."

CHAPTER 40

At the Cleft of the Rock

The march northward continued, even though danger from the evil ones seemed past. However, they did take longer rest periods. Partway through the night, Henda moved forward to lead the party while Keila took his place in the rear. This gave Akara a chance to drop back and walk with her, leaving Robin and Lanus to walk together.

After they had chatted for a few minutes, Keila said, "There's something I've been wanting to ask you. Back there by the cliffs, when the enemy soldiers were milling about below us, Lanus predicted that they would certainly see us. I heard you whisper 'perhaps they won't!' Amazingly, they didn't, but how could you have guessed that?"

"I didn't, Keila. That was just a hopeful whisper that slipped out!" She paused while they climbed over a fallen log that blocked the path, and then went on. "It had to do with the trumpet call I had just made."

"I saw you."

"Something made me use my trumpet just then. The rest of you all had your swords drawn, ready to fight the enemy. I had no sword or armor, but I felt I should help too."

"So you sent out a trumpet call."

Akara nodded. "Yes. And something told me to ask that the evil ones not see us. I don't know why, I just felt I had to make that request."

Keila stood still and looked at her friend. "The King answered your trumpet call in a wonderful way. You must tell the rest about this when we next stop to rest."

Akara shook her head. "I'd rather not tell anyone else. I believe it was the King who prompted me to make the trumpet call and told me what to ask for. This means a lot to me, but I don't want people giving me credit for it."

"I understand," said Keila.

A few minutes later, they stopped for a rest period. Robin gave Lanus a concerned look. "Is this journey making your leg worse?"

"Actually, I think the exercise has helped. My leg is still sore, but I'm able to walk better than when we started. I only use my crutch on bad spots in the path now." He grinned. "Perhaps by the time we've finished the journey, it will be as good as new."

To Akara, the night march seemed endless. But dawn came at last, and as she looked ahead, she saw in the distance a high rocky spire soaring upward from the mountain ridge. Henda turned back from the lead position. "There it is! The Cleft of the Rock!"

With new enthusiasm they pressed forward and at last reached the base of the rocky peak. A steep path led them up to a large cave near the top of the spire. Here the exhausted travelers dropped their packs, threw themselves down on the cave floor, and slept.

Akara awoke refreshed in the late afternoon to find her companions already up and spreading out food for a meal. Afterward, Lanus led Akara to the rear of the cave. Here he showed her an inscription that he said had been cut into the rock centuries before by the warrior David. It read, "Lead me to the rock that is higher than I, for you have been my refuge, a strong tower against the foe."

On one side of the cave was a small pool of fresh water. Lanus pointed to it. "This pool is fed by the rain that comes down through cracks in the rock, so the King's Soldier who rests here need never be thirsty."

Just then a cry came from Henda. "Look! There's a party headed this way from the direction of the King's Castle."

The others rushed to join him at the cave entrance. Sure enough, as they looked downward they could see through the trees the glint of sunlight on armor. As they watched, a group of the King's Soldiers came out into the open and headed toward the Cleft of the Rock.

"It's a large detachment," said Robin. "I count twenty-five."

Keila shaded her eyes. "And the leader looks like Jamin."

Indeed it was Jamin, and when he and his party had climbed the path to the cave, there was a joyous reunion. Tril was in the party, as were other women.

Later, when both parties were seated together on the cave floor, Jamin said, "We've had meetings each day in the Hall of the Trumpets asking that the King would bring you all back safely. Then, when Zemla and his delegation returned from Arn, we learned that Keila and Akara had escaped up the dark stream.

"We realized that you might have a confrontation with the enemy and decided to send two groups of soldiers south to help if necessary. The party I lead is the first group. A larger force plans to leave the castle tomorrow, for we were prepared to fight a major battle if required to bring you all back safely."

He smiled. "Now that we know rescue is not necessary, we'd like to hear about your adventures."

During the next half hour, the travelers told their story, beginning with Keila and Akara's escape from the miller, and ending with the miraculous deliverance from the enemy forces on the mountain slope. When they had finished, someone began singing a song of praise to the King, and they all joined in. Afterward, those in Jamin's party unpacked the fresh provisions they had brought, and there was a time of feasting.

Later, Jamin came to sit beside Akara. "I was delighted to hear that you made a decision to follow the King after you escaped from the enemy's valley," he said. "Are you still of that mind?"

Akara nodded firmly. "Yes. It was my commitment to follow the King that helped me cross the high bridge later in spite of my terror. Nothing since has convinced me to change. I want to become a real soldier as soon as I can."

"Good. I'm sure you will be given a warm welcome by everyone at the castle. One or two of us will talk with you to make sure you understand the decision you are making. Then you will be given your armor and will learn the name of each piece and why it bears that name."

This statement struck a cord in Akara's memory. "Garis told me there was a legend that each piece of armor worn by the Soldiers of the King had a name inscribed upon it, but that these names were invisible. He was not sure this legend was true."

"It is true," Jamin said. "When those who are now called the Hill Soldiers moved from the mountain down into the valley many generations ago, they lost the ability to see those names."

Akara leaned forward and stared at Jamin's breastplate. "You mean there is something written on your breastplate that I can't see?"

"That's right. I won't tell you what it is, but you'll be able to see it and the other names for yourself when you are given the King's armor to wear. At that time, you will also learn the meaning of these names."

Later, when Akara told Lanus and Keila about her talk with Jamin, Lanus beamed. "There will be many wonderful things for you to learn, my sister, and I hope to help you. We must train you in the use of the sword and in the study of the King's Book. Also, you'll have duties in and around the castle."

"I'm looking forward to all of that," said Akara. "I especially want to learn much more about the trumpet."

Keila looked across at Jamin. "Akara has already used her trumpet effectively. Her trumpet call helped us across the high bridge, though we were both terrified."

"Good," said Jamin with an approving nod. "One more thing, Akara. A person who becomes a Soldier of the King still has responsibilities as a citizen of the valley. One day soon, you must travel down and visit Zemla and Garis. I know you will want to thank them for the help they gave you. You should also tell them, as well as your other friends, that you have chosen to become a follower of the King."

Akara nodded vigorously. "Yes, I want to do that. Zemla and Dame Leck and Garis have all helped me. Zemla may be disappointed that I have not joined the Hill Soldiers, but I think he won't object to my becoming a Soldier of the King."

"I'm sure you're right. Zemla is a good man."

"Then, too, I want to see Blink and Skey and many of the others who have helped me and thank them all personally."

"I'm glad you feel that way," said Keila. "Once you take care of your valley responsibilities, your mind can be free to concentrate on serving the King."

They slept in the cave again that night. The next morning after breakfast, they prepared to leave for the King's Castle.

"How long a journey is it?" Akara asked Lanus.

"A day's march. We should arrive late in the afternoon."

"How is your leg this morning?"

"Better than yesterday. I should have no trouble keeping up with the group."

Near midday, they met the larger force under Gayne on their way south. The situation was explained to them, and they fell in behind Jamin's party to return to the castle.

Jamin sent a runner ahead to carry the news that the rescue party was returning. Sometime later, Akara got a distant glimpse of a castle turret. Then came the moment when they came out of the woods and the entire castle came into view.

The great castle gate stood open and a triumphant trumpet call greeted them from the battlements. Jamin called a halt and summoned the five travelers to the front of the formation. He spoke to Keila, Lanus, Robin, and Henda. "You have served the King courageously in completing your mission to rescue Akara. I want you four to march in front of the column as we approach the castle. You march with them, Akara."

The five comrades formed in a line. Akara was in the center, Keila and Lanus on either side of her, and Robin and Henda on the ends. Then they stepped out together toward the castle. Jamin and the rest followed.

As they neared the castle, a welcoming party came out to meet them. In the forefront was Latta, his white hair shining in the sunlight. As the two groups met, there sounded from a castle battlement high overhead the triumphant notes of a silver trumpet.

Akara felt a deep sense of contentment. Her days of wandering were over.

CHAPTER 41

With an Old Friend in the Valley

Northwest of Midra lies the village of Taravo. Near it is a low wooded hill. Early one morning the smoke of a campfire rose from a clearing near the summit of this hill. In the clearing, seated on a log beside this fire, was a tall man wearing a battered floppy hat. He had just finished his breakfast of roasted meat and bread when a figure appeared at the edge of the clearing.

The morning was chill, and the newcomer was wrapped in a hooded traveling cloak. The man was not certain whether his visitor was a man or woman, but he rose politely and made a slight bow.

"Welcome, whoever you are. Come join me at my fire."

The figure threw back its hood, releasing a mass of dark hair.

"Akara!" The man dropped the stick with which he had stirred the fire and came striding forward. "How wonderful to see you!" He enveloped the girl in a hug.

"Good morning, Wenk," said Akara. "I'm glad I found you."

Wenk led her back to the fire. "Tell me what you have been doing and how you came to be here."

"I've found a new life for myself, Wenk." Akara threw back her traveling cloak, revealing a suit of gleaming armor. Her head was bare, but on one side of her belt was fastened her silver helmet, while on the other side hung the King's sword. On her back under the cloak was her shield.

Wenk stared in amazement. "I recognize the armor. I think it was I who first described it to you. So you're now a follower of this person called the King?"

Akara nodded. "You started me in that direction when you gave me my silver trumpet. It helped me find the King's Castle."

Wenk waved her to his seat on the log, then dragged up another to sit on. "And that trumpet now hangs from a silver cord around your neck, I see. I want to hear about everything that has happened to you, as well as how you found me, but first may I make you some breakfast?"

"Thank you, no. My friend Keila and I breakfasted in the village. We've been traveling in the valley for the past week. She had an appointment in Taravo, so we stayed at the village inn last night. This morning I saw the smoke from your fire above the trees, and one of the village folk described the person who was camping here. I knew at once who it was, so I came to spend a little time with you."

"Well, time is something I have. Please tell me your story."

Akara recounted her adventures since she had last seen him. Wenk listened attentively, then said, "So you have found both a brother and a home. I'm happy for you. Do you like your new life?"

"Oh yes! It's the most wonderful life in the world."

"And now that you have a mountain castle to live in, what are you and your friend doing here in the valley?"

"Keila travels the valley with the King's message."

"And you, what is your mission?"

"I too have a responsibility to tell others about him. I want to start with my special friends: you, most of all, then Blink and Baslin. Then there are other acquaintances, Skey, Zemla and Dame Leck, the people at the House of the Hill Soldiers, and Dame Dessit and the folks at her orphan home."

Wenk grinned at her. "How about the miller of Arn — the one who chased you and later took you captive? Do you plan to visit him too?"

Akara knew she was being teased. She smiled and shook her head. "I don't think I'm quite ready to face him again."

"Well, I envy your enthusiasm, and I hope you succeed." Wenk paused for a long minute, then continued. "You have honored me by listing me first in your group of friends, and it is truly an honor. But I must tell you, Akara, as I did long ago, that I'm content with my life of wandering."

Akara sighed inwardly. She wanted so much for Wenk to know her King, yet he was evidently not interested. She was silent for a moment, staring at the fire. Then she said, "Wenk, do you recall telling me how much you enjoy watching the stars?"

"Certainly. The stars are my companions at night."

"What is it about them that attracts you?"

Wenk raised his eyebrows. "You're the only one who ever asked me that. I'm not sure. Perhaps I like the stars because they are so bright and beautiful, and they are in the sky, far above the valley. I like to imagine that somewhere among the stars are lands better than this one."

"I too like to look at them. I believe my King put them in the sky. We see the stars from the mountaintop. They look even brighter and closer up there."

"I suppose they might. I hadn't thought of that."

"When I was working in the library at the House of the Hill Soldiers, I read a poem about the stars, written many years ago." She closed her eyes for a moment, trying to remember, then quoted:

Though my soul may set in darkness
It will rise in perfect light
I have loved the stars too fondly
To be fearful of the night.

"I've never heard that. Whoever wrote it had the right idea, though I'm not sure what my soul is, or whether I have one."

Akara leaned forward earnestly. "The King's Book tells us that our souls are a part of us that lives on after we die, and those who follow the King will live with him forever when our lives here are over. I believe the King used the trumpet you gave me to draw me to himself. Perhaps the stars are his way of calling to you."

When Wenk said nothing, Akara took a deep breath and continued. "Wenk, would you come and visit me at the King's Castle? I'd like you to be able to see the stars from the mountaintop. If you come, my brother, Lanus, and I could meet you in Midra and guide you up the mountain. You needn't stay more than one night, of course, unless you wish."

Wenk was silent for a long time. Then he turned to her with a smile.

"You are very persuasive, Akara. Yes, I will come. A trip to Midra will also let me visit my friend Zemla. But I must first keep some other promises I have made. Three days from now I will meet you at Zemla's home in Midra."

A little later, Akara told Wenk good-bye and left the hilltop. She went down the path through the woods and out onto the open field at the bottom. A short distance away was the road that ran from Midra to Taravo. As she looked in the direction of the village, she saw Keila's horse and two-wheeled cart coming to pick her up as they had arranged.

Like Akara, Keila was wearing her traveling cloak over her armor. She answered Akara's wave, then drew the cart to a stop at the point where the path and the road intersected. As she watched her friend crossing the field toward her, she thought of the many changes she had seen in Akara since their first meeting a few months previously. Then, Akara had been a frightened girl, lost on the mountainside. Now the person coming toward her was a happy, confident Soldier of the King, one who was fast becoming skilled in the use of her shield and sword, and who was eager to serve.

Akara reached the cart and swung herself up into the seat. "You're right on time, Keila," she smiled.

Keila gave her an answering smile. "So are you." She shook out the reins and the horse moved off at an easy trot. "Did you find your friend?"

"Yes! And Keila, he's promised to come to the castle. Isn't that wonderful?"

"Yes, I'm so glad for you!"

"Did you finish your business at Taravo?"

"Yes. I met this morning with a family who had asked to see me. Now I'm ready to head for Midra. We can reach there by mid-afternoon, in time to stable the horse and climb the path to the castle before sundown. I brought some food so we can lunch along the way. Does that plan suit you?"

Akara smiled and settled herself comfortably on the seat. She raised her eyes to the Great Mountains, which rose bright and beautiful under the morning sky. "That suits me. It has been nice visiting the valley again, but I'm ready to go home."

The End